Anarchy Road

A Jake Caldwell Thriller

D1366632

JAMES L. WEAVER

WOLFPACK
PUBLISHING
— EST 2013 —

WOLFPACK
PUBLISHING
— EST 2013 —

Wolfpack Publishing
5130 S. Fort Apache Road 215-380
Las Vegas, NV 89148

Paperback ISBN 978-1-64734-743-7
eBook ISBN 978-1-64734-742-0

ANARCHY ROAD

DEDICATION

For Becky, Madison and Max (and yes, Dixon
too)—my family,
from whom all good things flow.
Love you guys.

ACKNOWLEDGMENTS

I'm extremely fortunate to have a bevy of people in my corner who provide contributions to my work both large and small but all vital to crafting the books I write. Anarchy Road is no exception, so I'd like to extend my gratitude to the following folks. If I left anyone out, my humblest of apologies. I'm getting old, after all.

My lovely bride Becky for putting up with me when I continually disappear upstairs at night to pound the keys. I hope you know how much I appreciate and love you.

Fellow writer Barry Brakeville who keeps me honest and never fails to throw a punch when it's needed in the story. Those punches hurt like shit sometimes, but the truth behind them makes the story better. Barry suggested the therapy angle in Anarchy Road. I ran with it and am proud as hell at how it turned out. If you liked it, it was the writing. If you hated it, it's Barry's fault for making me do it.

Author extraordinaire Jodi Gallegos who makes me laugh daily through social media. She provided some great insights for Anarchy Road and I so appreciate having her on my side. If you haven't checked out her High Crown Chronicles series, you are missing out.

Editor and author Rebecca Carpenter for her meticulous red pen and suggestions throughout the manuscript. She still talks to me even though I STILL can't seem to get commas right. If you need an editor, look her up. If you want a great read, check out her metamorphosis series starting with Butterfly Bones.

Fellow author Kate Foster for managing to work in a beta read in the middle of launching her own book. Jake Caldwell would not exist without her and I so appreciate having her continue to be a resource for me. Check out her latest book - Paws!

Doctor Alan Reeves, the best damn brain surgeon I know. Well, to be truthful, I don't know that many but I do know I've seen him on TV and know he's is well-respected in his field! Thank you for brainstorming potential head injuries with me over a couple beers and walking me through the signs and symptoms of the one we settled on. If I messed anything up in the final version, it's totally my fault! Don't blame Alan.

Doctor Danielle Skirchak for rolling through the therapy sessions in the book and letting me know where I veered off course. It was such a huge relief to have a professional let me know I didn't have to start from scratch! Thanks, Danielle.

My brother-in-law Brian Luce for his expertise regarding how cell phone towers work. The internet gave me some basics of what I needed, but Brian was invaluable in providing the details and putting it in terms that even I could understand. Thanks, man!

Great friend and forever beta reader Jim McKernan for continuing to read my work and giving me feedback. Very much appreciate your insights. We need to go swing the sticks sometime soon.

My dad who is a loyal fan and is always the first to read the rough draft and give me feedback. Thanks, Pop!

The fine folks at Wolfpack Publishing for their support, promotion and getting the Jake Caldwell series out there for public consumption. Appreciate everything you do.

And last, but certainly not least, to the readers out there who continue to follow the antics of Jake and Bear. My writing only means something to me if it means something to you. Based on your reviews, it looks like we're hitting the mark for most part. Thank you, thank you, thank you.

NOW

CHAPTER ONE

Jake Caldwell's goal had been to squeeze the murderer's throat until one of two things happened—the last molecules of oxygen evacuated, or his head popped off. Jake would have been okay either way. He'd pressed the murderer into the polished wood floor, clenching his hands around the leathery skin of the man's throat until the muscles in his forearms rippled and ached. Jake's attention was focused on choking away the son of a bitch's crazy grin and didn't see the gun butt that cracked into the back of his skull. The blow ended his short-lived attempt at justice and landed him in the office of Dr. Danielle Tate. Apparently, trying to strangle someone was a cause for concern for the powers that be.

"Jake?" Her voice was soft, like a breeze.

The face of the man rippled away like a stone thrown into a reflection on a pond. Jake paused in the doorway of the doctor's Kansas City office, eyes sweeping over the dark wood and polished leather. He inhaled the cinnamon stick scent of the air freshener plugged into the wall on the far side of the room. Jake had once read that merely smelling cinnamon can improve performance in memory recollection. He wondered if Doctor Tate bought into that psychobabble bullshit.

"Would you like to come in?" she asked.

Jake pressed his hands against either side of the door frame, fingers digging into the wood as if clinging to the last vestiges of freedom. "Do I have a choice?"

Leaning against her desk, she folded her arms. "Not according to Judge Cooper. I don't think you want to do a stretch in county for assault."

Jake crossed the threshold with all the enthusiasm of a death row inmate stepping up to the electric chair. He'd never been to a therapist before and wasn't anticipating the experience to be much better than getting strapped to Old Sparky. He'd much rather be watching the scumbag he'd tried to strangle get strapped into the chair. Jake would trample people for the opportunity to yank the switch himself. But that wasn't going to happen, so he stepped inside the office.

Sunlight spilled across her desk and backlit the amber strands of Dr. Tate's shoulder length hair. She was an attractive woman, the lines on her creamy skin marking her around fifty years old. She sported an athletic build under tan slacks and white blouse. Jake crossed the office and strolled past her desk, sensing her eyes tracking him.

Jake noted a pair of trophies resting among volumes of psychology textbooks in a built-in shelf on the far wall. Gold tennis rackets above matching plaques reading "Club Champion" two years in a row, though those two years were a couple of decades ago. A pair of diplomas from Kansas State University and Johns Hopkins took up the remaining free space along with a photo of her and another woman in an ornate carved frame sitting cheek to cheek from the lower level of a Chiefs game. Looked like her sister. No pictures of a man or kids anywhere in sight.

Dr. Tate cleared her throat and Jake turned toward her. She motioned to the center of the room which held a couch too expensive to sit on. It was bookended by a pair of leather chairs with rows of beaded gold stitched on the arms. A mahogany coffee table holding a bowl of peppermints rested in front of the couch. Jake took one and popped it in his mouth.

"How do we do this? Should I lay down?" he asked.

She flashed a hint of teeth. "Are you tired?"

Jake rolled the mint around his mouth. "Not really, no."

"Then maybe just sit."

Jake eased himself onto the couch, afraid if he sat too hard he'd crack the leather. He wiped his sweaty palms on the legs of his jeans, unsure why the nervous energy crackled through his body. His wife, Maggie, said even though therapy was the last thing Jake wanted to do, maybe it would be good for him as he carried around enough baggage to open a luggage store.

A strange concoction of anger and fear mixed, forming a rock hard ball in his stomach. Jake had his doubts and planned to participate just enough to get Dr. Tate to give him a clean bill of mental health and out from under the thumb of Judge Cooper. He tried not to think about the level of control she had over him. With one stroke of her pen, she could ensure Jake would spend some serious time behind bars. He couldn't imagine not being able to see Maggie, and his kids Halle and Conner.

Dr. Tate plucked a notepad, pen and a manila folder from her meticulous desk and settled in a chair across from Jake. Crossing her long legs, she leaned back. "How are you doing?"

He fixed a level gaze. "I'm in court-ordered therapy. What do you think?"

"Other than that."

"I'm peachy."

She ticked her chin to his wiping hands. "There's no need to be nervous."

Jake fixed the offending hands in place and dug nails into his palms. "I'm not."

"If we're going to get anywhere with this process, you have to be honest. This is a safe space for you."

"Is that so?"

"It is," Dr. Tate said. "What's said in here stays between the two of us."

"And Judge Cooper."

"Nope. Just you and me. My job is to evaluate your mental state and make a determination if you represent a danger—"

"A danger? To who?" Jake crossed his thick arms against his chest and narrowed his eyes.

"Well, I suppose, in Judge Cooper's eyes, the man you tried to kill last week for one."

"The prick should sure as shit should consider me a danger. Sorry."

"For what?"

"Cussing in front of you."

Dr. Tate laughed. "I work predominately with cops and have two older brothers, so I have a thick skin." She let her statement sit for a beat. "So, you are a danger to him? That's not helping your cause here, Jake."

"I didn't say I was a danger. I said he should consider me one." Jake tightened his crossed arms and looked away to the far wall.

"Do you want to talk about it, or should I write up my report to Judge Cooper now?"

Jake chewed on his bottom lip. "You don't beat around the bush."

She shrugged. "We can go through the formalities of the idle chit-chat if it will make you more at ease. But, most of my clients don't want to be here and like to get down to business. You strike me as the same."

"You're not wrong."

"Tell me what happened at the courthouse."

Jake could still see the asshole's cocky grin slipping across his iron jaw as he'd turned and locked eyes with Jake. Soulless eyes and devil's smile. Jake would kill the man in a heartbeat given the opportunity. But that wouldn't help him get out of therapy.

"I regret my actions," Jake lied. "It was rash and impulsive."

She lifted a plucked eyebrow and cocked her head. "Do you? Regret them?"

"Why would I lie?"

"To get out of therapy."

"If you knew the facts, you'd understand why I did what I did."

Dr. Tate leaned forward and placed her elbows on her knees. "You're not getting off that easy, Jake. I know what you went through and what he allegedly did."

Jake rubbed the three-inch scar running across his forehead below his scalp line. "Fuck allegedly. Pardon my French."

Dr. Tate paused, the corners of her mouth drifting

up. "I don't think that's French. I believe the etymology is German."

Jake was unsure if she was joking or a word nerd. Maybe both. "You have no idea what happened."

"Maybe I don't know everything, but I talked with some people I know in the KCPD about you. I do counseling after officer involved shootings, traumatic events and so on. I know a few of them pretty well."

Jake shifted in his seat. "Isn't that unethical? Getting the skinny on your patient from the local cops?"

"I didn't let them know I was treating you."

"How'd you pull that off?"

"You were in the news, Jake. It wasn't hard to bring up in casual conversation."

God, he wanted out of her office. "Don't believe everything you hear."

"Talking with them, I know this isn't your first violent episode."

"Episode? You make me sound like some uncontrolled psycho."

She settled back in her chair. "I don't think that at all. Some of the officers I talked to were, how do I say this, almost admirers. You have quite the reputation."

Jake scrolled through his mental Rolodex. He'd stepped on a few toes in the Kansas City Police Department over the years. "I bet it wasn't all unicorns and rainbows."

She laughed. "No. Some don't appear to care much for your tactics. It's the why that interests me."

She thumbed through the pages in the manila folder. Jake recognized his handwriting from the probing questionnaire. There was no way for him to be honest on the thing and get out from under Dr. Tate in the next century.

"Should we discuss why you did what you did?" she asked.

Why? Jake cranked his neck from side to side, the nervous energy raging like someone opened the dam. He reached forward and grabbed another mint, resisting the urge to fling the bowl across the office. Why? Jake knew the problem wasn't what he tried to do to the murderer, it was when he chose to do it. But he couldn't say that to Dr. Tate.

"Jake?" she asked. "You want to tell me why you did what you did?"

Jake sank back in the couch and ran his hands through his cropped brown hair. She was smart, astute. Jake was an excellent reader of people, too, and this woman wouldn't be swayed by any bullshit. She reminded him of his wife, Maggie. "This is a safe space?"

She dipped her chin. "Yes, it is."

"Justice. That's why I did it. It's why I always do what I do."

She tipped back in her chair and closed the folder. "Tell me more."

THEN

CHAPTER TWO

"What's your target body count?" Mara Wilder asked. She perched in a thinly padded seat by the office window down the street from the T-Mobile Center in downtown Kansas City. Her bony fingers pulled back the drawn curtains, sneaking a look to the rain-kissed pavement below. Street light spilled through the opening and cast a razor line of white across the worn carpet of the office.

Hunter Brenner bit his bottom lip to hold back a response. Mara asked too many questions at the wrong time. More than a quarter century had passed since high school, and she still demonstrated the annoying habit.

Mara wrinkled her nose and swept her eyes across the dim room. "This place smells as stale and dated as the furniture. I woulda thought a lawyer would have a nicer office."

"Maybe you should've asked him before you strangled him," Hunter said.

She smirked. "Maybe he should've worked harder on my case three years ago."

Hunter twirled a jigsaw puzzle piece between his thick, calloused fingers. "The protestors still there?"

She pressed her head against the glass. "Yeah, but I can't make out what their signs say."

"It doesn't matter. They're lunatics. Now, get away from the window, Mara."

Mara drew her thin lips to a pout and dipped her chin toward her ample chest. "Nobody can see us. I was just taking a peek."

"You can peek when Lance calls. Until then, stay the fuck away from the window. Sweet heart."

She let go of the curtain and slid to the desk where Hunter had the jigsaw puzzle half-assembled. The puzzle rested on a black roll-up mat for easy transport. The picture would eventually be an F-14 Tomcat flying above a layer of pink-hued clouds. Hunter loved puzzles. Eddie used to make fun of Hunter for doing them. Such mind-numbing piece work fell far below Eddie's idea of fun, but they relaxed Hunter. This puzzle depicted a scene from Top Gun, the movie he and Eddie watched on base the night before the ill-fated mission. But even Hunter started to regret this thousand-piece choice. He'd finished the fighter jet and now struggled with the clouds and monochromatic blue sky. All the shit looked the same.

Mara picked up a cloud piece and studied for a place to put it. "So how many?"

"How many what?"

"People."

Hunter snapped a piece of sky in place. "I don't know. Place seats like nineteen thousand."

Mara jerked upright. "You wanna kill all of them?"

Hunter crunched his tanned face. "Jesus, no. I'm not an animal. It's how many the place holds. Just take out enough to make our point."

"More than Seattle?"

An even dozen sheep slaughtered at a protest rally. "Seattle was more than we needed to make the point. Tulsa's body count was better, even if it wasn't us."

"Was Tulsa Mister X?"

Hunter ground his teeth together. "I told you not to talk about him, to me or anyone else."

"You know anything about this guy? Other than he's rich?"

Hunter knew everything about Mister X, along with the other surviving members of the Six Horsemen, but it would be healthier for Mara if she remained in the dark. "Drop it, Mara."

She ran her finger along the edge of the puzzle. "Well, I don't care what we do, as long as it's no repeat of Dallas. I don't wanna do that shit again."

He stroked her hand. "Executions are more dramatic, but you're right. Let's wait and see how things turn out here. Would you make me another drink, sweet pea?"

Mara kissed his lined cheek and plucked his empty glass from the desk. She liked it when Hunter called her pet names. He supposed he could throw the word sweet in front of any object and she'd like it. Mara was uncomplicated and wholly dedicated to him which made things easier. Especially considering what he was trying to do. Mister X had his own specific power-grab agenda and Hunter had his.

She plinked ice in the glass from the lawyer's minibar and poured a healthy measure of Woodford Reserve bourbon. She added a splash of soda water and stirred it with her finger. Swinging her hips and sucking on her finger seductively, she locked eyes with Hunter. "Maybe we could do something other than a puzzle to pass the time?"

He took the drink from her hand and considered the proposal. When she was ten, Mara was diagnosed with histrionic personality disorder which included inappropriate seduction and an excessive need for approval. She often exhibited sexually provocative behavior like she was doing now. While it sometimes caused problems, who was Hunter to complain at the moment? He pulled her to his lap and popped the first two buttons on her blouse when his burner cell rang. He answered and put it on speaker.

"People are starting to come out," Lance said through the speaker. Car horns beeped and tires droned on asphalt in the background.

"Where are you?"

"South side with Artie, like you told me."

Hunter covered the phone and told Mara to pack up and wipe the place down. He eased her from his lap and moved his two-hundred and twenty pounds to the window. Like everything else he told her to do, she did it without question. Not because he abused her or treated her poorly, but because she was terrified he'd leave her.

Peeking through the crack with a pair of binoculars, Hunter's bullish eyes searched the pyramids of light from street lamps up the road until he spotted Lance and Artie. Both wore ballcaps and light jackets. Lance had the backpack. Given his Marine experience with the contents of the backpack, it made sense he carried it. Until now.

"Give Artie the payload," Hunter said.

Lance turned back toward the office building, his face pinched. "But, I thought I was going to get to—"

"Don't think," Hunter interrupted. "Give Artie the backpack, hand him the phone and get your ass to the parking garage. Mara and I will meet you there."

Hunter watched Lance hand the phone and black backpack to Artie with the enthusiasm of a toddler asked to give up his favorite toy.

Artie's high-pitched voice wavered as he took the phone, his eyes widening as Lance limped away down the street. "Wh-wh-where's Lance going?"

"I'm giving you the honor, Artie. You've earned it. You ready?"

Artie's beady eyes darted around. "I guess so, boss."

Hunter's grip tightened on the phone. "You guess so? You believe in what we're doing, right?"

"Hell, yes," Artie said, stiffening. "Of course. Just a little nervous, that's all."

"Understandable," Hunter replied, keeping his voice calm and even. "I want you to start walking toward the arena. Slower. Casual. Now, wait until more people start coming out, walk into the crowd, drop the backpack on the ground near the protestors and walk away. I'll take care of the rest. Head north and we'll pick you up at the rendezvous point. You're going to be a legend, Artie. Can you handle it?"

"Yes, sir. I won't let you down."

"I know you won't. Looks like people are starting to come down. Once a decent crowd exits, make your move. Remember, walk. Don't run. Act casual."

Artie stopped, turned and offered a thumbs-up in their general direction. "For Anarchy Road."

"For Anarchy Road," Hunter replied. "Good luck and see you soon."

Hunter swept his binoculars to the front doors of

the arena as people trickled into the Wednesday night air. Most appeared in their twenties or thirties. He'd planned to do this a couple of months ago, but the concert in question was some new boyband which would attract too many kids and their mothers. The two dozen holy roller protestors screamed and pointed at the concert goers. One of the signs read "God hates fags" and another read "The United States is going to Hell." Hunter snapped his fingers and held out his hand.

Mara placed the detonator in his calloused palm. "All packed up and ready to go. Can I watch?"

"Sure thing, baby doll," he said, kneeling his six-foot frame and pulling the curtains wide enough for her to get a view of the arena. They were a full block to the south, but the glass-walled monstrosity of corporate greed blasted back the darkness of the April night. They waited a few minutes as the bulk of the crowd streamed through the doors. He swept back to Artie who made his way through the throng of concert goers, edging toward the protestors near the street. A team of cops hung close by to keep the crowd in check.

Mara stroked his caramel hair before resting her chin on his broad shoulder, her hot breath caressing his cheek. Her tawny arms wrapped around his flat stomach. "You think the bomb will shatter all that glass covering the arena? It would be pretty to watch it rain down."

Hunter didn't answer. He watched as Artie moved in on the protestors.

Mara's breath quickened, her heart thumping into his back as her hand slid down from his stomach. The closer Artie drew to the protesters, the harder she rubbed the front of Hunter's jeans. Bombs exploding got her hot and bothered. This was the first time Hunter would watch the carnage first hand and had to admit his pulse raced as well. Hunter pressed against her, responding to her touch and raised the detonator.

Artie weaved through the crowd toward the street, walking too fast, head darting around as if on a swivel. Like a guy carrying a backpack full of explosives.

"Slow the fuck down, Artie," Hunter whispered.

Ahead of Artie, a blue-uniformed Kansas City police officer tracked him with a scowl. The cop talked into his shoulder mic and walked toward Artie.

Hunter hung his head. Fewer people than he hoped, but it would have to do.

The last explosion he'd seen firsthand was years ago. Flashes of the night in Ramadi rolled through his mind as his finger hovered over the red button. The shithole building they were ordered to storm to set up a useless combat outpost. The screams of the wounded Marines. The deafening hail of gunfire. The explosions leaving his ears ringing and fillings loose. His best friend Eddie in jagged pieces, bleeding out on a debris covered floor seven thousand miles from home in the middle of Iraq. A nightmare of death and destruction at the hands of his own country that sent them there under a false pretense.

"Don't let them get away with this," Eddie had moaned before his eyes turned glassy and distant.

Hunter would set things right. His finger trembled over the detonator button.

"For you, Eddie," Hunter whispered.

CHAPTER THREE

The band sounded better on their studio album than they did live, not that he was a big fan of Perilous Plight in the first place. Jake Caldwell didn't give musical artists much leeway in concerts. In his opinion, most of them deviated too far from the original version when they played live. He supposed it must get boring playing the same songs night after night, and they had to do something to keep it interesting for themselves. He could relate. Seemed like his PI business fell into the same monotonous rut. If he had to spend one more night following a cheating spouse or chasing down a deadbeat dad, he might be forced to change things up, like the frenetic, long-haired band members on the T-Mobile stage.

The crowd of fifteen thousand roared as Perilous Plight throttled down the last of their encore riffs. The drums thumped slower to their inevitable last beat which would be synced with the lead singer landing from a jump off the raised portion of the stage holding the drums. The finale would be an explosion of pyrotechnics. Ten seconds later, the group executed the move to perfection. Guitar pics and drum sticks were thrown into the cheering audience. The group waved farewell and walked from the stage. The arena stayed dark and the audience roared in the fleeting hope of another encore before the lights blasted on.

"That was freaking awesome, Dad," Halle exclaimed, a smile blasting across her face as smoke drifted across the arena crowd, a hint of weed in the air. "What'd you think?"

Jake was the benefactor of the extra ticket his daughter had after her college roommate bailed on the show. Since it was a last-minute cancellation and her mother made it clear she would rather shove bamboo sticks up her fingernails than go to the concert, Jake was offered as the sacrificial lamb. Maggie officially owed him one.

Jake edged forward toward the aisle, keeping Halle in front of him. "Considering I only knew a few songs, it was okay."

"Okay?" Halle's jaw dropped as she spun around. "What about the drum set spinning upside down while Gunter did his solo?"

"Tommy Lee and Motley Crüe did it back in the eighties. Color me unimpressed."

She reached the aisle and they climbed toward the exit. "I acted more enthusiastic when you took me to the Alter Bridge concert."

"Alter Bridge is a hell of a lot better than Perilous Pussies."

"Plight."

Jake squeezed her shoulder. "Right. But thanks for taking me."

"You're paying for your own ticket, you know? I'm a broke college student."

They made their way to the concourse, a wide-expanse of concrete flanked by steel-shuttered concession stands and vendors waving over-priced t-shirts to fans of the band. Thankfully, Halle didn't want one. A rowdy group of twenty-something guys sloshed past, the last one pausing to do a double take at Halle.

"Hey, baby," he slurred. "Where you heading to?"

"Not with you, dick brain," Jake said, pulling her close and giving the guy a glare which would melt steel. "Move along."

The guy's eyes swept over Jake's six-foot-three-inch build and his chiseled arms and decided it would be in the best interests of his health if he caught up to his friends.

"I suppose you get that a lot?" Jake asked.

Halle rolled her eyes. "Too much. No better way to shut a woman down than to call her baby. Kudos to you, by the way."

"For what?"

"For not pounding him into the concrete."

Jake grinned. "I only would've done it if he tried to touch you. Let's get to the hotel, and I'll buy you a beer."

"Dad, I'm a minor."

"You didn't bring your fake ID with you?"

A rush of blood flooded her cheeks. "You know about that?"

"Don't tell your mother. She'd have my ass and kick yours."

A few months ago, Jake busted in on a guy named John Plinsky making fake drivers' licenses with a machine he bought off the black market. They were impressive in quality, almost as good as you could get at the DMV. Plinsky made some identification and a passport for a bail jumper Jake was tracking down. After handcuffing Plinsky to a pole in his basement studio, Jake scanned through his computer for his bail jumper. That's when he found Halle's picture along with her college roommate's.

He considered busting Halle with the information, but she made close to straight As at the University of Nebraska. She'd graduated high school a semester early and jumped into her freshman year of college in the Spring, so she obviously had a good head on her shoulders. He let the ID slide, but punched Plinsky in the face for the effort. Maybe more than once. At least he'd busted the bail jumper three nights later in Little Rock.

The cool April night air greeted them as they emerged from the arena. Shouts from protestors from a wacko church in Topeka were too far away to make out what they said but close enough that Jake still wanted to club the hateful bunch.

Halle took his arm. "Thanks for bringing me."

"My pleasure, baby girl. Not too embarrassed by your old man?"

She drew her head back, face scrunched in surprise. "Are you kidding me? You're one of the coolest dads I know. Seriously, you should see some of the schmucks who come visit their kids. The truth is, I've always been proud of you."

Jake blushed as they strode toward the street. She'd never said that to him before. "Proud of what?"

"How you go after the bad guys, no matter what. Even when it pisses Mom off. You do it because it's the right thing. It's admirable and makes me happy to be your—"

The world ripped apart with a deafening crack. An invisible fist punched Jake square in the chest, blowing him off his feet, careening back in a wave of pain and heat. Gravity kicked in and he slammed to the ground.

His vision blurred. His ears rang. The world shimmered.

Jake wiped his forehead and drew back bloody fingers. He blinked the swimming world away until it steadied.

Halle. Where was Halle? Groaning, he propped himself on his elbow, his ribs protesting. He scanned the mass of figures on the ground. People stumbling, wearing screaming masks of bloody panic.

Where was she?

"Halle!" He screamed her name but the ring in his ears drowned everything else. His eyes swept the bodies littering the ground around him. No, no, no. Please God, no. Screaming her name again, he rolled over, pain like a thousand knives stabbed in his chest. Then he saw her.

His heart stopped.

Ten feet away, she lay on the ground on her side, an older man with half his face blown off draped across her torso. Her eyes were closed, her pale cheeks streaked with dirt, blond hair matted with crimson across her angelic face.

Jake's chest felt like it was caving in, a million unthinkable thoughts flooding his brain. A tombstone etched with Halle's name. Maggie screaming in agony, clawing at the dirt around their daughter's gravesite. The perpetual empty place at their dining room table. Jake rolled to his stomach, drawing his knees under him. As he pushed himself up, the world wavered.

His legs failed to cooperate, and his face scraped the rough concrete.

"Halle." Jake choked out her name and dragged himself toward his daughter, digging his bloody fingers into the debris covered concourse, praying to God she was still alive.

CHAPTER FOUR

Jake managed to crawl to his daughter, calling her name and tapping her cheeks when he reached her, but she didn't respond. He checked for a pulse and dropped his head with relief when little thumps tickled his fingertips. Around him, sirens wailed, people screaming and crying. Jake forced himself to his knees and checked the man lying on top of Halle. Despite the glassy-eyes and bloody half of a face, Jake still felt for a pulse. Nothing. He rolled the body off Halle, careful to keep her still. No obvious wounds other than a nasty cut across her forehead and a scrape from the top of her right ear and up the flat part of her skull where the skin met her hairline.

He stood and scanned the sea of carnage, searching for help. Bodies lay scattered along the ground, some intact, others in pieces. It was like a war zone. Acrid smoke stung his eyes. Bodies and concrete rubble intertwined, creating a mangled, bloody walkway.

A weak voice croaked behind him. "Dad?"

Tears welled behind Jake's eyelids. He spun and

crouched beside her as she pushed onto her elbow. "Oh God, Halle. You okay?"

She wiped her mouth, blinking slowly, her gaze flat as it rose. "Huh?"

"I said are you okay?"

"I think so. Head feels like it's full of cotton. What happened?"

Jake stroked her arm. "An explosion of some kind, maybe a gas line. We were caught in the blast."

"An explosion?" She spoke slowly, shaking her head as if to clear the cobwebs and winced from the effort. She tried to sit up.

Jake helped her upright as Halle probed her head and studied her fingers. "My face hurts. Is that blood?"

Her skin was cold and sweaty, her breathing irregular. Jake removed his torn jacket and draped it over her shoulders. His mind raced, unsure what to do. Afraid to move her, afraid not to.

Wiping away the blood dripping into his eye, Jake yelled at an approaching cop who staggered in his direction. Ragged strips of flesh dangled from the left side of the officer's face. His name tag said "Madsen".

Madsen's eyes locked on Jake for a moment before sweeping across the bodies at his feet. "I saw him."

"Who?" Jake asked, pressing to his feet on wobbly legs.

"The kid with the backpack. The bomb."

Bomb? Jake's mind raced at the implication as Madsen swayed and his eyes rolled back. Jake grabbed him by the arm and helped him to the ground, finding an empty spot between two dead men who appeared to be in their early twenties. One of them clutched a tattered, black Perilous Plight t-shirt in his right hand. It was the drunk kid who hit on Halle.

"I saw him," Madsen repeated.

Jake scanned the crowd and spotted a trio of cops running toward the arena. He was more concerned about Halle than Madsen but knew the best way to get help quickly. "Officer down!"

The cops broke their way at a run, jumping over bodies like they played a perverse version of hopscotch. One peeled off to help a screaming woman. The other two reached them in seconds, one black, one white. The white cop stood chest high to Jake with a blond crew cut and a name tag reading Howe. The black guy was bald with wide, rheumy eyes. Jake knew him from bringing in bail jumpers. Wilson.

Wilson's eyes bulged. "Holy shit, is that you, Caldwell?"

"Unfortunately. I need some help with my daughter. She's conscious, but shaky with a nasty cut on her head."

"Speaking of nasty cuts," Wilson said, holding out a white handkerchief and gesturing to Jake's head. "You okay?"

Jake took the handkerchief and pressed it to the source of the bleed. "I'm fine. I need someone to check on Halle."

Jake dragged Wilson to Halle. The officer did a cursory check and called for help on his shoulder mic.

"She alright?" Jake asked.

"I don't know. I'm not a paramedic."

Jake scowled. "That's my daughter, man. Do something."

Wilson raised his hands apologetically. "Sorry, Caldwell. Hang on, help is on the way. What happened here?"

"I don't know, man. We walked out the doors and blam. The cop said he saw a kid with a backpack. A bomb."

"Jesus Christ," Wilson muttered, rubbing a heavy hand over his sweat-slicked dome. "This is just like Tulsa."

A couple of EMTs ran through the arena doors. Wilson flagged one of them, a Hispanic girl with raven hair pulled back in a ponytail. Jake directed her to Halle, and the EMT went to work.

The EMT checked Halle's cuts, the scrape on the side of her face, her pupils and ran through a series of questions—how she felt, her name, age, where she lived. A minute later, a cacophony of sirens blew into the area and uniformed cops and paramedics flooded the common area outside the arena. They juked through the debris, searching for survivors.

"We need to get her to the hospital, she probably has a concussion," the EMT said, staring at Jake's forehead. "You need to get checked out, too."

"Like I'm going anywhere without her." Jake's eyes stung from smoke and tears threatening to spill over, worry for his girl crushing his heart.

Wilson patted Jake on the arm and meandered around bodies toward Madsen who sat up but wore a blank, catatonic stare.

The EMT waved her partner over with a gurney. As he worked his way through the wreckage, Jake squatted next to Halle, stroking her arm. "It's going to be okay."

Her dazed eyes found his face. "Why did this happen?"

"I don't know, but I'm gonna find out."

"I mean, we were just walking when…"

Halle's voice trailed off and her eyes rolled over white. Jake caught her as she slumped toward the ground.

"Oh oh," the EMT said. She dropped to the ground with Halle. "How long since the blast?"

"I don't know. Maybe fifteen minutes. What's going on? She was fine."

The two paramedics worked quickly. Jake's heart thrashed in his ears as the woman intubated his daughter right there on the ground. Jake asked again what was happening but didn't get a response. They loaded Halle onto a backboard, securing her neck in a brace before wheeling the gurney through the wreckage. They had to lift the wheels over body parts and chunks of blasted concrete in places before they made it to the sea of ambulances and news crews waiting on Grand Avenue.

Jake climbed in after the gurney, clutching Halle's hand as the doors slammed shut. The woman paramedic jumped on the phone. "Incoming victim, teenage female, head trauma. Was alert and oriented but I witnessed rapid decline. Possible epidural hematoma. We're en route."

The diagnosis caused the walls of the ambulance to close in on Jake and his skin clammy. "How bad is it? What is an epidural hema whatever you called it?"

"Hematoma. It's when bleeding occurs between the brain and the skull, more or less," the EMT said. "It's bad, but if we can get her to the hospital in time…"

Jake didn't like the "if" part of her statement. He leaned forward and took Halle's hand, pressing it to his forehead, praying.

With his eyes closed, the scene from minutes before played.

"I saw him," Madsen said. A kid with a backpack.

"This is just like Tulsa," Wilson said.

A news report floated across Jake's mind. A bombing outside a right-wing rally killing a baker's dozen and injuring dozens more. A search still ongoing for a man who dropped a backpack and left the scene before the explosion. That's all he could remember.

As the ambulance rumbled forward, sirens blasting away the night, a thought rolled through Jake's thumping head. This bombing was the work of the same people. He would find out who and flay the skin from their bones.

CHAPTER FIVE

Screams and shouts, moans and groans and the coppery scent of blood littered the air as they wheeled Halle into the chaos of the Truman Medical Center emergency room. A team of doctors and nurses met them at the door. They transferred Halle to a different gurney and wheeled her into the ER. Around them, shell-shocked patients stacked the waiting room and treatment area. The EMTs disappeared on a run, heading back to the arena. They'd be busy tonight.

A twenty-something doctor with olive skin and bright eyes swept to the gurney, running a check on Halle while Jake told her what happened. They ordered Jake to go to another bay to get checked out, but he waved them off. The doctor told Jake they were taking Halle for a CT scan and asked him to wait there. While he waited, a PA took the time to give him six stitches along his scalp line while he sat on a stool and tried to slow his heart rate. He kept waiting for the doctor to emerge through those doors, head hung low to tell him they'd done what they could, but it was too late.

His phone blew up with texts and missed calls from Maggie who must've heard about the bombing on the news. A nurse directed Jake to an alcove with four cushioned chairs covered with a mosaic pattern. He thanked her and called Maggie back.

"Jesus, Jake." The worry in Maggie's voice nearly rendered her breathless. "I saw the news. What's going on? Where's Halle?"

"Mags," Jake said, struggling to keep his voice slow and even. "Take a breath. We're both still in the land of the living."

Her relieved exhale rattled the receiver. "Oh, thank God. When I heard about the bombing, I was terrified."

He sucked in a lungful of air. "Well, the explosion happened near us as we walked out. Halle got hit in the head with some debris. They just wheeled her off for a CT scan."

"A CT? Oh God, what do they think's wrong?"

"They said maybe some kind of hematoma, but I don't remember."

Maggie's volume caused Jake to jerk the phone from his ear. "You don't know?"

"I'm sorry, babe. Things are a little fuzzy. Don't worry, I'm staying by her side and I'll call you as soon as I know something. We're at Truman Medical Center."

"I'm coming down. I'll drop Connor off at the Parley's and I'll be there."

"That'd be great. Maybe Bear can drive you down since he's going to come anyway" Jake said. He didn't want her driving Mach Ten trying to get down there and end up in a bed next to Halle.

Her voice cracked with emotion. "I'll get a few things together, get the baby taken care of, and I'll be there in a couple hours."

She clicked off. Ten seconds later she called back. "Jake, are you going to be okay?"

"I'm fine, sweetheart. Nasty cut across my forehead they stitched up along with a few bumps and bruises. I've had worse."

Her voice choked. "I'm a horrible wife. Can't believe I didn't even ask."

"Don't even go there. You knew my head was hard enough to withstand even a bomb and you're worried about our daughter. Get going. Love you."

"Love you, too."

Ten minutes later, the olive-skinned doctor found Jake confirming it was an epidural hematoma, like the EMT said. "The impact to her head caused a skull fragment to lacerate the middle meningeal artery which is causing the bleeding."

Jake's legs weakened and he dropped to a chair. "Is she going to be okay?"

The doctor squatted in front of him. "We're going to take her into surgery immediately and drill a hole to relieve the pressure."

Jake cringed at the image of Halle's head getting drilled. "Will it work?"

The doctor patted Jake on the leg. "She's young and in good health. We have every confidence she's going to be fine."

A nurse escorted Jake to a waiting area near surgery. He thought about calling Maggie back with the update, but it would only freak her out. It was news best delivered in person. While he waited, he watched footage of the carnage on the television mounted to the wall. A left-wing group called DTR which stood for Death to Religion claimed responsibility for the bombing. Jake had a vague recollection of the same group setting fire to some old Catholic church in Washington DC last year. He made a mental note to do some research. Something didn't pass the smell test.

Thirty minutes later, another doctor emerged in green scrubs. He spotted Jake and the angst on his face and displayed a thumbs-up as he approached. Jake bowed his head and let loose the deep breath he'd been holding.

"I'm Doctor Reeves," the man said. "Everything went fine. We relieved the pressure and inserted a drain tube. She's sedated and we'll leave the breathing tube in until tomorrow. We'll know more when she wakes up."

"How long will that be?"

"Probably in the morning. If all goes well, she'll spend three to four days in ICU and will be able to go home. She's not out of the woods yet, but it's good news. Someone will take you to her room in a few minutes once we get her settled in."

Jake called Maggie and relayed the news. After a minute or two of relieved sobs, his wife said she and Bear were on their way and would be there in a couple of hours. Jake was glad his best friend was behind the wheel and not his emotionally shaken wife.

A half hour later, he stroked Halle's hair and kissed her forehead, willing her to wake up and let him know she was okay. The right side of her scalp was shaved and a bloody tube slinked from her head. She sucked in through a breathing tube as machines beeped and whirred behind her. Though the doctor was optimistic, fear raked Jake's guts while he waited for her to wake. It could've been much worse. But the vision of her lying dead in rubble mixed with a macabre scene of her funeral haunted his thoughts. His vision shimmered and he planted another gentle kiss.

With his mouth next to her ear, he whispered, "Daddy's going to take care of this."

CHAPTER SIX

"Caldwell?"

Jake wiped his eyes and took in the rail-thin black man in front of him, wearing jeans and a navy pullover emblazoned with KCPD. The man ran a hand over his shaved head and stepped into the room. The clock on the wall read eleven-thirty.

"Detective Ogio. It's been a while. What're you doing here?"

A couple years prior, Jake had chased after a mysterious silver briefcase containing a bioweapon. The Chief of the Kansas City Police Department was involved with the bad guys and wanted Jake out of the way. Though Ogio worked for the guy, he steered Jake in the right direction. From his brief encounters, Ogio seemed like a good man.

"It's all-hands-on-deck. Two cops from my precinct were caught up in the blast."

"How are they?"

Ogio pumped his skinny shoulders. "One's in surgery now and the other didn't make it. How's she doing?"

"She had an epidural hematoma. I'd feel a lot better if she woke up, and I could forget I ever learned that term. How'd you know we were here?"

"Saw the list of people being treated. I volunteered to talk to you. You have a sec?"

Jake waved toward a chair in the corner of the room. "Don't know how much I can tell you. One minute we're walking. The next the whole world explodes."

"You didn't notice the guy with the backpack? Some of our guys reviewed the surveillance footage. He wore a ballcap, so we didn't get a good angle of his face. He was white with dark hair."

Jake closed his eyes and replayed the scene in his mind, trying to rewind back to the time when they walked out of the arena. Glimpses of the crowd, flashes of faces. He was focused on Halle and the shouts of the protestors, not the people around him. Images of the dead and the wounded kept interrupting his vision. Needles jabbed his brain as he tried to remember the name of the cop who spotted the bomber.

"I didn't see anyone with a backpack," Jake said, gingerly touching his forehead stitches. "We know what caused the blast?"

"Feds are guessing C4. They talked to an Iraq vet who was there. Said he used it enough to know that's what it was."

"The FBI's here?"

"FBI, local police, some jerk weed with the ATF and Department of Homeland Security is heading our way. Like I said, all-hands-on-deck."

Jake didn't have personal experience with C4. He just knew it had the consistency of modeling clay and it could be triggered with a simple detonator or blasting cap. The question was where did they get it? "Anything else from the footage?"

"Not much. At one point he turned from the camera outside the arena, looking down the street, and made a gesture we can't quite make out."

"Any guesses?"

Ogio's lips pressed together. "If I had to make a wager, I'd guess he's giving someone nearby a thumbs-up. He looked upward—maybe someone in a nearby building was watching."

Jake really wanted to check out the footage, the gears in his head turning. "So not a lone wolf?"

Ogio's bald head swept slowly side to side. "I'd say no. You got nothing else for me?"

"Sorry, man. If I think of anything, I'll give you a call."

Ogio fished a business card from his wallet, holding it out to Jake between two bony fingers. "Hope your girl is okay, Jake. Good to see you outside of an interrogation room."

Jake took his card and snagged one of his PI cards from his own wallet. A plain white card with his name and cell number. "If you hear any more details, let me know."

Ogio nodded and left.

Jake sat at Halle's bed and took her hand, kissing her scraped knuckles.

Guy with a backpack.

C4 explosive.

The bomber himself may be spread in a thousand pieces across Grand Avenue, but whoever sent him was still out there.

Pressing his forehead against the cool skin of Halle's hand, he closed his eyes and relived the moments before the explosion, wondering if there was something he could have done to switch places with his daughter.

CHAPTER SEVEN

Mara grinded against Hunter, palms pressed against the top of the headboard, a sheen of sweat coating her pale skin. She let loose a primal groan, the first tones that her crescendo approached. It was a good thing she was closing in on her orgasm, because he was nowhere in the ballpark. Hunter grabbed her ass and pumped his hips faster, hoping it would help his failing erection. He knew Mara had sixty seconds to come or she would end up finishing herself off with the vibrator she kept in the nightstand.

He hoped the concert bombing might generate the same heat in his loins that it did in Mara's. Maybe the prospect they were one step closer to their goal would excite him. But he was numb. He'd killed at least a dozen people with the push of a button, and yet the same numbness rolled through him as if he'd popped a balloon with a pin.

He also thought the bombing might appease Eddie's ghost and allow Hunter a moment of peace without his best friend's dead eyes showing up uninvited yet again and boring a hole into his soul.

It didn't. Eddie was still there, his face coated with fine sand from that Iraq hellhole, a trickle of blood snaking its way from his fractured skull to his flat nose. Hunter jerked his head from side to side, trying to shake the image that wouldn't leave. The farther they traveled down this road, the more unwelcomed appearances Eddie made.

Maybe he should've blown himself to smithereens after Eddie died. Hunter built the suicide vest after learning how to make them from a local interpreter assigned to accompany him while on light duty. The plan had been to avenge Eddie and assuage his guilt by blowing up President Bush when he came to Iraq. But the trip was cancelled, and the doctors had noticed something unsettling about Hunter. He was discharged. Borderline antisocial personality disorder they'd called it. Shrinks.

Mara's ecstasy-laden scream bounced off the brick walls of their bedroom and sucked Hunter back to the present. She came, her body quivering as she collapsed against Hunter's bare chest, panting a jagged rhythm against him. He slipped out of her and rolled to the nightstand, grabbing his cigarettes, despite the fact he'd quit ten years ago. The stress of the last few months moved his intake far beyond the once in a blue moon when he drank. The alarm clock read one in the morning.

"You okay, baby?" Mara asked.

He collapsed back against his pillow and blew a plume of smoke into the whirling ceiling fan blades overhead, watching the smoke disperse. "I'm fine."

She twirled the hairs on his chest, her cobalt blue eyes turning up. "Don't I turn you on anymore?"

He took another drag, focusing on the dark wood

of the slow, spinning blades of the fan. "Of course you do. I just got a lot rolling around my head."

"Should I be worried?"

"It's not you, it's me. You let the local media know about Death To Religion being responsible?"

"Sent them some pics and the video we shot last week," she said.

Mara was a master with Photoshop and video editing software. A handy skillset to have when you're trying to influence the media.

"We should've bought stock in burner phones the way we go through them," she continued. "I never heard of DTR, but made it sound like I did. Where'd you come up with it?"

"I didn't. He did."

"Mister X?"

"DTR's an east coast group who have more of an affinity for fires than bombs," Hunter said. "But they fit the bill of a group who'd go off on a bunch of religious nuts."

"But if they—"

"Goddamn it, I don't want to talk about it. Jesus. What's done is done."

Mara studied Hunter's face before she pinched her eyes shut and breathed deep, her fingers pulling on his chest hair. He'd pushed too hard. When her eyes opened, he offered a weak, apologetic smile. She hopped off the bed and disappeared into the bathroom, yellow light spilling across the hardwood floor. The toilet flushed a minute later.

He shouldn't have been so abrupt with her. It rarely sat well. She was loyal but rash if crossed. Her old boyfriend from college learned the hard way after she drove his car into the front yard of his fraternity and set it on fire. Got her kicked out of school but reunited her with Hunter and Eddie. He remembered the first time he saw Mara and Eddie together and the ache in his soul it had caused. Everything circled back to Eddie.

In Iraq, Eddie dubbed their group The Horsemen. A group of six soldiers that sprouted from Eddie's vision. Using their military contacts to smuggle drugs out of Iraq made them a lot of money and operated like a well-oiled machine. Until Eddie wanted out.

Don't let 'em get away with it. Those were the last words Eddie said to him before the lights went out in his eyes and blood streamed across his stubbled face. Right before Eddie ran headlong to his death, the two fantasized what they would do when they got back home. Get absolutely annihilated in the Westport bars, eat too much Kansas City barbecue and get lost for a week in the Bermuda triangle of some hot twenty-something coeds.

Eddie had wiped his grimy, sweaty face with a towel, his M240B resting against one broad shoulder. "Hell, I might camp between her legs and never come up for air."

"The only thing that's going to be camping is your hand on your dick as you cry alone in the bedroom of your shitty apartment," Hunter said.

Eddie threw the towel at Hunter. Fuck you, muchacho. I'll always have Mara as a backup. Ten minutes later, he ran across the road and the world blew apart.

Mara returned and plucked the cigarette from Hunter's fingers. Hunter relaxed. Her return meant she wasn't going to spin into one of her depression cycles where she locked herself away for days. From the sultry look in her eyes, she had something else in mind. He wasn't in the mood with Eddie holding court in his mind.

Mara took a drag and stubbed it out in the ashtray on the night stand. Plucking an ice cube from Hunter's drink, she ran her tongue over the edges and rubbed the cube on the nipples of her perfect breasts until they were stiff enough to hang clothes on. She knew Hunter liked it.

"No more tonight, babe," he protested, pushing to get up.

Mara pressed him back to the pillows and straddled him, her long legs locking him in place. "Don't think of Eddie. Think of me."

She knew him too well. "Mara, I'm serious. I don't—"

"I'm serious too," she whispered. She ran the ice cube across his lips and kissed them, tugging at his bottom lip with her teeth. She slid her wetness against him, back and forth, soft and silky, and his resistance melted like the ice cube against her tongue. "No more Eddie tonight. Look at me and tell me the plan."

Hunter turned his head. Eddie sat in the chair in the corner, clad in blood-stained fatigues, eyes smoldering, blood trickling down his face like a tear.

Mara grabbed his face and forced his eyes to hers. "Tell me the plan. Step one."

"Sow chaos," he gasped, responding to her forceful touch.

She moaned from somewhere deep and dark, pressing harder against his crotch, grabbing his hands and placing them on her breasts. "Step two."

He rolled her nipples as she liked. "Let the pressure build."

She dug her fingers into his powerful pecs. "It's

definitely building. Step three?"

Hunter was at full attention now. "Let them kill themselves in the crossfire."

"Ooooh, now we're talking, baby." She drew her cold tongue down his body, grasping his steel in her hand. "And the final step?"

He locked onto her azure eyes. "Burn the whole fucking thing to the ground."

She smiled, drawing the tip of her tongue over blinding white teeth. "Anarchy."

She slid both the ice cube and him into her mouth.

The light, pink birthmark on the back of her neck bobbed. Some confused it for a bad tattoo. Hunter thought it now looked like a bird in flight. He locked his hands behind his head, his biceps bulging as he tracked the blades on the ceiling fan again. He flicked his eyes to the chair in the corner, but Eddie was gone. Mara always knew how to make him feel better.

CHAPTER EIGHT

A cool hand at the back of his neck drew Jake from his restless slumber in the uncomfortable chair perched at the side of Halle's bed. He rubbed sleep from his eyes, casting away a dream about his father Stony chasing his fifteen-year-old self around the house with a broken bottle of Jack Daniels, threatening to cut Jake's throat. It was only a dream. In real life, the bottle hadn't been broken. He craned his neck to find Maggie standing over him, her blonde hair pulled back in a frazzled ponytail.

"Hey, lady," he said, standing to wrap his arms around her. Over her shoulder, he noted the clock. He'd been out for a good two hours and guilt washed over him.

Maggie began to tremble, then let loose, tears soaking through Jake's shirt. After a minute, the crying slowed, and she choked in a few deep breaths. "How's she doing?"

Jake winced as he arched his back. Leaning over Halle's bed for the last few hours did him no favors. "No change as far as I know. I must've crashed."

Maggie moved to the bedside, brushing Halle's hair back. She bent and kissed her daughter on the forehead, a tear drop falling to Halle's cheek. Maggie wiped it away with a gentle swipe of her thumb.

"The doctors haven't said anything?" she asked.

"Not since midnight or so. She's sedated and probably won't wake up until morning."

Maggie swept a stray lock of hair from Halle's cheek, her fingers trailing over the stubble near the drain and surgical site. "She's going to be pissed they shaved her head."

Jake laughed. It felt good. "She is. What's it like out there?"

"People are flying around out there. Bodies everywhere. The ER's like a war zone."

"You drive yourself?"

She shook her head. "Bear. Audrey came over and is staying with Connor. Can't believe the little guy didn't wake up the way I stumbled around."

Jake yawned wide enough to pop his jaw. "Kid sleeps like a hibernating bear."

"I resemble that remark," Bear said, filling the doorway of the hospital room clad in jeans and a leather jacket. His best friend broke the threshold and wrapped Jake in a tight hug. "How you doin', partner?"

"Sore," Jake wheezed. "Don't squeeze the air outta me."

Bear released him and clasped Jake's shoulders. "Sorry, man. How's our girl?"

"Still out. Her hair will grow back, but the nasty cut on her forehead is probably going to scar which will piss her off."

"Bah. It'll give her character. She's gorgeous

enough to pull off a little scar."

Bear crossed to the side of the bed opposite Maggie and took Halle's hand. He dipped his head as he closed his eyes, his lips moving almost imperceptibly. Jake hadn't seen the county sheriff pray, but he supposed every little bit would help at this point.

"You talk to any cops out there?" Jake asked.

"That Detective Ogio cat. He flagged me down. Must've remembered me from the Ares bioweapon briefcase clusterfuck."

"Feds?"

Bear's lip curled. "Recognized a few faces, but nobody I'd want to talk to. Been trying to call our FBI buddies. Foster's phone goes right to voice mail. You should call Snell and let her know what's going on. This shit's a full-on Federal case now. We need every bit of intel we can get."

Jake dipped his head in agreement. "I'll call her when the sun comes up."

"What the hell happened?" Bear asked.

A nurse came in to check vitals and add a new saline bag. When she left, Jake told him and Maggie the story. "You know a cop named Wilson? Black guy, eyes like an owl?"

Bear chewed on his whiskers for a beat. "Doesn't ring a bell. Why?"

"He helped us out at the scene. I pointed out another cop named Madsen who said he saw the guy with the backpack. Madsen looked like someone took a filet knife to his face. Was wondering how he was doing."

"And what he saw."

Jake nodded. "That too."

"Want me to poke around?"

"That'd be good. I'm staying here until her eyes open."

Bear kissed Halle's forehead. He whispered something in her ear and walked toward the door, wiping his eyes. When he disappeared, Jake wrapped his arm around Maggie's shoulder and they stood, Halle's hand in both of theirs, praying for her to wake.

*****

Moonlight snaked through the blinds of the room and across Maggie's sleeping form as she slumped in the uncomfortable chair Jake slept in earlier. Their RN wheeled a bed into the room a few hours ago, but Jake couldn't sleep. Instead, he spent the hours lying on the thin mattress, running the scene through his head and watching the footage on television, flipping the muted channels between CNN, Fox News and the local stations. The Feds had raided the house of some guy with DTR and found nothing. Another group called God's Avenging Angels vowed retribution on the DTR and any other gang they were affiliated with.

With each click of the remote and each new angle of the blast scene, his anger and frustration built. He paced the floor of Halle's room as he watched the montage of different cities mobbed with protestors who pillaged, burned and screamed to the sky over bombings, fires, police shootings. You could almost hear the social fabric of the nation tearing apart.

Jake's face grew hot at the thought of the sheer cowardice of the monster who did this, his fists wanting to strike out at something. Jake was old school. You looked a man in the eye when you took him down because taking a person's life had to be a personal thing and you'd better have a goddamn good reason for doing it. There was nothing personal about a bomb dropped off in a crowd. His vision blotted red as watched his unconscious daughter, uncertain if she would live or die.

Whoever was behind this was a psychopath. A psychopath with a reason. Jake had to figure out what it was. If he could figure out the reason, maybe he could find him. He pounded the thick wooden bathroom door with a clenched fist, biting back the urge to scream until Maggie wrapped herself around him and told him it was going to be okay.

CHAPTER NINE

Knuckles rapped on the door to Halle's room a few minutes past seven the next morning. His second favorite FBI agent stuck her head through the door. Jake waved her inside. Foster had let her dusky hair grow to her athletic shoulders. She managed a weak smile, lifting the dark bags camping under her eyes. Bear trailed in behind her.

"Hey, stranger," she said.

Jake knew she wasn't much of a hugger, but she wrapped her strong arms around his waist anyway. "I take it Bear found you?"

"Rescued me is more like it," she said, releasing him. "I can't do another interview with another person who didn't see anything. It's frustrating as hell."

Maggie stirred and sat up in the chair. She blinked the sleep away and squinted at Foster. "What time is it?"

Jake swept an arm toward his wife. "Foster, this is Maggie."

Maggie stood. She hid a deep yawn behind her fist and crossed the room to shake Foster's hand. "I've heard a lot about you."

Agent Foster nodded. "How's your girl?"

"She's going to be fine. I know it in my bones. I'm going to find a cup of coffee. Would you like a coffee, Agent Foster?" Maggie offered.

Foster waved her off. "I'm fine, thanks. I drink any more and my heart will explode."

"I'll let you three talk. Nice to meet you."

Foster tracked Maggie as she headed out the door. "She's too pretty for you, Jake. You outkicked your coverage."

Bear huffed. "More like kicked it out of the stadium."

"Don't remind her," Jake said.

Foster glanced to the bed. "What do the doctors say?"

"She's going to be fine. I hope. You talk to Snell?"

"She's on her way down from Omaha. Should be here in a couple hours. You want to talk here or go somewhere else?"

"Here's fine," Jake said. "What do you know?"

"Not much. We've pulled every piece of security footage we can get our hands on from the arena and street cameras. Have a dozen techs combing through it for anything useful, but whoever did this covered their tracks pretty well."

"Cops said there's footage of the bomber," Bear said. "Any chance of making an ID?"

"It's grainy footage. He emerges from the building shadows on the east side of Grand. Starts walking while talking on a cell phone. At one point he stops and turns. Even then, his hat was pulled low, and we don't get a good face shot. Still, we blasted the image across the networks to see if anyone recognizes him. Tips are pouring through the local police station, but you know how it goes."

Bear grunted. "A bunch of unreliable tips from people hoping to get a reward. A needle in a haystack, if you're lucky."

"Even though we can't see the guy," Foster continued, "we're trying to back track his movement through street cameras. Unfortunately, KC doesn't have as many as we'd like. Looks like he snaked his way to the arena from the south, stays in the dark where he could and keeps his head low. The thing is, when we picked him up on the cameras from the south, he doesn't have a backpack."

"It means someone met him there with it or they planted it somewhere beforehand," Jake said. "Anyone walking with him?"

Foster rubbed her eyes and yawned. "Not that we've seen. There were thousands of people crawling around the outside of the arena before the concert. We're combing the footage, but it's going to be tough to pin anyone down."

"What about security footage from local businesses?" Bear asked.

"Checking that, too. The bomber turned and gave a thumbs-up to somebody. If we can triangulate where he was looking, maybe it'll give us a hint where to start. We have footage from a few of the businesses, but others haven't opened yet. Some don't have cameras and a tattoo parlor said theirs wasn't working."

Jake closed his eyes and mapped out the area. The bomber came in from south of the arena along Grand Avenue. I-70 ran east to west under a bridge just before Truman Road, a good distance from the arena, but still within a line of sight. The Power & Light District was a few square blocks of bars and restaurants bustled across Grand Avenue. The guy was looking south, down the hill. There was a furniture store, record shop and a restaurant on the west side of Grand and a diner, vape shop and the tattoo shop Foster mentioned on the east side. Jake knew the guy who ran the place. There were a few lofts and offices above the businesses. Past that, you'd be too far to see much of anything.

"You think this is related to the recent bombings in other cities?" Bear asked. "This DTR group?"

Foster shrugged. "Could be related, though this DTR may be a dead end. Someone blew the head off an activist in Dallas, someone responded in Tulsa and wiped out a few on the right. Seattle took out some left-wing nuts and an abortion clinic was bombed in Chicago, the group called God's Avenging Angels claimed it was their handiwork. Now someone wipes out the religious nuts from Topeka."

"Seems like these extremist groups retaliating against each other," Jake said.

"I agree," Foster said. "Army of God, Proud Boys, Antifa have all been in the area and active in the riots but deny they were involved when questioned, which isn't surprising."

"It's fun being in the spotlight until the government comes knocking," Bear said.

Foster sighed. "Everyone's a suspect. The House Intelligence Committee is digging into it, exerting a lot of pressure to produce records of what we know and when we knew it."

"The committee's full of snakes," Bear snarled. "I wouldn't piss on any of them if they were on fire."

"I don't know. Something doesn't feel right," Jake said, thinking out loud. "Those groups like to announce their presence with authority."

"But they also won't step up claiming they blew up a bunch of people," Foster said. "You'll know what I know when I know it. I'll give you a holler when Snell gets here and we can touch base. I'm going to head back and kick over some more rocks."

"Maybe Bear and I will do the same once Halle wakes up," Jake said. "Can you get us the security footage of the guy with the thumbs-up?"

"You trying to get me fired?"

"I was thinking promoted. I know these streets, the people. Maybe I can find something you can't. You can have the glory."

She sighed. "I could use a little glory. Let me see what I can do, but no promises."

Foster took one last look at Halle's sleeping form and patted Jake and Bear on their arms as she left the room and disappeared down the hall.

Bear's eyes narrowed. "You think Maggie is going to let you leave here and kick over rocks?"

"Unless you have a better idea. I sit here much longer with my thumb up my ass and I'm going to start climbing the walls."

"But Maggie will—"

"Whoever tried to blow me and Halle to bits are still walking around out there drawing oxygen. It ain't right. Plus, I got a feeling they're going to strike again."

Bear slipped a tobacco pouch between his cheek and gum. "You're going to get us in trouble again, aren't you?"

Jake's hands dropped to his sides, a familiar gleam in his eyes. "Now, when has that ever happened?"

NOW

CHAPTER TEN

Dr. Tate set the manila folder with Jake's skimpy questionnaire on the floor at the base of her chair. "You used the word justice. Can you define it for me?"

Jake rolled his palms up. "Aren't you the one with the PhD, doc? It's a pretty simple word."

"With a variety of meanings depending on who is using it," Dr. Tate said.

"How do you mean?"

"Well, in Afghanistan a few years ago, the Taliban tracked down a woman who was forced to marry against her will and ran away with another man. After a couple of days, they caught both of them. They buried the woman in a hole leaving her head showing and stoned her to death for adultery. Hurled rocks at her head at close range until she died. The Taliban would no doubt call it justice for her crime. But would we?"

Jake shifted in his seat. "Jesus, no. It's goddamn medieval."

"But not to them. It's part of their culture, the way they were raised. It's their justice. What does justice mean to you, Jake?"

Jake searched the ceiling for an answer, trying to think of a way to explain it to her so it made sense. "It's kind of like porn."

Her eyebrows drew together. "I don't follow you."

"I was watching some news show a few months ago, and they talked about some semi-famous guy who was brought up on pornography charges. The porn guy's lawyer said his guy's stuff was a form of free speech protected by the first amendment. The prosecutor said obscene speech is unprotected speech according to the Supreme Court, so the first amendment didn't apply."

"How does this apply to your definition of justice?"

Jake snatched another mint. "The prosecutor quoted a Supreme Court justice. Said something like, I won't attempt to define what's obscene, but I'll know it when I see it. The same applies with justice for me. I know it when I see it."

Jake reclined and popped the mint in his mouth, clacking the candy against his teeth. He let a wry grin creep up, proud of himself.

Dr. Tate wasn't impressed with his knowledge of Supreme Court precedence. "If you're going to quote Justice Potter Stewart and know it when you see it, then you should be able to give me a definition of your criteria for meting out justice."

Jake's grin melted. Potter Stewart. It sounded like the name of the justice the documentary gave. This woman was smart. His eyes combed her bookshelves, trying to conjure an answer to her question without implicating himself. He didn't think she'd be able to or even would turn him in for admitting to any crimes he may have committed in his past, but it'd be best to avoid pushing the theory to the limit.

"If you talked to the cops," Jake began, "I'm assuming you heard what I used to do."

"If you mean being a leg-breaker for our local mobster Jason Keats, then yes. I heard something."

Being an enforcer for a local mafia heavy wasn't high on Jake's list of proud achievements. The less people knew the better. But her admitting she knew about his past made the telling of the tale easier.

"I haven't told anyone this before," Jake said. "Not Keats, my wife or even my best friend, but I think it'll give you what you're looking for. A few years back, Keats sent me to Overland Park to pick up five grand from a lawyer who had a gambling problem. I go to his house and knock on the door. No answer, but I hear a woman scream and something break inside. I pound again and this guy flings open the door, eyes bloodshot, shirt half-untucked, chest heaving. I tell him who I am, and he mumbles he doesn't have any cash on him, and he'll get me something next week. Then he tries to slam the door on me. Big mistake."

"What'd you do?"

"Bust the door open hard enough to crack the schmuck in the face. He screams and hollers I can't be in there, a heavy stench of bourbon seeping from his pores. I get, um, persuasive, say he'd better produce something, or I'm going to break things, starting with his kneecaps and work my way up."

To her credit, Dr. Tate appeared unaffected by the story. Then again, Jake supposed she'd heard all kinds of things if she counseled traumatized cops.

"Did he give you anything?"

"I followed him into his office where he had a safe hidden in a bookshelf," Jake said. "He handed me four grand and promised to have the rest in a couple of days. I verified it was all the cash in there and turned to leave. That's when I saw her."

"Who?"

"The wife. She sat on the kitchen floor, a shattered vase surrounding her, a bruise the size of Texas on her cheek. An old, yellowed bruise that had been there for a while and a fresh, red one on the other side. I grew up with that shit and nothing sets me off like a wife beater. I ask her if she's okay, but she stares at the floor and wrings her hands. The guy says 'She's fine, Superman.' I crowded him back against the bookcase and told him she'd better be fine. I manage to hold back the urge to use the guy's head to break those fine oak bookshelves and leave."

"And that's justice? Verbally standing up for her?" Dr. Tate asked.

Jake clenched his fists. "Two weeks later, the wife is found dead in a shallow grave down in Swope Park. Beaten to death. The husband is cleared pretty quick. Was supposedly out of town at the time of the murder and, being a lawyer, he has friends. He walks away from it."

"But you think he did it."

"I know he did it. I'd bet my life on it."

"But how do you know for sure?"

Jake chewed on his upper lip. "I ran into him at Hollywood Casino a week later. Asked him how his wife was."

"Why?"

"Because I'm a dick and wanted to see how he'd react. He winked and said, 'Where she deserves to be, Superman'."

Dr. Tate blew out a breath. "Jesus."

"There's people in this world who can't ask for justice because they're too afraid or can't demand it because they're dead. Then there's people like me who do it for them. I do it because it's the right thing to do and nobody else will."

"Did this lawyer get his justice?"

Jake took another mint and rolled it in his fingers, eyes locked on the swirls of red and white. "I heard he was found dead in his home a few days later. Shot in the forehead."

"You heard?"

He shrugged. "What can I say? The world is a dangerous place."

She cocked her head, studying his face. "Justice."

"Sometimes her scales tilt in the right direction."

THEN

CHAPTER ELEVEN

Jake and Bear traversed the sidewalk outside the hospital, getting some fresh air. Cars flashed by along the street during the morning commute.

"You find out anything from Wilson or Madsen?" Jake asked. "The cops I asked you about?"

"Found Wilson. He said Madsen died two minutes after you left. Didn't give a description of the guy with the backpack."

"Damn. Standing on square one still."

"Square one is food. Maybe there's a downtown diner we could hit up," Bear offered.

"There's a cafeteria here."

Bear winced.

"You'd pass up hospital food?" Jake asked.

"I'd pass a kidney stone over hospital food."

Jake's cell vibrated. Maggie.

"I need you to come back to the room," Maggie said, her voice quivering. "Now."

"Jesus, Mags. What is it?"

The words caught in her throat. "Just get here."

The call ended and Jake stared at the phone, a

thousand negative thoughts and images flooding his brain. He jerked his head up. "Something's wrong with Halle."

Jake and Bear darted toward the elevators. Jake jammed the up button a dozen times, panicked eyes locked on the descending numbers.

What horrible news could the doctors have brought while he was gone? Had Halle taken a turn for the worse? Oh Jesus, did she die? The incessant buzz of a monitor registering a flatline bounced around his brain, the accompanying image of Halle lying motionless beneath the machines as doctors hovered over her shaking their heads. He rubbed his temples with his fingers, willing the image to go away, but Halle's pale, motionless face remained, lips parted as if they'd failed to hold back her last breath.

"Easy, partner," Bear whispered, patting Jake on the back.

The elevator doors opened at last and Jake split the crowd of people exiting, smacking the button for the fourth floor as if the more times and harder he pressed it, the faster the doors would close. An old woman shuffled on with a walker, fuzzy yellow tennis balls lodged in the base to help it slide across the linoleum. Bear followed in behind her. What was he thinking? Leaving Halle before she woke up and Maggie alone to bear the brunt of the bad news. Tears stung his eyes.

As the elevator lurched up, a gentle hand laid on his arm. He glanced at the old woman. She bowed her snow-topped head, lips moving silently. The paper-thin skin of her gnarled hand clutched Jake with surprising strength. The door dinged and slid open at the third floor.

The old woman released him and craned her long, thin neck to Jake. "Looked like you could use a little help from above."

"I could," Jake said, holding the door open before it closed on her. "Thank you."

The woman offered a slow wink as she pushed the walker forward. "The Lord works in mysterious ways. I have a feeling he'll be working for you today."

Jake watched her shuffle until the doors shut. He hoped she was right.

Outside of Halle's room, he inhaled a lungful of the sterile hospital air, steeling himself for a moment before crossing the threshold. A doctor in a white, knee-length coat stood at the side of the bed with his back blocking Jake's view of Halle. Maggie stood on the opposite side of Halle's bed, her arms clutching herself, eyes full of tears.

Jake's heart stopped.

The old woman's prayers weren't enough.

He was too late.

He latched onto the door frame, digging his fingers into the wood. Memories of Halle crashing his brain like waves on a rocky shore. Running the hills of Warsaw together, watching her track meets, teaching her to shoot guns and moving her into the dorms.

A groan escaped his lips, the sound causing the doctor to turn. When he did, it revealed Halle's angelic face looking across the room at him. Relief swept through him at her open blue eyes and the time-stopping smile crossing her face.

"Hey, Dad," she said, her voice cracked and strained, but still the most beautiful two words to ever grace his ears.

Jake's knees buckled. He made it to the side of

the bed and grasped Halle's hands, covering her forehead with kisses. A hot tear dripped onto her cheek. "Oh, thank God."

Maggie took Halle's other hand. "I'm sorry if I worried you with the call."

"Scared the shit out of me is more like it."

"Doctor Williams came in with the test results... the look on his face freaked me out and I didn't want to hear what he had to say without you here. After I hung up, this little bugger opened her eyes."

"How you feelin', kiddo?" Jake asked.

"Like I drank a gallon of vodka last night." She shot her eyes to Maggie. "Not that I'd know what that's like."

"I'll bet," Maggie said.

Halle turned back to Jake, wincing from the effort. "Where'd you go?"

"Stepped outside to get some fresh air and Bear some food. Man, it's good to see those blue eyes again."

"Did you figure out who did this to us?"

Jake ran a hand along her forehead. "Not yet. Been too worried about you."

Halle pressed her lips in a line and squeezed Jake's hand. "Whoever did this is the one who should be worried. Half my head is shaved and I have a tube coming out of my skull. Nobody does this to a Caldwell."

Jake had never been more proud of his daughter.

CHAPTER TWELVE

"You're leaving?" Maggie said, venom dripping from each whispered word. "Our daughter just woke up from major brain surgery. You must've gotten whacked in the head harder than you thought if you think you're stepping one toe of those boots out of this hospital."

"I'm not going far, just downtown," Jake said, hands on her shoulders. Halle had fallen back asleep, but the doc said it was normal. "Bear and I are going to poke around and see what we can find. You call me the second you need anything, and I can be back here in less than fifteen minutes."

Maggie opened her mouth and Jake winced at what would to come out. She closed it, sucked in a deep breath through her nose and blew it between her thin lips. When she spoke, her voice was edgy, but controlled. "There's a hundred law enforcement agents and local cops combing the area and the hospital. What exactly are you and Grizzly Adams going to figure out that they can't?"

Bear muttered, "No offense taken."

Maggie glared. "Stay out of this, Bear."

Bear stepped back, slowly, like he was afraid he would step on a land mine. Given the look in Maggie's eyes, it wasn't far from the truth. "Listen, I'll head out and start poking around. If I hear anything, I'll call you."

"Bear, wait," Jake said, but Bear was already out the door. He turned right and disappeared.

"We were going to check around and ask some questions," Jake said. "And you're right, there's cops and feds crawling around the area like white on rice, but I know the people in the area. They don't. These people will talk to me, but not the police. We'll be careful. I gotta do something, Mags."

Bear passed by the door again, his face crunched in confusion, muttering to himself.

Maggie ran her fingers through her long wheat-colored hair and lowered herself to a two-seat couch along the wall by the window. "You had to do something when Snell's daughter was kidnapped. You had to do something when a Russian spy shot up your cabin. Or when Shane Langston escaped. Or Keats waved a wad in your face to find his missing money laundering cash. It's always something."

"And I come through every time."

"After a lot of shit gets broken. Your daughter's broken now, Jake. She needs you. You can't fix everything."

Bear appeared at the door, opened his mouth to say something, but Jake waived him off. He walked off to the right again.

Jake sat by Maggie and took her hand. "You know what Halle told me as we walked out of the concert? The last thing she said before the explosion? She told me she was proud of me for going after the bad guys, for doing what's right even when it makes you mad."

Maggie's chin dipped. "She told me the same thing after your little adventure in Nebraska. But—"

"You know me, Mags. You know how I'm wired. I can't sit here and do nothing while the madman who almost killed me and our daughter is out there running loose. I'm going to start punching holes in the wall if I don't do something. Maybe I can't fix everything, but maybe I can play a hand in fixing this. I have contacts on these streets. Maybe one of them heard something that'll lead us to these people. Maybe I can play a hand in stopping this from happening somewhere else."

She stroked the back of his hand. "That's a lot of maybes."

"I'm an optimist. Maybe means it's possible."

"Or maybe you want revenge for Halle."

Jake sandwiched her hands between his. "I'd consider that a win-win scenario."

Bear stepped into the room. "Sorry to interrupt, but where the hell is the exit? Been walking around in a circle. This place is fucking confusing."

Maggie bit back her amusement and waved Jake to the door. "Jesus, go before this dumb galoot gets so lost we'll never find him." Her eyes rose to meet his. "No more than fifteen minutes away?"

"I'll come running the second you call."

"No drama?"

An ongoing joke between the two of them. Jake always promised no drama. Sometimes he was able to keep the promise. Sometimes people forced him to break it. And when it broke, it tended to get bloody.

"No drama," he said, kissing her on the forehead.

"Bear?" Maggie asked. Bear turned from the

doorway, hands shoved in the pockets of his leather coat. "No drama. Jake promised. If he breaks it, I'm holding you responsible."

Bear scowled. "Well, that hardly seems fair. Jake's a dick. I can't be held responsible for how people react to him."

"Then don't let him act like one. Be careful, you two."

Jake planted a gentle kiss on Halle's forehead and followed Bear out the door. They walked in silence toward the elevator.

"You like how I faked like I was lost to spring you?" Bear asked.

"Sure, let's go with 'you faked it'."

"I was, kind of." Bear rubbed his ample belly. "Any chance we can grab a little grub first at some place other than the hospital cafeteria? My stomach is eating itself."

"I know, I can hear it. You're lucky a doctor didn't tackle you thinking you had some gastrointestinal disease."

"I need some bacon."

"We don't have time to eat. Too many questions to be answered."

Bear batted his statement away. "So long as you have bacon in your mouth, you have solved all questions for the time being."

"Fine. There's a breakfast place down the street from the arena. We should hit the area anyway."

The elevator doors slid open and they climbed inside.

"Is it a real breakfast place?" Bear asked. "Or one of those that serves organic, free range eggs from chicken who get weekly massages or avocado toast on artisanal bread. My body craves grease."

Jake pressed the lobby button. "It's a real place with real food."

Bear growled. "It better be real or I'll whine your ass into next week. What about after breakfast?"

Jake's mental map of downtown displayed. The Feds were focused on the bombing site, and Jake and Bear wouldn't be able to get close to it, anyway. Jake was more interested in the path the bomber took to get there. Foster said they already had footage from street cameras and businesses. Except one. The tattoo shop.

The doors opened and they crossed the crowded lobby. "After we stuff your never-ending gullet, we start at a distance and work our way back toward the bombing site. If the bomber looked back and signaled someone, the person couldn't be anywhere beyond I-70."

"The Feds already have the footage," Bear said.

"Not all of it. The tattoo shop."

"Let me guess. You know they guy who runs it."

"I do. And he's the type who wouldn't cooperate with the cops out of spite. He's had issues. I have to make a call first to get some information."

Bear groaned. "If you say you're gonna call Jason fucking Keats, I'm going to knock your teeth out."

Jake slid his cell from his jeans. Jake's reliance on his old mob boss was a continuous source of tension between Jake and Bear. "Fine. I won't say it."

"You are such an asshole, Caldwell."

CHAPTER THIRTEEN

Jake and Bear headed toward the diner, passing the Lit Ink Tattoo and Body Piercing Shop on the way. The inside of the shop was dark, and the sign on the door said they didn't open until ten o'clock. Jake scanned the front of the building. A security camera hung from one end of the emerald awning, pointed toward the front door. He scanned the underbelly of the awning and spotted a black wire coming through the front wall and running to the top corner. Stepping back to the street, he noted the camera pointed toward the building across the street. He turned his head toward the red-bricked building—nothing but darkened windows.

Bear studied the window of the tattoo and body piercing shop. "What do you think the 'Lit' in Lit Ink means?"

"Lit is slang for exciting or cool," Jake said, returning to his side. "As in that party was lit last night."

"I thought it was slang for being hammered. As in I got so lit at the party last night, I puked in the punch bowl."

"I don't think people use punch bowls any more, old man. Besides, the last thing you want is for your body piercer to be drunk lit."

"I think I'd have to be drunk lit to let some dude shove a needle into my body. Did you hear Johnny Huener got his dick pierced?"

Jake shuddered. "Jesus, why?"

"Exactly. Makes me want to throw up thinking about it."

Jake patted him on the shoulder. "Well, trust me. Nobody wants to see any part of your body pierced. Especially that one."

"Hey, I have the same chiseled physique you do, Caldwell. It's just hidden behind artfully crafted layers of fat."

They continued past a vape store to the Grand Avenue Diner. Jake held the rustic red door open for Bear. Aromas of grease and the sizzling pops of frying meats kicked the starter switch of Jake's appetite. The place held a dozen or so tables covered with butcher paper. Booths lined the smudged windows giving view to the street. Half the place was occupied with cops whose faces dragged with weariness. A twenty-foot counter with red-leather-topped bar stools was manned by a plump, grandmotherly type who snagged food from the kitchen window and passed it to a middle-aged, slinky waitress in jeans who had every table under her charge.

They dropped into a booth in the back. A minute later, the waitress worked her way to them with a coffee pot and two mugs in hand, a couple of laminated menus clasped under her arm pit.

"Hi, I'm Bev. Coffee for both of you?" Her almond eyes darted between the two of them waiting for a response.

"God, yes," Bear sighed. "Bless you."

Bev dropped the menus on the table and poured. "You two here because of the bombing?"

"Unfortunately," Jake said. "My daughter and I were caught in the blast as we left the concert last night."

Her mouth fell open, leaning in as she noticed the scrapes on Jake's face. "Jesus, you guys okay?"

"Daughter's at Truman with my wife. She's going to be fine. You hear anything from the cops coming in?"

"No. Think they're too exhausted or shell-shocked. You know what you want to eat?"

"I'll take the left side of the menu," Bear proclaimed.

Bev grinned. "How do you want your eggs?"

"Over easy. Maybe let's start with the eggs, hash browns and two sides of bacon. We'll get to the rest later."

Jake ordered pancakes with hopes he could steal a slice or two of Bear's bacon without getting his hand bitten off. When Bev left, he stood and moved toward the door, pulling out his phone and telling Bear he'd be back in a minute. To his credit, Bear glared but remained silent.

Jake stepped outside and dialed Keats's cell. It was eight in the morning, and there was a ninety-nine percent chance he'd be waking his old boss up. He wasn't wrong.

"Caldwell," Keats mumbled. "What time is it?"

"Morning time. Sorry to wake you."

"What in God's name do you want this early?"

"Information. You have a late night?"

Keats yawned. "Stayed up watching the arena bombing news. Svetlana and Alina went to the concert last night together."

Svetlana was Keats's girlfriend and Alina was a girl he and Jake helped out of a sex-trafficking ring last year. Keats had both of them living at his house.

"They good?" Jake asked.

"Luckily they went out a different exit."

"They are lucky. Halle and I went out the wrong one. We both were hit."

Keats paused. "Aw, I'm sorry. She okay?"

"They had to insert a drain in her skull, but she's awake. In ICU but should be out in three or four days if all goes well."

"Jesus. Well, I'll say a prayer for you guys."

Jake didn't know Keats to be a religious man but figured it couldn't hurt. "Bear and I are grabbing some chow at the Grand Avenue Diner before we start trying to figure out who did this."

"You and every cop and fed in the four-state area."

"I'm going to find these fuckers and string them up by their balls for hurting my girl."

"What can I do?" Keats asked.

"Bear and I are getting ready to go into Lit Ink and talk to Skinny. We're hoping he has some footage off his security cameras that might help us. He still have a gambling problem?"

Keats grunted. "He owes me a grand. It's not due for a couple weeks, but feel free to squeeze his shoes if it helps you out."

"If I squeeze any cash out of him, I'll pass it along. Thanks, Jason."

"No problem. And Jake? If you need anything, I mean anything, to help catch these guys, you let me know. I don't like people blowing shit up in my town. I'll keep my ears open, and if I hear anything, I'll let you know."

Jake ended the call and headed back inside. Bear wolfed down his breakfast like he hadn't eaten in a month. "If you choke from eating too fast, I'm not giving you the Heimlich."

Bear folded a piece of greasy bacon into his mouth. "Like you could get those puny ass stumps of yours around my waistline. What'd Keats say?"

"Skinny, the guy who runs the tattoo parlor, owes him a grand. We have the green light to lean on him."

"Like we needed that crooked motherfucker's permission to do that."

Jake coated his pancakes with butter and syrup and dug in. "But Skinny will probably know I don't collect for Keats anymore. Invoking Keats's name will grease the skids."

"Speaking of grease, this bacon was soaked in it."

"Too much?"

Bear moaned. "Hell, no. It's perfect. And don't think you're getting any of it, either. I see you eyeballin' it."

Twenty minutes later, Jake shoved his plate away as Bear finished a piece of cherry pie. Bev came over and cleared empty plates. "Anything else, gentlemen?"

"Just the check," Jake said.

"It's been taken care of."

"By who?"

"Mr. Keats. He's a regular. He called and told you boys happy hunting."

Jake asked, "You guys have any security cameras out front?"

"Don't need 'em."

"Why not?"

"Keats is a regular, remember?" she said. "Nobody with a brain would hit this place."

As she left, Jake took in the scowl on Bear's mug. "What's the matter? You hate Keats so much you want to turn down a free breakfast?"

"I do hate the guy that much, but if I knew the asshole was buying, I would've ordered a lot more food."

CHAPTER FOURTEEN

Bear tugged on the door handle to Lit Tattoo and Body Piercing, but it wouldn't budge. It was still a while until the store opened, but he cupped his hands around his eyes and pressed his nose against the glass to see past the gleam from the morning sun breaking between the buildings across the street.

"There's a light on in the back," Bear said. "Don't see anybody, though."

Jake reached out and rapped his knuckles on the glass. They waited, but nobody came. "Let's go around back."

They walked down the narrow alley between the tattoo shop and the vape store, stepping over boxes and a sleeping homeless guy who smelled like he'd bathed in cat piss. The alley opened up to a six-space parking lot marked private. A red, vintage Camaro, with two black racing stripes down the hood, parked nose-in to a door labeled "Lit" in yellow stenciled spray paint.

Bear whistled. "Sweet ride, man. A '69?"

"'68, I think. Skinny's had it for a while."

"What's this guy like?"

"A bit of a perv, but he's a great artist. If I was ever going to get inked, Skinny is who I'd come to." Jake tried the handle to the locked back door. "I'll knock, you stand in front of the peephole. Tell him it's a delivery."

Bear ran his hand along the fender of the Camaro, admiring the lines. "You two don't get along?"

"I might have been a little rough retrieving Keats's money from him a few years back. He spots me, he probably won't open the door."

Jake slid to the brick wall to the right of the door. Bear stepped up, thumped on the metal and waited.

"Yeah?" a voice sounded from the other side.

"Got a delivery," Bear said.

"Where's Charlie?" the voice asked after a beat.

"Called in sick today. You want the box or not?"

"Deliveries only accepted during business hours and through the front," the voice said.

Bear rubbed his temples. "Listen, I got a route to run. I tried the front door and nobody answered. You have to sign for it, or I leave it here for the homeless guy in the alley."

The deadbolt snapped back and the door swung open. Jake slid into view and pushed Skinny into the building. The man's girth filled the narrow hallway, his owlish eyes wide with surprise.

"C-Caldwell?" Skinny sputtered. "What the hell are you doing here?"

Bear followed Jake inside and pulled the door closed behind him.

"Let's go to your office," Jake said.

Skinny turned with the speed of a sloth. "You sneaky son of a bitch. Why didn't you wait until I opened and come in through the front door like a normal person?"

They walked ten feet and Skinny squeezed sideways through a door, breathing heavy from the walk. Jake followed him into a ten by fifteen office occupied by a cluttered desk with dual computer monitors and file cabinets crammed with papers. Drawings of tattoos wallpapered the office. Skinny waddled around the desk and dropped into a swivel chair that groaned from the effort. Jake and Bear stationed themselves in front of the desk.

"This is nice," Jake said, fingering a picture of a dragon tattoo Skinny displayed on his wall.

"'Course it's good. I did it." Skinny smoothed the tendrils of thin hair over his balding scalp. They looked like tiger stripes. He scratched the patchy stubble on his cheeks, still wheezing from the walk down the hall. "Whatcha want, Jake? I got a serious shoulder job coming in at ten-thirty, and I know you ain't workin' for Keats anymore."

"Maybe I want a tattoo."

"You woulda come in the front door."

"Still playing poker at Harrah's?"

"Yeah and I've been on a good run of bad luck. What. Do. You. Want?"

Jake tapped the top of the computer monitor. "I want the security footage from your cameras from last night."

Skinny showed off yellow teeth. "Already told the cops the camera ain't workin'. Repair guy was supposed to be out last week and didn't show."

"You know why you lose money at poker, Skinny? Because you're a horrible liar."

Skinny's teeth disappeared. Thankfully. The visual

made Jake's stomach turn. "Piss off, Caldwell. You got no standing around here no more."

Jake leaned in. "You think I won't beat it out of your fat ass, Skinny? Try me. I've had a shitty last twelve hours."

"I pay Keats a monthly fee for protection. You keep hasslin' me and I'll call him."

"Go ahead. I talked to him a few minutes ago, and he said while I'm here, I might as well collect the grand you owe him."

Skinny slumped. "I still got a week."

"Give me the footage and I'll make sure it stays that way. Dick me around anymore and I'll collect it from you right now, one way or another."

"Jesus Christ," Skinny muttered, pounding keys on his computer. He fished a thumb drive from his desk and downloaded the file. He handed it to Jake. "There. After the bombing, I skimmed through it and didn't see anything, but knock yourself out. Now will you get outta here?"

"What about the footage from your other camera?"

Skinny's eyes shot down. "What other camera?"

"The next time you lie to me I'm going to find out how many layers of your gut fat I can punch my fist through. The camera aimed across the street you tried to hide in the awning. Why do you have one pointed over there anyway?"

"I'm telling you, there's no—"

Jake raised his clenched fist and started around the desk.

"Okay, okay!" Skinny's face flushed. "There's a girl up on the third floor. She's a painter."

"So?"

"She likes to paint naked in front of the window,

and she has a rack to die for," Skinny said, white spittle forming at the corners of his mouth. "I mean, my dying wish would be for her to lean over my coffin. I'm telling you, these things are—"

Jake flashed his palms. "I get the point."

He wouldn't be surprised if Skinny had an entire archive of this woman. He had a history of doing crap like this. What was it Detective Ogio said in the hospital? It was almost like the bomber was looking up. "And I suppose you have her on video from last night?"

"Why do you think I told the Feds the cameras weren't workin'?"

Bear stepped around the desk. "Show us."

Skinny twisted his head around, the fat folds bunching up like an ugly Shar-Pei. "Who are you?"

Bear clamped his hand on Skinny's head and forced it back to the monitor. "Your worst nightmare if you don't pull up the footage."

Jake crowded around the desk by Bear who wiped his now greasy palm on his jeans, lip curled in disgust. Skinny groaned as he punched up the security feed. The camera was trained on the east side of the building across the street, zoomed in to pick up a framing shot of four windows. The video feed was already cued to the woman in question. Her dark hair stopped at bare shoulders as she painted a canvas by the window. Skinny might be a scumbag, but he wasn't a liar. The woman was topless, attractive and had high, firm breasts as she worked her brush back and forth. The quality of the video wasn't high definition by any means, but it was good enough. A Mona Lisa smile perched on her face as her head flicked toward the window on occasion.

Bear whistled. "She knows she's being watched."

"And doesn't care," Skinny said. "When she's painting, guys hang out in front of my store."

Jake checked the time stamp on the bottom of the video feed. The bombing happened at 10:42 last night. It was a long shot they'd find anything helpful on the video, but it was worth a look. "Fast forward to ten-thirty."

Skinny's brow bunched. "Fast forward? You'll miss the best part. Besides, she's gone by then. She only paints for an hour."

"Just do it, numb nuts."

Skinny slid the slider bar on the video forward. The four windows shown in the video were now dark, except for one which displayed a sliver of light between curtains. It sat diagonal from the painter's window.

"Fast forward, slowly," Jake said.

"Fast forward slowly," Skinny said. "Isn't that one of them oxy...oxy...what do ya call it?"

"Morons," Bear said, poking Skinny in the shoulder. "Like you. Do it."

Jake and Bear kept their eyes on the sliver of light. At 10:35, the curtains widened and a woman's head came into view—blonde and pale. The footage was a bit grainy. The woman's head turned toward the T-Mobile Arena, hand pressed against the glass. After a few seconds, she raised binoculars. After another minute, she glanced over her shoulder and the curtains closed again.

"What do you think?" Bear asked.

"Could be anybody."

"Could be somebody. Who looks out a window with binoculars?"

Bear was right. The binoculars made it feel like

somebody. The video continued to roll, the seconds ticking off on the counter.

"What's in the building across the street?" Jake asked.

"Record store on the bottom floor next to some hipster bar," Skinny said. "Offices up top, I think. Haven't been in anything except the record store. I have a thing for old vinyl."

"And peeping in on naked women through windows," Bear said.

Skinny spread his hands wide. "Hey, I ain't made of stone, man."

Jake folded his arms. "Didn't you think this looked suspicious? A woman peering out a window with binoculars after someone bombed the arena and killed twenty people?"

Skinny's grin dissolved away. "Man, I stopped the video when Big Tits turned out the light. I never seen this. Oh man, am I in trouble? Like hiding evidence?"

Jake held his palm out. "Slow your roll, Skinny. We don't know if this means anything yet."

At 10:38 PM, four minutes before the bombing, the curtains opened again. This time a man's head appeared, mostly obscured by the curtain. He had a beard and wore a hat pulled low. He was lower than the woman, like he was kneeling, but he was holding up the binoculars, looking down the street. The woman's head appeared over his shoulder. They stayed in that position until 10:43 PM. A full minute or so after the bomb exploded. Then the curtains slid shut. A minute later, the sliver of light disappeared and nothing but darkened windows showed.

A knock sounded from the front of the store.

"That's my customer," Skinny said. "You want me

to get rid of her?"

"Go take care of business after you put this video on the same thumb drive as the other."

Skinny took the thumb drive from Jake, copied the file and wiggled his way out of the office, leaving Bear and Jake alone.

"Holy shit," Bear said. "That has to be them."

"But what are the odds?"

"Not great, but it has to be. We should call Foster. Or Snell."

Jake's pulse tapped quick as he slipped out his cell phone. Foster answered on the third ring. Jake explained what they found and suggested she get down here. Foster wasn't as optimistic as Jake but said she and Snell would be there in thirty minutes.

Jake and Bear stepped into the tattoo parlor where Skinny showed a design to a young woman with more ink showing than bare skin. She needed another tattoo like Jake needed a root canal without anesthesia.

"Listen," Jake said to him after waving him away from the girl. "At some point this morning, some Feds are going to come knocking."

Skinny's owl eyes shot wide with panic.

"Calm down," Jake continued. "You aren't going to get in any trouble, unless you delete any of the footage. It might be nothing, it might be something. You get any bright ideas about deleting it or editing out Big Tits so you don't look like a pervert, then your ass is grass. If it is something helpful, you might get a reward which would help square you up with Keats."

Skinny's dry mouth smacked open as he struggled to form words. "Um…okay. What are you guys going to do?"

"We're going to go across the street for a few minutes," Jake said.

Bear's eyes blinked rapidly. "We are?"

"Yeah. Which window is the painting woman?"

Skinny waddled to the front of the store and pointed. "Fourth floor, third one from the right."

The two suspicious characters were one floor down and catty-corner to the painter. Third floor, fourth from the right.

Jake and Bear stepped out into the warming morning air, holding their hands over their eyes to cut back the glare.

"We really going over there?" Bear asked. "Shouldn't we wait for Foster and Snell?"

"We have thirty minutes. Let's go take a peek. Aren't you professionally curious?"

Bear cut his eyes to Jake. "You know your wife's holding me responsible for whatever stupid shit you do."

"No drama," Jake said. "I swear."

"When karma comes back to punch you in the face, I want to be there in case it wants help."

CHAPTER FIFTEEN

Dim bulbs pushed back the darkness in the garage where Hunter double-checked he'd loaded his range bag into the rear of the truck—three pistols, eight pre-loaded magazines and two-hundred extra rounds ought to be plenty if things went wrong. But, if everything went right, he wouldn't need more than one magazine.

Hunter worked to focus his mind on this mission and not the one Mister X discussed an hour ago. A new opportunity which might render the planned main event a moot point. Hunter's mind worked through the possibilities as he packed the truck.

Mara sulked along the back wall, resting against the storage shelves crammed with boxes and tools. When Mara sulked, every muscle in Hunter's body tensed.

Hunter tossed a bag in the truck bed and sat on the tailgate. "What's on your mind, Mara?"

She picked up a wrench and thumped it against her palm. "Lance is worried."

"About what?"

"You blew up Artie. Guess that worries me, too."

Hunter sighed. "I told you both, he was running his mouth about us. If he would've talked to the wrong people, he'd screw us all."

She bit her bottom lip as her eyebrows shot to the ceiling. "You sure?"

He walked over and plucked the wrench from her hand before she decided to swing it. "I'm sure. You and Lance have nothing to worry about. I can't do any of this without both of you. It was a mistake to even bring Artie in the loop. I can own that one."

"So, you're good with Lance?"

Hunter tossed the wrench back on the tool bench. He kissed her. "I'm sure, baby." He snatched the last bag from the floor and threw it in the back of the truck bed. "Lance is fine, and he worries to damn much. Where is he now?"

"Scanning the downtown map. How do we know this is even going to happen?"

Hunter slammed the tailgate of the truck closed. "Oh, it's happening. Cops shot a black teenager. Situation's getting ready to blow. We gotta get up there to get set up before dark. The protests last night were mostly peaceful, but it won't last, especially when we get there."

"They say if the kid was armed?"

Hunter walked past her toward the door. "Does it matter these days? He could've been pointing a bazooka at the cop and there'd still be riots."

She followed him back into the house, past the door to Lance's basement bedroom and up the stairs to the main living space. Lance hunched over the dining room table with a red pen in hand, a map of downtown St. Louis spread in front of him. He'd circled several spots in a five-block radius around the police precinct where the cop in question worked.

Lance's hungry eyes tracked Mara as she walked across the room and Hunter noticed. He trusted Lance with his life out on the street, but not so much when it came to Mara. Hunter knew how Lance desired her, had even found a picture of her in Lance's room a few months ago under his mattress. Hunter said nothing. Lance's wife started sleeping with his neighbor a month after Lance deployed to Iraq. The guy deserved to at least look. Besides, it kept him loyal, and maybe those feelings could be put to good use somewhere down the road. If it crossed a line, Hunter would deal with it.

"I think any of these would be good locations to stage something," Lance said, adjusting his round rimmed glasses over his wide nose. His coffee skin contrasted with the white pullover he wore, a bulldog on the breast from his high school which was less than twelve miles away from the shooting site. "Cops will be gathered to protect the precinct. Governor is talking about calling up the National Guard but hasn't yet. That would be an unnecessary complication."

Hunter studied the map. "You know the area well? Any friends we could call on if needed?"

Lance tossed the pen on the table and rubbed his shaved black skull. "I grew up in Ferguson. Was in high school when Michael Brown got shot. My school was ninety-percent black. I know two dozen angry motherfuckers I could call off the top of my head to rally to the cause. But, we should be fine. Our friend is staging the area as we speak."

At other protest sites across the country, Mister X arranged for pallets of bricks, frozen water bottles and signs for the masses. For the more serious of the group, light body armor and gas masks which Lance and Hunter didn't require. They packed their own gear.

Lance pointed to a spot he'd circled a block from the police precinct. "Remember in Ramadi when the group of ISIS insurgents came at us on the market street? We could set up the same thing here."

Hunter pointed at a spot on the map two block from the precinct, a retail strip across the street from a church. "Mister X said an Antifa group is going to start rioting here. You and Mara draw them toward the church like we talked about and I'll take care of the rest. By the time the cops sort out what happened, the city will be on fire, everyone will be at each other's throats and we'll be long gone."

"I hope it goes smoother than Seattle," Mara said.

"It will." Lance sat at the table, removed his glasses and rubbed the scarred tissue on the side of his face, courtesy of an IED near Ramadi. "How's the main event planning?"

"Construction is going smooth," Hunter said. "But, we have another alternative. How much weight can your drone carry?"

Lance pursed his lips and thought for a moment. "Depends. How fast does it need to move?"

"Doesn't have to be max speed, but quick. Maybe sixty, seventy percent."

"Ten to fifteen pounds, then. What's the target?"

"A hospital. I'll know more tomorrow. It's still a bit up in the air."

"Instead of the rally?" Mara asked.

"This would be easier," Hunter said. "I'm worried the dogs will smell the RDX in the C4, even with the precautions we've taken. We'd be screwed before the targets got anywhere near the kill zone."

Lines popped on Lance's forehead. "Shit's getting real, man. End game's approaching fast."

"You having doubts, soldier?"

Lance stiffened. "No, sir. Not a one. But, killing the President and Vice-President of the United States…"

"Will tear the country to pieces," Hunter finished, his jaw set. "You have to crack a few eggs to make an omelet."

Lance clucked his tongue. "Or blow up the whole fuckin' hen house."

"Either way works for me. Let's pack up and hit the road."

Hunter turned and walked toward the bedroom to grab his clothes. He didn't acknowledge Eddie sitting in the corner watching him, but his creepy grin sent a shudder down Hunter's spine.

CHAPTER SIXTEEN

Jake and Bear crossed the four lanes of Grand Avenue, a simple feat given the fact the bombing at the arena had shut down traffic coming from the north. They walked along the darkened front of the record store until they found a door recessed in the brick building. It opened to a compact lobby with a staircase leading up and an elevator adorned with an "Out of Order" sign.

"Well, that's fucking great," Bear grumbled, glaring at the sign as if he could change the wording to "Welcome Aboard" by sheer will.

"Looks like we're taking the stairs. You want to end up like Skinny? It's only two floors."

Bear lumbered like his feet were bogged down by a ball and chain. "Says the skinny, little shit with some semblance of cardio."

"It could be worse, they could be on the fourth floor with the naked painting woman."

"But I'd at least have some incentive."

Jake figured he could have made a half dozen trips up and back in the time it took Bear to reach the third floor. His best friend sucked oxygen from the climb but was better than Jake expected, hands on his hips instead of his knees or keeled over on the floor mouthing for Jake to dial 9-1-1.

The hallway was painted ash blue and tiled with black and cold grey tiles in a herringbone pattern. Jake knew it was a herringbone pattern from the many unfortunate hours Maggie had forced him to watch home renovation shows on HGTV. "How many doors from the end of the building is the office?"

Bear held up four fingers rather than expend needed oxygen.

"Want a minute to catch your breath, old man?" Jake asked.

Bear showed Jake his longest finger.

"Fine, one more minute," Jake said, waiting until Bear stopped gulping air.

The fourth door from the end of the hallway was an old-school opaque-glass square set in the upper half of the door. Black stencil against the glass read "Walter Nichols, Attorney at Law".

"Why do they say Attorney at Law?" Jake asked. "Why not just attorney?"

"An attorney is someone acting in place of another person and providing representation for their best interest. Like a power of attorney which is an attorney-in-fact. An attorney at law is someone who actually does stuff in court and has to be licensed in the state to practice law before the court."

Jake drew back. "I'm impressed."

"Don't be. I was stuck in a room with the county attorney a few months ago on a case. He bored the crap out of me with useless trivia like that."

"Lucky you."

Jake reached for the door and Bear grabbed his arm. "Wait. What's our story? Why are we here?"

It was a good question. "I suppose 'we want to look out your office window and search your office for clues' would be a bit on the nose."

"That and he's an attorney—"

"At law," Jake reminded him.

"And if we should find anything incriminating, he'd shred it to pieces."

Jake thought for a moment and snapped his fingers. "You're thinking about retiring and joining my PI business, and we need a lawyer to draw up a partnership agreement, or something."

Bear scoffed, "And you think you could afford to pay me?"

"You'd make more than you're making now as sheriff."

"Sadly, that's probably true. Fine, let's go with your bullshit tale."

Jake opened the door and walked into a waiting area. The musty smell and threadbare carpet told him Walter Nichols was a far cry from one of those five-hundred-dollar-an-hour attorneys. A pair of antique chairs sat in a corner under a fake tree and a bare coffee table. The mustiness of the office was overcome by the perfume of the woman behind the desk. A name plate on her desk read "Sharon McWilliams, Paralegal".

Sharon was a black woman a few years short of retirement, typing on a keyboard in front of a large monitor. Over her desk hung a series of pictures of an overweight white guy with slicked back hair the color of dirty snow, shaking hands with various people. Jake thought one of them was a former KC mayor and another was an old Chiefs player. On the opposite side of the room was a single, closed door which would look out over Grand Avenue—the view Jake wanted to check out.

Sharon had a thin, long face under tight yellow curls and glowered at Jake and Bear over the top of thick framed glasses like they were intruders. "Can I help you gentlemen?"

"We'd like to see Mr. Nichols," Jake said, assuming the man worked behind the door in question. He wrinkled his nose, the wafting perfume overpowering.

She frowned, exasperated she had to move, and spun sixty degrees in her chair to face them. "Do you have an appointment?"

"No, ma'am. We were just hoping—"

She spun back to her computer and clicked a few keys. "His calendar is full. His earliest opening is Monday morning."

"Is he here?"

"Not at the moment, sir, but he should be in shortly."

Bear asked, "How shortly is 'shortly'?" He flicked air quotes with his sausage fingers.

"I don't know, sir. He's usually here by now, so I'm guessing it will be…shortly."

"My wife says 'shortly'," Bear continued, using the air quotes again, "But that could mean an hour."

Jake sat and tugged Bear's sleeve to draw him down into the chair by him. "It's fine. We'll wait."

Sharon rubbed her brow, her foot tapping as if a headache was coming on, and it had the names of the two guys in front of her on it. "Suit yourselves. But, he won't talk to you without an appointment."

She turned back to her computer and clicked away as Bear sat.

"We just going to sit here? You and I both know shortly could be goddamn forever," Bear whispered.

"Might as well. If the lawyer shows up before Snell and Foster get here, we can check out his office. If not, they flaunt their FBI badges, and we get inside. Relax."

"I can't relax," Bear said, pinching his nostrils shut. "I'm going to pass out from the stench of her perfume. Eau de Old Lady."

After ten minutes, Sharon stood and moved toward the door. "I'm going to the restroom."

"You want us to answer the phones or anything while you're gone?" Bear offered.

Sharon glared over the top of her glasses. "Don't touch anything."

The second she disappeared from sight, Jake jumped up. "Guard the door. Let me know if she's coming back."

Bear stood, brow pinched. "What are you gonna do?"

Jake tried the handle to the lawyer's door. Locked. He moved to the woman's desk and opened drawers searching for a key.

"Are you crazy?" Bear whisper shouted. "I'm supposed to keep you from doing stupid shit, remember? This is beyond stupid."

"Only if we get caught," Jake said. He found a loose brass key in the center drawer. He slipped it into the lock on the lawyer's door and clicked it open. "Let me know when she comes back."

He slipped inside the office and scanned the room which smelled as stale and dated as an old library. A credenza on the nearest wall was covered with knickknacks next to a closed door, a bookshelf on the far wall filled to bursting with law books and a wet bar. In front of the window, an orderly desk with two chairs in front of it. The open curtains provided a view of Grand Avenue. Jake strode to it and peered down toward the T-Mobile arena. He wanted the view from the bad guy's perspective, if indeed those were the bad guys in the video. Outside the arena, his eyes locked in on the spot where he and Halle stood when the bomb went off. Heat flushed his body as he realized he could be standing in the same spot as a psychopath who nearly killed his daughter along with twenty other people.

Who were these people?

Why were they in this office?

He turned from the window and a smudge on the glass caught his eye. Jake leaned in closer. A handprint. Petite. Like a woman's. Pulling out his cell phone, he snapped a few pictures, trying to get a good angle where the print showed up.

His internal clock blinked red, his brain working through how long it would take an older lady to shuffle to the bathroom and back. His gaze swept over the desk for anything helpful before moving to the floor. He spotted an odd shape on the floor by the desk and picked it up. A puzzle piece. If nothing else, the lawyer was probably the same level of uptight as his secretary, and it would drive him crazy to finish whatever puzzle he worked on, so Jake pocketed the piece.

"Jake, hurry up," Bear sounded from the other room. "She's gotta be close to coming back."

Jake stepped around the desk, eyes sweeping over the bookshelf and credenza. One last thing. He opened the door next to the credenza which led to a bathroom.

White porcelain sink.

Mirror that needed cleaning.

Half-filled trashcan.

Dead body of an old man in a suit. His blood-red eyes pointed at the ceiling, lips swollen, and deep bruises ringed his neck. Same snowy hair as the guy in the lobby pictures.

"Oh shit," Jake whispered.

He closed the door and used his shirt tail to wipe the handle, eyes darting around the room playing back his time in there. He didn't touch anything else.

"She's coming," Bear yelled. "You got fifteen seconds."

Jake darted across the room, pulled the door shut and turned the key he'd left in the lock.

"Ten seconds."

Jake used his shirt to wipe the door handle and the key before dropping it in the drawer and slamming it shut. He put three steps of distance from the desk when Sharon returned. Her eyes narrowed and flicked between Jake and Bear.

"You boys okay?"

Jake pulled farther away from the door. "Listen, we'll come back another day when Mr. Nichols is in."

"You want to make an appointment?"

Jake snagged a business card from a holder on her desk. "We'll call ya."

Bear waited until they reached the stairs. "You must've found something good. What about the lawyer?"

"We'd be waiting a hell of a long time to talk to him."

"Why's that?"

Jake loped down the stairs. "Someone strangled

him and dumped him in his office bathroom. Why did you think I wiped everything down?"

Bear tromped down after him. "So much for no drama. Maggie's gonna skin me alive."

CHAPTER SEVENTEEN

Jake and Bear stood on the sidewalk outside the record store, waiting for their FBI friends Foster and Snell. Jake pressed against the storefront window while Bear sat on the brick lip. He extracted a tobacco pouch from a tin in his coat and slipped it against his gums. They watched a handful of cars pass in silence.

"That was the place," Jake said. "Those bastards strangled an old man and blew up twenty people right from that office."

"Did you go through special training or something?" Bear asked.

"For what?"

"On how to perfectly jump into the middle of a giant steaming pile of shit, because you have a particular knack for it. If it was an Olympic sport, you'd be a gold fuckin' medalist."

"We got what we needed and found a dead guy before he stinks up the building."

Bear chuckled. "Sharon in there wouldn't smell him for days over her obscene amount of perfume." He glanced to Jake. "What's up? Your jaw is set so hard you're gonna crack your teeth."

Images flickered. The explosion. The bodies strewn across the ground. Blood. Guts. Halle lying in the hospital bed. The dead lawyer with his purple tongue protruding through swollen lips.

His fists ached from the tension. "These motherfuckers have to go down in a most serious and painful way. I don't know what their goal is, but I'm sure as hell going to find out. If it means jumping in a steaming pile of shit, then so be it."

Bear stood and draped an arm over Jake's shoulder. "She's gonna make it, man. You can't take down a Caldwell that easy."

Jake blew out the tension. "Thanks."

A black Ford Fusion pulled to the curb in front of him. Agent Foster climbed out the passenger door and Special Agent Victoria Snell ejected from the driver's side. A few months had passed since Jake saw her last. She wore black slacks under a waist length, dark leather coat, her ash hair spilling over the collar. Her pale skin was clear of the cuts and bruises from when she was kidnapped in Nebraska.

"We interrupting something?" Snell asked.

"Jake and I are sharing a moment," Bear said, shaking Snell's hand. "Good to see you."

There was a time in the not too distant past when Bear couldn't even say Snell's name without letting loose a derogatory term or three. Some bad blood over a joint task force between the FBI and the local PD over Jason Keats of all people. The two seemed to have made amends which was good for everyone involved.

"You have some video to show us?" Foster asked.

"We have a lot more than that," Jake said. "You

got a laptop?"

"In my car," Snell said.

"Let's get in and fire it up and I'll explain everything."

"Any reason we can't do it out here?" Snell asked.

"I don't want the whole world to hear you chew my ass out."

Jake and Bear crowded in the backseat, Snell and Foster took the front and swiveled around to face them. After he showed them the video, he prefaced the debrief with a disclaimer to hold scathing judgments until the end before laying out everything. The tattoo shop, the two sets of videos, the woman in the window and the lawyer's office. Snell was moments away from biting through her tongue when Jake reached the part of stealing the key and breaking into the lawyer's office. She pressed her palms into her forehead as if to keep her brain from exploding when he mentioned the dead body in the bathroom.

Jake finished and let the tale breathe for a moment. "Any thoughts?"

Snell dropped her hands to her lap, blinking fast above a red-hued face. "Any thoughts? Other than you're an idiot? Jesus Christ, Jake. If this is the staging location of the bombers, which it appears to be, any evidence we recover would be thrown out of court. For starters."

Jake drummed his fingers on his legs. The thought of evidence crossed his mind about the time he twisted the stolen key into the lock of the lawyer's office. The thought faded during the ten seconds it took him to cross the office to look out the window, seeing the same view as the bomber who nearly killed his daughter a little more than twelve hours before. Once he spotted the handprint, he didn't give a damn whether the evidence was admissible or not. If these were the people responsible, they wouldn't make it to the inside of a courtroom if Jake had anything to say. But he couldn't say this to two FBI agents, no matter how good of friends they were.

"Sorry," he said. "I was caught up in the moment."

Snell narrowed her eyes. She knew Jake well enough to smell bullshit when the bouquet filled her car. "The question is, how do we legally get access to the office so we can find the handprint and the dead body? We don't have enough of anything to get a warrant."

Foster jumped in. "What if we go to the tattoo guy? He shows us the footage of the windows across the street and apologizes for failing to provide it when we first came knocking. Which leads us to the building across the street."

"Where the perfumed paralegal will tell us to take a hike," Snell said. "No way she's going to let us root around in her boss's locked office."

"Tell her you want to look out the window to verify the site lines to the arena," Jake said. "That's it and you'll be out of her hair."

Foster piped in, "And if she gives us any lip, we'll threaten a warrant. She'll try to call her boss, but he won't answer. Maybe we get lucky and his ringer is on and we have probable cause. I'll bat my Bambi eyes and remind her we just need to check off the box and we'll be gone."

Bear said, "You do have nice eyes."

"Thank you, Bear."

"My wife says I'm too much of an asshole and should complement people more."

"Anyway," Jake interrupted. "Skinny at the tattoo

parlor will slide over a bed of razors for you if you bat your eyes at him, but it won't work on this lady. Stress how inconvenient you're going to make her life, or she can give you fifteen seconds to look out a window."

Snell studied Jake and Bear. "You two think this is legit?"

Jake glanced at Bear who nodded. "Yeah. I could feel them, like people describe the cold sensation of ghosts."

"Foster and I will start with this Skinny and then go talk to the paralegal," Snell said.

"What do you want Bear and me to do?"

"Absolutely nothing. Go shop in the record store or something. Find me some old Waylon Jennings vinyl. My dad's birthday is coming up."

Bear clucked his tongue. "Your old man has good taste."

The tension that washed away from Jake's shoulders with the news Halle would pull through crept back with the knowledge the monsters responsible for this were still out there. The dead lawyer added one body to the count, and Jake would bet there would be more to come if he and Bear didn't act fast.

After Foster and Snell disappeared inside the tattoo shop, Jake scanned the street, gaze following the road to the arena. The Feds had the video from the arena, and they couldn't get ahold of that. He and Bear wouldn't be able to get within a block of the bombing scene. The C4 used in the bomb. The ATF would be all over that angle, but...Jake's brows shot to the sky. He might know a guy.

"What are you thinkin' about?" Bear asked, his brow wrinkling. "You're wearing your mischievous expression, which scares the shit out of me."

Jake turned to Bear. "You really want to go shopping for vinyl?"

"I'd rather pluck my pubes out with tweezers."

"Let's cruise the streets and shake some trees. I'd like to see if we can find some C4."

Bear shucked his eyebrows. "That would be an explosive development."

Jake rolled his eyes. "Jesus, that was bad, even for you, Bear."

NOW

CHAPTER EIGHTEEN

"Have you ever lost someone close to you?" Dr. Tate asked. Jake marked the passage of time by the afternoon sun's movement as it crept across the contents of her desks—the paper weight, a pen, a coffee mug with Dr. Tate's strawberry-colored lipstick along the rim. He wasn't sure if it was the sun blasting through the windows or her questions that heated things up.

Jake tugged at the collar of his t-shirt while he thought how to answer. "Haven't we all? The only two certainties in life are death and taxes."

"Who have you lost?"

"Why?"

Dr. Tate let the question sit. "Is there a reason you don't want to talk about it?"

Jake twisted on the couch, his hands dancing above his legs, uncertain where to place them, knowing wherever they landed would be wrong and interpreted as some type of hidden feeling or emotion he repressed. Nothing good could come from scraping scabs off old wounds. Jesus, it was hot in this office. He scanned the wall for a thermostat he could turn down.

"Tell me one person, Jake," Dr. Tate said. "Just one."

"Can we be done after that?"

"We'll see. One for starters."

Jake exhaled a long breath through his nose, pressing his hands into his lap. "Fine. My brother. Nicky."

"Younger or older?"

Nicky's mop head of dark hair and deep dimples all the girls swooned over swam into focus followed by memory flashes. The two of them dry walling the hallway because Jake had put Nicky's head through the plaster while they wrestled. They scrambled to fix it before their father came home from whatever bender he was out on. The image of Nicky's haunted ten-year-old eyes when Stony made him go pick out the dress to bury their mother in. His big brother curling himself into a ball under the incessant assault from their father's belt while being called a pussy. Fishing together at the pond by their house with fat worms as thick as your pinky that they dug out from the muddy banks. The same pond where they found Nicky's body years after Jake left. Nicky's coffin being lowered into the ground while Jake watched from Poor Boy Road, rather than get within spitting distance of his father.

"Older. By two years."

"How did he die?"

Jake wiped his nose with the back of his hand. "Heroin overdose."

Dr. Tate pressed her lips in line. "I'm sorry."

"Why? You weren't the scumbag who hooked him on the poison."

"Do you know who it was?"

Jake ground his teeth. "I did. Thanks to me, there's one less drug dealing murderer in the world."

"Prison?"

"We tried prison, didn't work. He escaped, tracked me down and came at me with a knife. Fatal mistake on his part."

She jotted a note on her pad. "Another case of justice, I suppose?"

"Justice for Nicky, justice for Halle and Maggie who he kidnapped, and justice for every person in Benton County. Believe me, there wasn't a single tear shed at the death of Shane Langston."

"How does that make you feel? Knowing you took the life of the man who killed your brother."

The desire to flee the office in a cloud of dust rippled through Jake again like a shiver. Feelings. Why were his feelings after he blew the back of Shane Langston's head off important? But she wasn't letting him off without an answer.

"I don't know," Jake said, crossing and uncrossing his arms, twisting his ass against the expensive leather of the couch. No matter how he moved, he couldn't get comfortable.

"Let's pretend 'I don't know' are three words that don't exist. Come on. Good? Bad? Happy? Sad?"

Jake jumped to his feet and paced the floor behind the couch. "The truth? All of them. I felt every one of them. Good his evil brains slid down the cabinets in the kitchen where I shot him. Bad that it took that long for me to get to him. Happy he wouldn't be able to terrorize me or my family any longer or poison people like my brother. Sad? Scratch my answer of all of them. I wasn't one bit sad that piece of shit was dead."

"How did you feel when you received the news Nicky died?"

Jake linked his hands behind his neck, pulling his elbows in tight while he walked. "Devastated I hadn't seen him for a few years, but he was still my big brother."

"And what was your first thought when you found out how he died?"

Jake rolled his eyes to the ceiling, trying to remember the call. "My first thought was Nicky, you dumb shit. My second was I'm going to get the person responsible for giving him the heroin in the first place."

"And you got him."

"Four years later. The wheels of justice sometimes turn slow."

"What about your mother? You mentioned she died when you were little?"

Jake dropped his chin to his chest, his pace slowing. "I was eight."

"How did she die?"

Jake stopped. "Heart attack in our kitchen."

"She have a bad health history?"

"She had a bad husband. Alcoholic, abusive. Drove her to an early grave."

She tapped her pen on her notepad. "How did you deal with that emotion? Believing your father was responsible for her death?"

Jake let his arms fall and shook his hands out, like a runner readying for a race, letting go of the building tension. "I didn't kill Stony if that's the link you're shooting for."

"You called your father by his first name?"

"I certainly wasn't going to call him Dad. He never earned the right. I didn't kill Stony. Cancer did. But I was envious of the cancer, the way it got to eat him piece by piece, to cause him pain he could do nothing about, until it rotted him away from the inside."

Jake sat in silence, a memory stirring.

"I almost killed him once," he said, his voice soft and low.

"Tell me about it."

Jake gripped the back of the couch. "The night I left Warsaw. Nicky was out with his friends, my younger sister Janey was in her room. Stony came home, blitzed as usual on cheap ass whiskey. He staggered in the house and stopped, wavering on those skinny ass legs of his, like he couldn't get his eyes to focus. He slopped across the room and backhanded me to the floor for no reason. I'm lying there, blood trickling down my nose, when Stony stands over me and slurs 'Go make me something to eat, you dumb bitch. What kinda wife are you anyway?' Then he staggers to his chair, falls into it and passes out."

Dr. Tate's voice was soft, soothing. "How old were you?"

"Eighteen and a lot bigger and stronger than him. He thought I was my mom. That's how drunk he was. And I was filled with this…this white-hot fury when I realized the crap she went through over the course of their marriage. What he did to her night after drunken night. Beating her down. But she took the beatings to protect us, just like I took beatings to protect Nicky."

Jake hung his head as he tried to recall the times his mother stood up to Stony to protect her children or how many times Jake jumped in the middle of a Nicky beating for something stupid like leaving a wrench out in the rain or leaving the kitchen a mess. There were too many to count, and they blurred together into a pulsating, painful fog that squeezed his heart.

"Men like Stony never stop themselves," Jake continued, "Because they don't think they're doing anything wrong. If he couldn't stop himself, I was going to do it. I got to my feet. Walked across the living room to his tool belt and grabbed his roofing hammer. I stood over his chair with the hammer raised as he snored, wanting to crash it into his liver-spotted skull with every fiber of my being, but at the same time terrified to do it."

"What stopped you?"

A memory of bouncing red curls and freckles hit him. "Janey. My little sister came out of the bedroom, book in her hand and...God, that horrified look on her pretty, little face, wondering why I was standing over our passed-out father with a raised hammer. She knew Stony was a mean drunk, but he never touched her, and she still loved him for some reason. She didn't have the scars Nicky and I did."

"What did you do?"

"I dropped the hammer. Went to my room and packed a bag, kissed Janey on the forehead and left town, taking Stony's car. Abandoning Stony and stealing his car gave me a weird power, like I was getting back at him in some small way."

Dr. Tate scribbled a few notes. "Shane Langston for your brother, your father for what he did to your mother. Justice?"

"I think so."

Dr. Tate crossed her legs and leaned back in her chair. "To be honest, Jake, it doesn't sound like justice to me. It sounds more like vengeance."

To that, Jake didn't have an answer.

THEN

CHAPTER NINETEEN

After spending an almost fruitless hour hitting up a few of the informants about the bombing, C4 or any chatter they'd picked up on the street, Jake and Bear returned to the tattoo shop with a lead from the last informant, a fireplug named Dodge whose skin hadn't kissed a bar of soap in a week. The unfortunate smell lingered in their noses, but at least they'd scored a name. Chester Coates. Jake knew the guy. Bear jerked to the curb in front of Lit Ink. Across the street, two black SUVs and a couple KCPD squad cars camped in front of the record store. Uniformed cops, and men and women in blue jackets with FBI emblazoned on the back moved from vehicles to the door leading to the law offices.

"Guess they got in," Bear said, flapping his jacket open and closed like wings. "Man, we're gonna smell like that Dodge guy all day long."

The bell on the door to the tattoo shop tinkled as Skinny stepped out into the sun.

"Speaking of smells," Jake said.

Skinny chewed on a king-sized Twix candy bar as

he gestured across the street. "What the hell have you got me into, Caldwell? Word gets out I helped the cops, and my business is gonna tank."

Jake folded his arms across his chest. "Twenty people were killed, Skinny. If this turns into something and we catch a madman, how's that gonna hurt your business? Might even be some reward money."

Skinny finished off the candy bar and shoved the wrapper in the pockets of his sweats. "Hey, you think Agent Foster would give me her number?"

Bear stifled a laugh.

"Sure," Jake said. "If you think less than zero's a chance."

Skinny closed his eyes. "Man, that lady is smokin' hot. You shoulda seen the way she batted her big brown eyes at me."

"Lemme guess. Right before you gave up everything you had while wiping the drool off your chin."

Skinny jabbed a fat finger in Jake's direction. "You owe me one, Caldwell. I think getting her phone number for me would be a good start."

"Fine. If you want to get shot down like a buck at the start of deer season, I guess I can't stop you."

"Thanks," Skinny said before lumbering back inside the tattoo parlor.

Across the street, Sharon the paralegal walked out the door with an agent and disappeared inside one of the black SUVs. She wore a pinched expression, like someone rubbed shit under her nose and wouldn't let her wipe it off.

Bear craned his head. "You really going to give him Foster's number?"

"Hell no. She'd kill me. Let's go see what's going on."

They crossed the street and weaved between the cop cars. A stoic uniformed officer posted by the door waived them off, so Jake texted Foster and let them know they were down on the street. They propped themselves against the hood of Snell's Fusion and waited.

Jake took the moment to check in with Maggie. Halle was asleep, but things still looked good from the doctor's perspective.

"How's your hunt going?" Maggie asked.

"Got a lead on a guy that Bear and I are looking into. You need anything?"

"It's almost five o'clock and I haven't eaten anything since breakfast. I'd kill someone for a cheeseburger and a strawberry shake."

Jake grinned. "I'll see what I can do."

Ten minutes later, Foster walked out the front door and shoved her hands in her jacket pocket.

"How's your girl?"

Jake gave a thumbs-up. "She's good. Thanks for asking. Any trouble getting in up there?"

She wrinkled her nose. "Once we waded past the perfume, Snell sweet-talked her into giving us a look out the window. Once we let her know about her boss's body in the bathroom, she fell apart. I'm guessing those two had something going."

"So she's in the clear?" Bear asked.

"I think so, but we'll still check her out. Based on rigor mortis, the lawyer's been dead since at least yesterday afternoon, and the paralegal said she was off yesterday."

"Convenient."

"She says she was in Omaha visiting her sister," Foster said. "We're checking it out now, but I can't see how she could've strangled the guy. A team is combing through the office for any other clues."

"What about the handprint on the window?" Jake asked.

Foster pulled a granola bar from her jacket and gnawed on it. "Got our team checking it now. It's a pretty good print, but not perfect. We'll run what we have through the system and see if it kicks anything back."

"How many prints does the system have to wade through?"

Foster brushed crumbs off her shirt. "Over a hundred and fifty million. Our techs will analyze the results and give us any hits."

"What's the chances we'll get something useful?" Bear asked.

Foster's eyes scanned the steel gray clouds above. "Success rate for latent prints is thirty percent, if you have good technicians."

Bear wrinkled his nose. "Thirty percent? That's not great."

"It's better than zero," Jake said. "What can we do?"

Foster crumpled the granola bar wrapper and shoved it in her pocket. "Nothing and you might want to keep it that way. Snell is not happy you guys went in that office."

"For the record," Bear said, "I stayed in the waiting room."

"Bet she won't be pissed if you get a lead out of what we found," Jake said.

Foster nodded. "Let's say it would help smooth the waters. Personally, I welcome any help we can get. Two more from the bombing have died in the last hour, so everyone's on point."

Jake didn't plan on giving up the chase but agreed with Foster it might be a good idea not to step on the FBI's toes. "What else are you working on?"

"Analyzing the video evidence, checking threats against the Topeka religious group, so that could take a while based on their list of haters. And we're combing the arena scene and tracking the C4 used in the bomb. If this turns into something, you already helped us find this place. Stay close and Snell or I will let you know if we hear anything. Hey, I'm glad your daughter's going to be fine. Why don't you go be with her?"

"Thanks," Jake said as Foster disappeared inside. "You ready to go back on the prowl? I want to find Chester."

"Can we shower and change clothes first? I want to wash that Dodge guy off me."

"Did you bring any clothes from home?"

Bear's face fell. "Shit. Maybe we can go walk around the lawyer's office and pick up the perfume scent."

"I'm not that desperate."

CHAPTER TWENTY

After dropping off the cheeseburger and shake Maggie requested and spending some time talking to Halle, Jake and Bear scoured the streets of downtown Kansas City in the search for Chester Coates, a man who knew how to get things. They hit up every back-alley informant he'd ever used, but nobody knew where Chester hid out these days. After a couple of hours, Bear's stomach howled.

"I need some chow, stat," Bear said. "I'm starting to hallucinate. The lines in the road are turning into bacon strips."

Jake rubbed the puzzle piece in his jacket pocket, fingers tracking the curved edges. Lines. Food. God he was getting old and forgetful. "I know just the place."

Ten minutes later, they took a seat in navy backed barstools at the Blue Line off Walnut Street, a red-bricked hockey-themed bar and grill in Kansas City's River Market district. Kansas City wasn't exactly known as a hockey town and Jake couldn't name more than a couple of professional hockey players, but the food was good and the beer cold.

TVs lined the top of the bar above shelves of liquor. Framed jerseys of Kansas City sporting legends Len Dawson, George Brett and Patrick Mahomes covered the walls. A group of customers chatted over a sea of empty bottles in one corner while two drunk guys argued sports in the other. Jake drummed his fingers on the bar top to Journey's Escape playing overhead, the smell of fried bar food wafting from the kitchen to their right, triggering his salivary glands.

A dark-haired bartender in a Royals jersey approached and set napkins and menus on the bar top in front of them. She was young, cute and the bar top hit her mid-chest. "Hey, Jake, long time no see. Where you been hiding?"

"Hey, Barb. Moved to Lake of the Ozarks, working my PI business from there."

"You still married?"

Jake waggled his wedding ring. "Happily."

Barb pouted her lips. "Too bad. I always hoped you'd ask me out."

"You're young enough to be my daughter," Jake said.

Barb's pout turned flirtatious. "Almost. Who's your friend?"

"Sorry, this is my buddy Bear."

Barb shook Bear's hand. "Nice to meet you. What can I get you guys?"

"Beer and fried pickles," Bear said. "The sooner, the better."

She waved her hands toward the taps. "Any beer in particular?"

"Surprise me."

Barb set them up with a couple of Dunkels from

the KC Bier Company and mozzarella sticks. Barb set their beers in front of them in tall frosted mugs and moved on to deliver food to the drunks in the corner who wolf-whistled as she approached.

Bear wiped foam from his bearded lip. "Is this unusual? Chester being this hard to find?"

"A little. He's the guy who can get you things, so his livelihood depends on him being available which makes me curious. Where the hell is he?"

Barb yelled from the corner. Jake turned to watch her slap the hand belonging to one of the drunks away from her ass. The drunk laughed and poked his buddy as she stomped back toward the bar.

"Still," Jake continued, turning back to Bear, "I'm pissed I didn't think about this place earlier. Chester is Barb's uncle."

Barb returned to the bar, adjusting her jersey, face flushed. "Jerkoffs."

"Hey," Jake said. "You know where we can find Chester?"

Barb sighed. "Good Lord. What's he done this time?"

"Nothing. We just need some info. The kind Chester's good at getting. The kind people pay money for."

Barb crossed her arms and narrowed her eyes at Jake. "You planning on hurting him?"

"Nope. Just want to talk to him."

"And here I thought you just came to see me." Barb flicked her eyes toward the drunks. "Well, Jake Caldwell, today might just be your lucky day. You see the douchenozzle in the corner?"

"You mean the one with his handprint on your ass?"

"Yeah. Our bouncer doesn't come in for another

couple hours, and those two can't keep their hands to themselves. I think it would be in their best interests to leave before I break a bottle over their heads."

"Let me guess," Jake said, standing up and stretching his arms, limbering up. "You want me and Bear to make them go away."

"If it's not too much trouble. You also pay me whatever money you were going to give to Chester for the information. He broke into my apartment and stole my TV last month. I was halfway through the last season of Game of Thrones and I'm pissed. You do that for me, and I'll tell you right where you can find him."

Jake drained a third of his beer while he considered her offer. The two guys were above average in size, but Jake could handle them in his sleep. With Bear at his side, he could do it in a coma. He slid a fifty dollar bill across the bar top.

"And you can't break any furniture this time," Barb added, stuffing the bill in her shorts.

Jake set the mug down and wiped his mouth with the back of his arm. "Deal. I'll get you another fifty if we actually find him."

Bear groaned as he slid from the barstool. "Here we go."

CHAPTER TWENTY ONE

The two drunks in the corner stopped arguing mid-sentence about the necessity for the designated hitter in baseball when Jake and Bear headed their way. Jake didn't walk around the chairs and tables, he moved the chairs and tables from his path, keeping his eyes locked on the drunk with the energetic hands. It was an effective psychological demonstration of power. Who would you be more afraid of, the guy who dodges through a crowd to get to you or the guy who causes people to jump the hell out of the way lest they get caught in his path?

The drunk with the affinity for Barb's ass was dark-haired and barrel-chested with beady eyes. A scar ran down his nose and disappeared around his cheek bone. He looked like an old hockey player, which would make sense since the Blue Line was branded as Kansas City's number one hockey bar. The other guy wasn't quite as thick but his muscular frame was defined under a University of Kansas t-shirt two sizes too small. His acorn-colored crew cut and bloodshot eyes flickered between Jake and

Bear as they approached.

Jake stopped in front of the table nearest Mr. Handsy while Bear slipped to the side, pressing against the wall behind Crew Cut. Between the two of them they looked like they could generate enough brain power to lightly toast a piece of bread. Overhead, Y&T's Summertime Girls switched to Def Leppard's Hysteria which wasn't exactly a fighting song.

"Can I help you with something, pal?" Mr. Handsy asked, cocking his high-domed melon, his tone low and menacing.

Jake clasped his hands in front of him. "You've been asked to leave the bar."

"By who?"

"By me."

Mr. Handsy thumped his beer bottle on the table, leaning back into his chair and alternating his focus between Jake and Bear. "And who the hell are you two?"

Jake stepped forward, his thighs pressing into the table. "The guys asking you to leave. The bartenders don't like it when guys grab their asses while they're trying to do their jobs."

"I was just having a little fun," Mr. Handsy scoffed.

"She wasn't."

"You her father or something?"

Jake was half-offended the prick would assume he was that old. He clenched his hands and set his jaw. "It's time for you to hit the road, bud. Whether you do it with your feet or face first is up to you."

Mr. Handsy exaggerated a neck roll to his buddy, locking eyes with him. Jake took a half-step back and to the side. He knew how this would play out. Mr. Handsy would fake being nice like he was going to leave and take a cheap swing at Jake. Which left Jake doubting he would to be able to keep his promise to Barb and avoid breaking any of the furniture.

Mr. Handsy rolled his head back to Jake. "Can I finish my beer first? You know, before I kick your ass?"

Jake smiled. "I think you've had enough. Let's go."

Mr. Handsy leveraged his weight against the table as he rose to his feet, wobbling for a moment. Standing a half-head taller than Jake, he pushed his fingertips into Jake's chest. "Listen, pops. You don't know who you're—"

In one smooth move, Jake slipped his palm under the guy's fingers, clamping his fingertips on the top of Mr. Handsy's digits. Pressing down at his knuckles and bending the fingers back, Jake applied pressure until the guy's eyes bugged wide, he gasped and dropped to his knees. It was a simple, yet effective move a black belt in jiujitsu taught him a long time ago.

Crew Cut rose, but Bear slipped behind him, jamming the line of his index finger under his nose and applying painful pressure to the nerve rich spot where the nose meets the upper lip. Crew Cut whimpered and followed Bear's direction toward the door.

"You're gonna break my goddamn fingers," Mr. Handsy groaned through clenched teeth.

"Agree to be a good boy and leave, and I'll let go," Jake said.

Mr. Handsy grunted. Jake let go and took a step back. Mr. Handsy rubbed his fingers, a snarl curling on his lip. He wasn't going to be a good boy, and Jake wasn't going to be able to keep his promise to Barb.

Mr. Handsy's upper cut was fast and hard but didn't come close to catching Jake. Jake pulled back and jabbed his fist into the drunk's exposed rib-cage, twisting his hips into the punch for a little added power. Air fled Mr. Handsy's lungs and he staggered back against the wall, crashing into a Miller Lite neon sign. As Jake moved in, Mr. Handsy grabbed his beer bottle by the neck and thumped it against the table twice, unsuccessfully trying to break the glass.

Jake cocked his head and waited. "Need some help there?"

"Fuck you," Mr. Handsy said, finally breaking the bottle and waving the jagged edges in Jake's direction.

Jake peeked to Bear who still had Crew Cut by the nose. Crew Cut had his arms raised to the ceiling in total surrender.

"You sure you know what you're getting yourself into, man?" Bear asked.

Jake pouted. "Thanks for the vote of confidence."

"I was talking to the idiot with the broken beer bottle. He's the one I'm worried about, not you."

Jake turned to Mr. Handsy. "Don't you think the broken bottle is a little much given the circumstances?"

Mr. Handsy swiped at him with the broken bottle, wincing in pain from his ribs. "I'm gonna kill you, man."

"Seriously, dude," Jake said. "Just drop the bottle and leave while you can still walk."

"You scared, pussy?"

"My man, you're about to experience a world of unnecessary pain. Last chance."

Mr. Handsy telegraphed his approach with a wild, wide swing of the broken bottle. Jake stepped into it, blocking the descending arm with his forearm, grabbing the guy's wrist holding the bottle, and headbutted him in the nose, blood spraying everywhere as it gushed from his nostrils. Mr. Handsy's eyes rolled back, the bottle slipping from his hand. Jake spun and slammed the drunk's head into the brass railing of a nearby booth. The man slumped to the floor.

Jake turned to Crew Cut whose eyes were as wide as full moons. "Would you like to leave now?"

Bear released the pressure from the man's nose, and Crew Cut jerked his head emphatically.

"Leave money for your tab on the table and take your dumbass friend with you," Bear said.

"B-b-but he's unconscious," Crew Cut stammered, pulling out a couple of twenties.

"Drag him out by his feet," Jake said. "And you'd better leave a good tip. Just empty your Velcro wallet, tightwad."

Jake and Bear watched as Crew Cut dumped all the bills from his wallet on the table, grabbed his buddy under the arm-pits and dragged him across the floor. A wide-eyed incoming patron held the door open for the bloodied duo as they passed into the early evening street.

After straightening the chairs and tables, Jake and Bear returned to the bar. Barb came over and poured three shots of Skrewball, passing two of them to Jake.

Jake raised his shot glass. "I didn't even break a table or chair."

Barb's mouth closed in a line. "But, you put a monster dent in our brass railing."

"I didn't do it, his forehead did."

The trio clinked their shot glasses together, and Jake savored the peanut butter whiskey as it worked its way down his chest.

"Now," he said, turning back to Barb. "Where can I find Chester?"

CHAPTER TWENTY TWO

The blue spring skies morphed to amber by the time Hunter and his crew reached the staging spot in the heart of St. Louis. The sky color matched the flames licking up the side of the Bed, Bath and Beyond on their right. Protestors laden with signs and boiling rage blocked off I-70 along with many of the major streets—Black Lives Matter, Defund the Police along with other signs depicting messages and images that would send the network television censors scrambling. Hunter was forced to back-track and send the GPS unit in his truck into a hysterical frenzy of routing and re-routing. He kept the truck in motion, even if he had to skirt around groups of people. He knew what could happen if he stopped and the mob took over.

"This is crazy," Lance said, his voice soft with awe as he inclined between the bucket seats from the back as they passed store fronts with broken windows and looters pillaging its contents. Some stores still smoldered in the day's fading light. The closer they drew to downtown, the worse it was. "All this because a cop shot a black kid."

"A black cop shot a black kid who pointed a gun at him," Hunter reminded him. "Not that it matters."

"This place was a powder keg already," Mara mused, drumming her knuckles against the window. "Mister X lit the fuse."

Light the fuse. Eddie used to say it all the time. In high school before every football game, Eddie would crank up Metallica so loud your ears would bleed. Lighting the fuse. If they were heading out on the town, they'd do pre-party shots to light the fuse. In Ramadi, Eddie kept smelling salts in his pack. He'd break one open and jam it under his nose, inhaling, grunting and jumping up and down. Lighting his fuse. Hunter checked the rearview mirror, and Eddie's bloodshot eyes stared back at him.

Lance craned his neck as they passed a movie theater. "I took my wife to that theater the day before I deployed. Our last date."

The last time Hunter had been to a movie was with his son, who was ten years old at the time. Drew was seventeen now and only spent time with Hunter on the occasional awkward weekend and holiday. He harbored no ill-will toward Cindy. He was never around and things fell apart. The fact Drew and his ex-wife lived less than ten minutes from where they were now wasn't lost on him, and he felt pulled toward them. Hunter pinched himself on the leg to bring his focus back to the moment.

Lance droned on. "I can't believe it was just—"

Mara snapped her fingers in Lance's face. She'd heard his wistful tone too many times. She and Hunter had talked about Lance slipping into the past. It was like a runaway truck down a steep incline and there wasn't a chance in hell you would stop him.

"Focus, Lance," Mara said. "This ain't no time for a trip down memory lane."

Mara smacked the Garmin unit as the directions changed again. Hunter wouldn't let them use their phones or the tracking app in the truck. "This GPS is crap, Lance. Where's this sister of yours live?"

Lance's sister lived a few blocks away from the area they'd planned the shooting. The sister was out of town and owned a house with a garage which made it a perfect place for them to stage and keep their get-away vehicle from being torched by the rioters. They'd be in and out of there without anyone being any wiser.

"Turn here." Lance pointed down a side street, and Hunter wheeled the truck left. After a series of twists and turns while the last of the day's light faded away, he jabbed a finger at a house on Mara's side of the truck.

Hunter's headlights spilled across the front of the white, vinyl-sided ranch. The tidy grass yard was trimmed, but the bushes along the side of the house stretched over the concrete as Hunter guided the truck down the narrow pitted driveway. He stopped in front of a free-standing garage separated from the house by a rusty chain-link fence housing a small square patch of grass.

Lance jumped from the back seat and tried the garage door. Locked. He jogged to the back door of the house, climbed a couple of wood steps and fished a key from under the top step. A light spilled over the driveway from the kitchen window as Lance disappeared inside. He emerged seconds later waving another key. In moments, the garage door was up and Mara hopped out. Once inside the garage, Lance closed the door.

The garage was narrow, enough for the truck and some yard equipment resting on blotchy oil stains above spiderweb cracks in the foundation. Light diffused from a cobweb crusted pair of naked bulbs attached to the ceiling joists. The smell of motor oil and rotting trash from a garbage can filled the air.

Hunter dropped the tailgate and passed out the black clothing they'd wear for the op, slipping a Glock 19 in a shoulder holster under his jacket along with a few extra magazines of ammo. He slid a knife into his boot and pulled the pant leg back down. He peeked up in time to catch Lance eyeballing Mara as she undressed, but Hunter let it slide. For now. Lance's pre-occupation with Mara was starting to be an issue and one Hunter would have to address sooner rather than later before Lance starting entertaining possibilities of what could happen between them.

Slapping an area map down on the lowered tailgate, Hunter went through the plan again, Mara and Lance nodding along. After it went down, they'd hightail it back to the house and get the hell out of Dodge.

"Lance, you handle the protestors, Mara gets the counter protestors. Wait for my signal," Hunter said, handing them new burner phones. "If you get busted before the shootings, don't resist. The worst they can do is delay things. If it's after the shootings, do whatever it takes to get away. Shoot a cop in the head, throw a baby in the street, I don't care. Get back here and make sure nobody follows you. Any questions?"

"What if we can't get back here?" Mara asked.

"Head east. When you get somewhere you can hole up, call me and I'll come get you. I'll be closer to the truck than either of you."

Lance bounced on his toes. "This is it. Last op before the big one."

Hunter clapped a hand on his shoulder. "Yup. Let's make sure we don't screw it up. Nothing stops us."

"Nothing stops us," Lance repeated.

Hunter turned to Mara and kissed her on the forehead. "You ready to make some history, sweetheart?"

"For Anarchy Road," Mara beamed.

CHAPTER TWENTY THREE

Barb the Bartender directed Jake to two probable locations for her Uncle Chester. If he had any money in his pocket, Harrah's Casino in North Kansas City. If he was broke, the house of a sometimes girlfriend who danced during the day under the stage name of "Midnight" at a strip club called The Shady Lady on the edge of a sketchy neighborhood east of downtown. Barb gave them the address of the house.

As they walked to Bear's truck, Jake called a security contact at Harrah's who was well acquainted with Chester. His buddy swept the casino floor, but there was no sign of the man.

"Hey, Gates Bar-B-Q is a few blocks away from the house," Bear suggested. "Fill me up with some burnt ends and show me a strip club, and I'd die a happy man."

"You just ate a basket of fried pickles."

Bear looked offended. "That was an appetizer."

"I'm good with the barbecue, but we're hitting the stripper's house, not the club. Barb said Midnight works days."

Bear pouted. "Killjoy."

"You can't afford that place anyway. Lap dances are like thirty bucks apiece."

"And you know this how?"

"Got hired to do a surveillance job by a wife who wanted proof her lawyer husband was cheating on her. Followed him into the club."

Bear slipped a tobacco pouch between his cheek and gum, spitting into an empty soda bottle. "Was he? Cheating?"

"Nailing one of the dancers and snorting coke off her tits out back in his car. I had video."

"Classy guy."

After filling their bellies with ribs and burnt ends, Bear followed his GPS to the address Barb gave them off Benton Boulevard. They listened to the radio along the way, news reports of rioting in St. Louis following a police-involved shooting. Kansas City had its own protests downtown, but they'd been relatively peaceful.

The neighborhood was dark with most of the street lights broken out. Shady characters trudged around the broken sidewalks, bundled up against the cool spring evening. A group of kids kicked a soccer ball in the street under one of the working lamps, Bear's headlights splitting them to the curb. Their ten-year-old eyes hardened as the truck passed, one pointing a finger and shooting at Jake.

"Jesus," Bear said, trying to find a house number. "Nice place to be from."

"We've got worse areas back home, but I know what you mean."

They climbed out of the truck in front of Midnight's tiny house. The front yard was all dirt with sporadic patches of dead grass encased by a chain-link fence with a section missing. A concrete sidewalk led to the faded red brick house, enough space for one room on either side of a canary yellow front door, reinforced bars over the door and windows on either side.

"Is Chester going to be armed?" Bear asked.

"Probably not, but he won't be happy to see me and might run."

"Why?"

"My elbow slipped during our last encounter," Jake said. "It ran into his nose. Broke it."

"Funny how that can happen."

"He did try to knee me in the balls."

Dogs barked and snarled across the street as the smell of something burning wafted in on a slight northern breeze. The sound of gunshots from several blocks away echoed as Jake ticked his head toward the driveway disappearing around the side of the house. Bear took the cue and faded into the darkness to cover the back. Jake checked the Sig Sauer on his hip and knocked on the outer door.

After a few seconds a dark face peeked out from behind a curtain to his right. He waved. The face disappeared and a series of locks clicked and thumped. The inner yellow door opened, and a woman in her early thirties dressed in pink sweatpants and a tight white t-shirt appeared. She had long hair spilling over her shoulders and skin so black it was blue. Midnight. She was pretty, but the hard lines on her face matched the steely glint in her eyes.

"Help you?" she asked.

"I need to talk to Chester." Jake found if you said you were looking for someone, it implied you didn't know where they were and it was easy for the other party to confirm it. If you said you need to talk to someone, it gave the impression you knew they were there. It was a subtle difference, but effective.

"You a cop?"

"Do I look like one?"

Midnight scanned him up and down. "A little."

"I'm not, relax. My name's Jake. I'm a private investigator and I need to talk to Chester. He and I are acquainted."

She lit a skinny cigarette the length of a football field. "Don't know no Chester."

"You dance at the Shady Lady?"

Midnight blew a plume of smoke through the door. "Not as much as I used to."

"Then you know Chester. His niece Barb sent me. It's important."

"Your name's Jake? You the guy that busted his nose a few months back?"

"I thought you didn't know him."

Midnight snorted. "He snores like a damn freight train now coz of you. Anyway, he ain't here."

"You sure?"

She plopped her hands on her hips and drew back. "Muthafucka, you callin' me a liar?"

A door slammed at the back of the house, metal trash cans clanged and shouts echoed in the night. Jake turned as Bear emerged from the corner of the house with Chester's scrawny ass in tow, one oversized hand twisting Chester's arm behind his back and the other clamped on his neck.

"Take it easy, man," Chester moaned as Bear shoved him forward. "You're gonna break my arm."

Bear presented Chester to Jake. "This little weasel took a swipe at me with a knife."

"A butter knife," Chester said. "I was makin' a

sandwich when I heard this asshole's name."

Jake stepped down to the sidewalk and ticked his head to Bear to release Chester.

Chester rubbed his freed arms and glowered at Jake. Standing five foot six, he might weigh a hundred and twenty-five pounds fully clothed and carrying an anvil. Excessive smoking and drinking lined his pale complexion, and Jake wasn't sure what to call the foul odor seeping from his pores. "What do you want, Caldwell? Wanna break my nose again?"

"C4," Jake said.

Chester barked a laugh. "You want C4? Go fuck yourself."

Jake reached out and squeezed Chester's nose. The skinny man howled and tried to back away, but Bear blocked his path.

"You said you just wanted ta talk to him," Midnight said from the open front door.

"That's before he told me to fuck myself," Jake said, releasing his nose. "Be nice, Chester or I'll break more than your nose."

Chester pressed his nose between his dirty palms, tears slipping from the corner of his clenched eyes. "Goddamn that hurts, you ass…never mind."

"I don't want C4," Jake said. "I want to know if you know where one could obtain it."

"What for?"

"Does it matter?"

Chester straightened, wiping tears away. "It does. You plan on blowing something up and it gets traced back to me, I'm fucked. I don't like to be fucked unless Midnight is doing it."

Midnight grumbled. "Glad one of us be enjoyin' it."

Jake pulled a c-note from his wallet. "Someone blew

a backpack of C4 at the T-Mobile arena last night."

"I don't sell the stuff."

"My daughter and I were caught up in the blast, and she's in the ICU with a tube coming out of her head."

"Hematoma?" Midnight asked.

Jake's eyes widened with surprise.

"I was studyin' to be a nurse before I ran outta money for school," she said.

Jake waggled the hundred-dollar bill in front of Chester. "If you don't sell it, give me a place to look. You're the man who knows how to find things."

Chester's eyes flicked between Jake and Bear. "That's it? A name and you give me a hundred bucks?"

"Two hundred if the lead pans out. But if you send me on a wild goose chase, I'll find you and pulverize your knee caps to powder."

Chester thought for a moment. "Only one place in the U.S. makes it. Army ammunition plant in Kingsport, Tennessee. You gotta purchase it through a legit explosive distributor and I don't know none of them."

Jake moved the bill toward his pocket. "So you're of no help to me whatsoever."

Chester's eyes locked on the bill and waved his hands. "Whoa, whoa, I didn't say that. I had nothin' to do with the Sprint Center shit."

"Didn't say you did."

"But I know a guy who might happen to have a certain supply of a certain said aforementioned military type explosive."

Jake raised the bill again. "Don't try and talk like a smart person, Chester. Who's the guy?"

"It don't get back to me? This guy's crazy, like 'rub my dick raw with a cheese grater' crazy if he found out I gave him up."

"I'll forget I know your name. Who is it?"

"Lenny Moritz."

Lenny Moritz. Jake knew him. Former muscle for Teddy Garrett, one of Keats's rivals who was serving a thirty-year sentence for drugs and weapons charges. Lenny turned state's evidence against Teddy and somehow avoided a prison sentence and a river-soaked cement block tied to his ankles. Last Jake heard, Lenny was in a pine box.

"Lenny's dead, Chester," Jake said, stuffing the c-note in his pocket. "Rubbed out in a drive-by last year."

Chester scoffed. "Bullshit. I talked to the guy last month. Lives out in Wyandotte County by the water park."

"You sure?"

"If I'm lyin', I'm dyin'."

"Would he talk to me?"

"He'd shoot you before he talked to you. But if I was with you…maybe."

"What about the whole cheese grater dick crazy thing?" Bear asked.

"I'll take my chances. A man's gotta eat," Chester said.

Jake poked a tongue in his cheek and exhaled. "Let me guess, for the right price, you'd be willing to make the introduction."

Chester rubbed his dirty fingertips together. "I think a cool thousand would cover it."

"Try two hundred. I'll throw in another hundred for hazard pay if he actually whips out a cheese grater."

Chester considered the offer. "You wanna drive or should I?"

Bear shuddered. "Can we put him in the back of the truck? I don't want to stink up my cab."

CHAPTER TWENTY FOUR

Chester didn't bemoan the fact he'd be riding in the back, especially when Bear said he'd break his face if he smoked in the cab of the truck. While they rolled down the highway heading toward Kansas City, Kansas, Jake called Maggie to check on Halle. Her head still hurt but she was more lucid as the hours passed. Doctors said they'd leave the drain tube in her skull but were hopeful she'd be able to walk out of the hospital in four or five days if there were no complications.

They crossed into Kansas heading toward I-435 as Jake called Snell for an update. He put her on speaker so Bear could listen in.

"No hit on the window print yet," Snell said. "We're running through the lawyer's client list to see if anyone matches the people in the video. Foster is working with the ATF on the C4 angle but haven't heard anything from her other than the fat ass across the street keeps calling her."

"Skinny's a quitter," Jake said. "He'll get discouraged and fade into the woodwork eventually. Bear and I are chasing a C4 lead as well."

"I don't suppose telling you to stay out of a federal investigation would do any good?"

"No," Jake said.

Snell sighed. "I didn't think so. A lead from where?"

"A guy I know."

"I forgot you know a lot of guys," Snell said. "Anything we should know?"

"Not yet."

"Why do you make always me nervous, Caldwell?"

"Beats the hell outta me," Jake said. "When have I failed to come through?"

"You always come through, but you tend to leave a gargantuan pile of chaos and destruction in your wake."

"I'll be careful this time. Besides, Bear's here to keep an eye on me."

"That doesn't make me feel better," Snell said. "You guys and Foster should connect. We're picking up some chatter about something big in the works."

"Chatter from where?" Bear asked.

"Some right-wing groups we've interviewed."

"How far right?" Jake asked.

"Off the scale," Snell said. "DTR, Liberty Keepers and the Armed and Ready Society, to name a few. We're especially concerned since we've heard the same thing from different sources. Talk to Foster."

Jake tapped his foot against the floor mat. "Let me see if this pans out first. Could be a wild goose chase."

After promising to call after their meeting with Lenny, Jake ended the conversation.

"What do you know about this Lenny guy?" Bear asked.

"Never dealt with him personally. The guy's a little long in the tooth, so it's been a while since I heard stories from Keats. They've crossed paths before."

"Big shocker. What kind of stories?"

"Like, he's one of those end of days guys," Jake said. "Lots of guns and ammo, enough food rations to make it through a nuclear fallout. Keats said if the zombie apocalypse hit, he'd camp out at Lenny's."

They exited north off I-70 onto I-435. The Legends shopping area, the Kansas Speedway, and Hollywood Casino where Jake played poker on occasion disappeared in their rearview mirror as they headed east down a four-lane road.

Chester tapped on the back window and signaled for them to pull over. Bear eased into a parking lot of a closed auto dealer. Chester clambered over the side of the truck with the grace of a sloth in a body cast, smoothing his windblown greasy hair as Jake rolled down his window.

Chester pointed up the darkened road. "Lenny's place is a half mile up ahead. Has one of them squawk security boxes in front of a gate. There'll be a camera, too, so don't look suspicious. Dude's paranoid."

"Will he recognize you?" Bear asked.

"Yeah, so let me do the talking. I'll vouch for you, say you want to buy some hardware. He makes his own AR-15s. You need to take him serious."

"The guy makes his own guns and sells C4," Jake said. "We'll take him seriously."

Jake and Bear wrinkled their noses while Chester climbed in the back of the cab. Two minutes later, they parked in front of a long, black, wrought iron gate with haphazard lines and angles. While the gate physically blocked the drive, whoever built it must have done it in an introduction to welding class. The camera system was no joke, and it took Chester a minute to convince the voice behind the controls to open the gate. After a brief pause, the wrought iron contraption squealed as it swung open.

Bear pulled up a gravel drive toward a long, ranch-style house in the distance. "Thought we were going to have to drive around the gate for a minute to get in."

"Bad idea," Chester said. "Knowin' Lenny, he'd have it mined or somethin'. Pull 'round to the garage on the right side."

The house sat on a spacious lot, a good quarter mile from the road. Jake couldn't spot another house in sight. Budding oak trees towered over the roof of the low-slung ranch, lit up by a myriad of spotlights slamming on as they approached. Bear's headlights spilled across the front of the grey house, past a pair of eyes peeking out through drawn blinds. The eyes disappeared as Bear's truck crunched over gravel and stopped in front of a cinder-blocked building thirty yards from the house. One of two large garage doors rolled up as a dark figure slipped toward them from the house.

"Go on and pull in," Chester said. "Lenny'll close the door behind us. He don't like to do business out in the open."

Bear bit his lower lip as he shot a worried squint at Jake.

Jake didn't like it either but nodded his head toward the garage.

Bear grumbled something unintelligible and slid the truck forward.

The garage was empty but for the dusty concrete floor, and sagging shelves holding parts and chunks of metal. Jars of screws and washers sat on a workbench under a peg board of hammers and saws. Cobwebs crusted the corners of the garage, and a wood railed staircase along the north wall led down.

Chester opened the back door of the truck and climbed out.

"I don't like this," Bear said, his voice low. "Something's off."

"I know what you mean," Jake said. "Stay on your toes."

They climbed from the cab as a side door to the garage swung open. A man in his mid-fifties with a shock of disheveled gray hair entered and kicked the door closed behind him. His caterpillar eyebrows were drawn together over wild eyes emitting a crazed energy. It wasn't the man's eyes causing Jake and Bear to stop in mid-stride. It was the AR-15 the man pointed at them.

CHAPTER TWENTY FIVE

In a normal setting, wearing a mask and black clothing tended to draw unwanted attention to yourself. It wasn't a problem with the protests sweeping the country—at least half of the crowd wore similar gear which allowed Hunter to blend in. He walked along with the chanting crowd, holding up a No Justice, No Peace sign from the stash of signs, bricks, and frozen water bottles Mister X arranged to be delivered a half mile from the gathering point by the church. A text went out to a handful of Antifa members in the crowd who passed along the message to those around them. He rolled his eyes at the talking networks heads who claimed Antifa was an idea instead of an organization despite the overwhelming evidence in front of them.

The St. Louis protestors were amped up, their energy of the injustice done in their community wafting off them like heat waves off summertime blacktop. They had no qualms at spitting on police, beating down anyone wearing the wrong hat, or breaking windows of nearby businesses using whatever implements were at their disposal.

Hunter didn't give a damn about their message or their cause. He made no judgements of the right or wrong of their actions. The protestors and right-wing counter-protestors were two sides of a corrupt coin, the fire in their bellies perpetuated and encouraged by the government entities they supposedly rose up against or protected. To Hunter, there was no difference between Right and Left—they both sought order in their own corrupt ways.

He marveled at how much he sounded like his old man. If there was one thing his dad liked to beat on more than his wife and children, it was the government. Get Arthur Brenner a few stiff drinks and he'd wax on for hours. The more he drank, the farther back people tended to retreat. The problem with being a child was there was only so far you could shrink away.

What would have happened if his father had been driving the car that day as planned instead of Hunter's older brother? Though he'd just been twelve years old, Hunter rigged the brakes on the car to fail with his father behind the wheel. He didn't count on his brother taking the car that day. The most surprising thing was the lack of emotion over his brother dying in the ensuing crash. Still, things would have been better with his old man in a box.

As much as he hated his father, Hunter recognized the influence his father wielded over him. Hunter's father's favorite quote was from Henry Adams, a historian and descendant of two presidents — "Chaos was the law of nature; Order was the dream of man." He made Hunter recite it on command. As much of an asshole as his father was, he wasn't wrong about the quote. Hunter learned long ago that the government fulfilled the law of nature of wreaking chaos in its pursuit of an order which was nothing but a pipe dream.

Hunter fingered the gun under his jacket as the anger of the crowd fueled its own flames and blossomed. It would take a mere nudge to send the mob over the edge, which was exactly what he and his team intended to do.

He linked up Mara and Lance via his burner phone. "I'm two blocks from the church, about to reach the target area. You two in place?"

"I'm ready," Mara said. "Let's do this thing."

Lance grunted. "Crowd's thick and tight, but I'll be ready in a minute."

"Leave the line open," Hunter said. "I want to hear it."

The crowd flowed toward the square, and Hunter flowed along with it, blending in as another anonymous face. The church lit up in the distance, flames from a nearby building reflecting against its golden dome. Smoke floated like a fog over the blacktop.

He edged toward the curb and stepped to the sidewalk in front of a pair of apartment buildings, their pitted bricks climbing five stories high on either side of an alley encased in shadows. He slipped into the darkness and crouched behind a dumpster a dozen feet from the opening. Over his shoulder, his escape route was clear with no sign of foot traffic or vehicles.

Across the alley, obscured by the shadows, Eddie crouched against the brick wall, dressed in camouflage, his bony knees drawn to his chest, doused with wet blood from the fateful night in Ramadi. What are you doin', man?

"Go away," Hunter said, grinding his teeth.

This is fucked up, Hunter, even for you, and I know what you did in Iraq.

Hunter squeezed his eyes shut, his voice weak. "It was Fletcher's idea."

Try and blame what happened on the Horsemen all you want, muchacho. This one's on you.

"Please go away," Hunter said, a pleading tone in his voice that he hated.

Gone, but not forgotten.

When Hunter allowed his eyes to creep open again, Eddie was thankfully gone.

"Holy shit," Lance shouted through the earpiece. "Cops shot another kid at the church. Cops just shot an unarmed black kid at the church. Let's go!"

In the background, the crowd noise went from a seven to an eleven. Screams of anger rattled the phone, growing as Lance repeated the fake news.

"We're moving," he panted. "Go, Mara."

Seconds later, Mara screamed. "Antifa's beat down a cop by the church. They're gonna lynch him from a light pole. They're gonna lynch a cop! Let's go."

The cries from the counter-protestors weren't as instantaneous or loud, but they grew quickly as Mara repeated her lies.

"We're moving," she said.

Ten minutes later, the crowd streaming past the alley opening thickened, the rage more palpable as the fake news filtered its way through the mob. Hunter stayed in the shadows behind the dumpster. Did the rotten garbage smell come from the container he hid behind or the souls of the crowd on the street?

A throat-shredding yell erupted from the street, and the mob heading toward the church turned their collective heads. Hunter slipped his gun from his shoulder holster and racked in a round, holding the piece by his side. The counter-protestors pouring in from the south met the protestors streaming from the east. The protestors near the church ran toward the commotion and a brawl ensued before Hunter's eyes. Punches were thrown, batons and bats arced through the air along with a bevy of rocks and bottles. The fainter at heart scrambled away from the melee, some falling to the ground before being trampled by the mob of bodies. A minute later, a swarm of police in full riot gear descended on the crowd shoving riot shields and batons, trying to split the warring factions.

Hunter half-considered letting things play out. It was a thing of chaotic beauty to watch.

"I'm clear," Mara crackled over the Bluetooth.

"Clear," Lance responded a moment later.

Hunter reached into his coat and extracted an Enola Gay CM75 Cloud Maker smoke grenade he bought online under a fake name. The beast would belch out ninety-thousand cubic feet of smoke over three minutes, providing abundant cover to conceal his shots. He waited for an opening, pulled the wire, and tossed the spinning grenade into the crowd.

Screams erupted as the black smoke belched from the canister.

Hunter took aim over the top of the dumpster, his finger tight on the trigger. He waited for some semblance of remorse at what he was about to do. It didn't come. His father's voice rattled in his head. Shit happens, people die, things get destroyed.

As the smoke cloud grew, he checked over his shoulder again.

Alley was clear.

The bodies of the mob disappeared behind the fog.

The radical left and the radical right, people who were nothing but sheep. Controlled by the system, spewing lies the media and internet trolls told them. Both sides wanted a justice that didn't exist. A justice they were manipulated into believing they deserved, but they didn't deserve a damn thing. Fuck them.

Hunter emptied his magazine, swinging the gun from side to side as he squeezed off shot after shot. At least four bodies dropped through the smoke before he turned and darted back down the alley toward the rendezvous point, slapping in a fresh magazine and slipping the weapon back in his holster as he ran.

Eddie waited for him on the street at the end of the alley, propped against the cool brick wall, his hooded brown eyes accusing. Hunter ran past him, unwilling to meet his gaze.

He knew what he did. He didn't need Eddie to remind him.

CHAPTER TWENTY SIX

Lenny stopped fifteen feet away, swinging the barrel of the AR-15 back and forth between Jake and Bear. "Who the fuck're you two and what do you want?"

"I'm Jake. This is my buddy James."

"Howdy," Bear said.

Lenny crinkled his nose. "Howdy? You some kinda cowboy or somethin'? Gonna do the two-step for me?"

"I can if you wanna watch me fall on my ass," Bear said, pointing to the rifle in Lenny's hand. "You mind pointing that barrel somewhere other than my dick?"

Lenny's teeth disappeared and the rifle barrel moved from Bear's crotch to his face. "This better, cowboy?"

"Not really, no. What the hell's going on, Chester? You said this guy was cool."

Out of the corner of his eye, Jake spotted Chester fading back to the workbench along the wall.

"You two cops?" Lenny asked.

"Not last time I checked," Jake answered, remaining still. Lenny's darting eyes and wide pupils caused his lizard brain to crack open the adrenaline valve. "You make the AR-15 yourself?"

"I make all my own stuff. Don't trust nobody but these two hands, especially since Colt stopped makin' 'em for the civilian market."

"We're looking to buy."

"How many?"

"How many you have?"

Lenny spit on the floor, swung the barrel of the AR-15 to Jake's head and edged forward. Jake shifted from Lenny's crazy eyes to the gnarled finger resting against the trigger guard. It would take a microsecond for Lenny's finger to slip down on the trigger, but knowing he had that time helped keep Jake's pulse from exploding out of his neck.

"Maybe I don't have any," Lenny spat. "I don't know you."

Jake chewed the inside of his cheek. "I used to work for Jason Keats. He'll vouch for me."

"Bullshit."

"You want to call him?"

Lenny flicked his eyes between Jake and Bear. "How come you don't work for him anymore?"

"Personal reasons. It wasn't easy to get out, but I did."

Lenny snorted. "I'll bet. You got money?"

Jake nodded, gaping down the cold black barrel of the rifle. He was sick of it pointing at his forehead. "Probably enough for several depending on what you're charging. If my friends like them, I'll be back for more."

"What friends?"

"The kind who wrap themselves in the American flag and believe the second shoulda been the first."

Lenny grinned, but the barrel of the rifle didn't

move. "A lot more of those guys comin' outta the woodwork lately. Two grand each. Those are friend prices, seein' how you know Chester and all. You got the money?"

Jake only had two hundred in his wallet. "Can I check them out, or are you going to keep threatening me with that one?"

Lenny took a half-step forward, the barrel a foot from Jake's head. Behind them, the distinctive click of a hammer being pulled back sounded. Chester. Bear's head pitched forward as Chester shoved a revolver in the back of his skull.

"Maybe you give Chester and me the money, and I'll let you walk outta here alive."

"What about the guns? You don't have them?"

Lenny showed off a crooked smile. "Oh, I got 'em all downstairs, but I ain't sellin' any of it to you. Give me the money."

"You think I'm bringing thousands in cash to meet with someone I don't know?" Jake asked.

The grin vanished from Lenny's face, and he pressed the rifle barrel into Jake's forehead. "You sayin' you don't have it? You don't put on a condom unless you're gonna fuck. Now, gimme the goddamn money before I put so many holes in you that you bleed like a colander."

Jake pinched his lips tight. He'd counted on verifying the guns, inquiring about the C4 and promising to come back later than night or the next day to complete the sale. He didn't want the stupid guns, he just wanted information. Now he and Bear were in a tight spot with guns at their heads.

"Bear?" Jake asked, "You remember how much I love Hawaiian fruit?"

A few months back in Nebraska while chasing down some money laundering cash stolen from Keats, Bear gave Jake the ridiculous signal word of "pineapple" to trigger the time for action. They joked about it often since the bar shootout, so Jake was certain Bear would get the reference.

"You feelin' a hankerin' to eat some?" Bear asked.

Lenny's finger slid toward the trigger, his face crunched up like he tried to remember the order of the planets in the solar system. "What the hell are you two babblin' about?"

"I'm hungry," Jake said. "Pineapple."

Jake ducked low and slammed his forearm up as he stepped into Lenny. The barrel of the AR-15 swung to the ceiling as bullets rained against the roof, the shots deafening inside the empty concrete structure. His ears ringing, Jake threw his elbow under Lenny's chin, and Lenny staggered back, the AR-15 clattering to the floor.

To his left, Bear pinned Chester's arm and engulfed Chester's skinny wrist in his paw, jerking the barrel of the .38 Special to the floor. He twisted Chester's wrist and, even over the ringing in his ears, the bones cracked. The .38 smacked to the floor by the AR-15 as Bear forced Chester to his knees or risk having his arm ripped from his socket.

Jake turned back to Lenny who staggered back a few feet and slipped a hunting knife from a sheath at his back. Wiping the blood from his mouth with the back of his forearm, he waved the eight-inch knife at Jake. "Come on, motherfucker. Show me what you got."

Jake jammed his hands on his hips. "Seriously, Lenny? You had your finger on the trigger of an AR-

15 implanted in my forehead and lost the battle. You think you're going to get me with a knife?"

Jake's calm gave Lenny a moment of pause as the knife stopped cutting the air in front of him.

Next to him, Bear had the rifle hanging at his side in his left hand and the .38 in his right, aiming it at Lenny. His giant, booted foot ground down on Chester's shattered wrist while Chester lay on the floor howling.

"You make one move with the knife," Bear said. "And I'll put a bullet between your eyes."

Lenny's chest heaved, his breath rapid and ragged. "You're gonna kill me anyway and steal my guns. Go ahead."

Jake raised his hands. "We're not killing anybody. We're looking for some C4 and heard you were the man to see."

"C4? Why the hell would I have any C4? You said you wanted AR-15s."

His response was slow and mechanical, his eyes darting away at his C4 comment. It was brief but there. Jake was a poker player at heart and knew Lenny lied.

"Listen," Jake said, eyes flicking to the knife. "I want some information. You put down the knife and tell me what you know, and you'll walk out of this unscathed. If you don't and come at me with that knife, I'll put you in traction for six months. That's if Bear doesn't shoot your dumb ass first or throw you in jail before we turn you over to the Feds."

"Jail? You two said you weren't cops."

"I'm not, he is," Jake said. "What's it going to be, Lenny? A little info and you walk away from this, or excruciating pain and you don't walk anytime in the near future?"

Lenny sucked his cheeks in tight, wild eyes darting around the garage. The one way out was through Jake and Bear to the door, and Bear had a gun pointed at him. He groaned and tossed the knife across the garage floor.

"Who are you two? For real." Lenny asked, crimson creeping up his pale neck.

"Concerned citizens with friends in high places. We're looking for the arena bombers and the source of the C4 they used."

Lenny shifted back and forth on his skinny legs. "You and every law enforcement dick in four states."

"You sell any recently?"

"I ain't sayin' shit. I want my lawyer."

Jake stepped forward and crowded Lenny back against the tool bench, battling against the halitosis rolling from Lenny's mouth. He pressed against the man, their noses touching. "You're not under arrest, but if you don't answer my questions, the only person anyone is going to need to call is the coroner to pick up your pulverized body. Whoever set off the bomb almost killed me and my daughter so I don't give a flying fuck what you do or who you sell it to until it nearly kills someone in my family. Now, did you sell some C4 to anyone recently?"

"No," Lenny said, dropping his head. Another lie.

Jake clamped his fingers around Lenny's throat and squeezed, not hard enough to cut off the man's oxygen, but enough that Lenny knew Jake could if he wanted to. "Don't lie to me, Lenny. I'll gut you like a deer right here in this garage with your own hunting knife. Leave you and Chester dangling from the rafters to bleed out. Slowly."

Lenny's lips disappeared in a line. "He'll kill me."

"I'll kill you. Right now. For certain. Give me a name."

"And you won't call the cops?"

"You have my word, as long as you don't lie to me again."

Lenny glared at Chester lying on the ground, forehead planted against the cold concrete. "Chester, you tell a soul about this and I'll—"

"Chester ain't gonna say anything," Bear said, twisting his boot on Chester's wrist. "Are you, Chester?"

Chester groaned and shook his head.

"Name?" Jake asked.

"Wallace Humphrey," Lenny said, eyes locked on Jake. "I swear, a guy named Wallace Humphrey."

"Who's he?"

"He's a member of the 2A Militia. Small group, but crazy as shithouse rats. Lives here in town off Leavenworth Road."

"You have the address?" Jake asked, releasing the pressure from Lenny's throat, and the man spilled the address. "How much did you sell him?"

"Everything I had. Sixty pounds."

Jake cranked his head to Bear and his wide eyes. Sixty pounds of C4 in the hands of some nuts. It would blow a hole in the earth.

"When?"

It took Lenny a few seconds to generate enough brain power to do the arithmetic. "Like five months ago. I swear I didn't know what they were gonna use it for."

Jake shoved Lenny toward Bear. "I'm sure that'll help your case."

Jake fished around in the drawers of the tool bench. In the second one from the bottom, he found a package of thick, black zip ties. After securing a protesting Lenny and Chester to the support pole in the garage with enough zip tie pressure to bulge their skin, they headed toward the truck.

"Let's call Snell and Foster," Jake said. "Tell them what we found and where these two assholes are."

"Who's Snell and Foster?" Lenny asked.

"FBI agents. You'll meet them in a few minutes."

Lenny's eyes blazed. "You promised you weren't gonna call the cops if I gave you a name."

"I'm not calling the cops. I'm calling the Feds," Jake said. "Enjoy your time in prison, dick head."

"What about my money?" Chester asked.

They ignored Chester. Bear opened the garage door and backed up the truck. Jake closed the garage door and slipped out the door Lenny came in. He hopped in the passenger side as Bear gunned it down the driveway.

"Sixty pounds of C4?" Bear marveled. "Jesus Mary Mother of Joseph."

"Snell said she's heard chatter of something big being planned. I have a feeling those sixty pounds might have something to do with it."

NOW

CHAPTER TWENTY SIX

"Vengeance?" Jake had described almost killing his father Stony with a hammer and stealing his car, taking out Shane Langston and strangling the psychopath in the courtroom as justice. Apparently, Dr. Tate thought it was the wrong word.

Dr. Tate crossed her long legs. "Those instances you described and your response to them doesn't sound like justice, it sounds like vengeance."

"Maybe sometimes they're the same thing."

She pondered the statement for a moment. "Maybe. But not always."

Jake plopped back on the couch, weary from the mental exercise she put him through. He'd bet she'd never gotten her hands dirty in her life beyond tending a garden and certainly not the way Jake had. He pressed his hands into his thighs to keep from throwing something. Her naiveté about the real world was getting old.

Jake scowled. "Why don't you give me your definition of justice?"

"You still haven't given me yours."

"Maybe I'm too dumb to put it into pretty words, but I gave you a sufficient number of examples for you to figure it out."

Dr. Tate doodled on her notepad, swirling her pen tip in circles. "Fine. Justice is the principle that people receive that which they deserve within the confines of the law. Vengeance is retribution or retaliation for a wrong. I'd like for you to tell me how what you did doesn't constitute vengeance."

"Why?"

"Because a just man isn't dangerous to others. But a vengeful man is."

Jake met her penetrating gaze as she waited for his response. He still didn't understand the point of tilling up the past like a farmer's auger ripping through the hard, packed soil. He didn't understand why she pushed this vengeance angle so hard, and it caused him to carve half-moons into his palms from his fingernails.

She waited patiently. She had a demeanor that left Jake unbalanced. On one hand, she was easy to talk to. Lord knows he hadn't even told Maggie some of the things he told Dr. Tate. But, at the same time, those bronze eyes that were the color and shine of a new penny locked in on you like a fighter jet during a dogfight. No matter how much he banked and spun, she had a missile lock on him and wasn't going to let him off easy. He forced himself to take a few calming breaths.

"Are you married?" Jake asked.

She tapped her pen against her notepad, her voice pinched. "We're not here to talk about me, and it's inappropriate of you to ask."

Jake threw his hands up, surrendering. "Relax,

Doc. I'm not asking you out or anything. I was thinking how I bet people don't get away with much with you on the questioning side of things. You have this soul-searing stare."

A giggle erupted from her thin lips which she covered with her hand. "Excuse me."

"Nothing to excuse," Jake said. "You have a good laugh. But what's so funny?"

She hooked a lock of hair over her ear. "It's just my girlfriend says the same thing, about my stare. Especially when she comes home late after being out with her co-workers."

"She the one in the picture over there?" Jake asked, flicking a thumb toward the bookshelves.

"Yes. She says I should've been a lawyer."

"You would've been good."

She wiped the emotion from her face. "Which is why I won't let you deflect this justice definition versus vengeance anymore. I think it's important we establish you know the difference."

Jake chewed on the inside of his cheek. "Since I'm considered a danger and all."

"Only to the man you strangled. And this Shane character. And the guy who killed his wife."

"We're going to be here a long time if you keep adding to the list."

"Be serious, Jake."

He slid to the edge of the couch. "I am. There's a problem with your definition of justice."

"And what's that?"

"You said with justice people get what they deserve within the confines of the law. But you know it isn't a realistic definition."

"It's not?"

A hot flush crept up his neck. "Our criminal justice system may work most of the time, but it's not flawless. And your definition doesn't account for the stuff that doesn't make it into the system. My mother getting beaten twice a week for no reason, my father shattering my knee with a lead pipe, the prick who killed his wife and buried her in a shallow grave, Shane Langston killing my brother. Those are all things that never made it to the inside of a courtroom where those righteous scales of justice sat idle. And this psycho made it through those scales and broke through those confines of the law without a scratch on him other than the ones I put there. You tell me how that's justice."

Dr. Tate's eyes softened. She opened her mouth to say something, then closed it again.

Jake stuck his elbows on his knees and pointed a finger at her. "But you were right about vengeance. It's punishment or retribution inflicted for a wrong that's been done. People get hurt or killed, and those who did the deed get to walk away. The psycho in the courtroom killed and he walked away. He sat on the scales of justice with his legs casually swinging before sliding off and leaving a free man. The truth is, when justice fails, someone has to step up and balance the scales. Sometimes, when justice fails, vengeance is all that's left."

Now it was Dr. Tate's turn to not have a reply.

THEN

CHAPTER TWENTY EIGHT

After Jake and Bear called Snell, it took the FBI ninety minutes to get to Lenny's, question him, and get a search warrant on Wallace Humphrey. In the meantime, Jake and Bear took a trip to the address Lenny provided. Bear stopped the truck at the mouth of a driveway protected by a rusty gate attached to warped wood posts. He killed the lights but left the engine running.

Humphrey's two-story house slumped a hundred yards off Leavenworth Road on a patch of acreage split by a deep-rutted dirt road leading to the abode. It was too dark to make out any detail leading to the house, but lights from the lower level bit back the night. A dark shape hulked to the east of the house, maybe a barn.

Jake raised a pair of night vision binoculars Bear kept under the seat and trained them on the house. No sign of life other than the lights.

"See anything?" Bear asked.

"Lights are on but can't tell if anybody's home. A dark F150 in the driveway in front but that's it. Should we take a closer look?"

Bear snagged the binoculars from Jake and looked for himself. "Let's do the smart thing for once and wait on the warrant and Snell."

"Smart is boring."

"True, but anyone who buys sixty pounds of C4 is going to be on edge. I'd rather have a squad of cops and Feds storming the castle than us. I'm trying not to push my luck when it comes to dodging bullets."

Jake scratched his chin. "Good point.

They pulled down the road and turned north down a pitch-black country road. Bear called his wife and Jake checked in with Maggie. There was no change in Halle's condition, but the doctors were still optimistic. Jake then checked in with his informants, but it was a fruitless exercise. They were happy to see the convoy of cars snake behind Bear's truck. A half dozen dark SUVs and another half dozen Kansas City, Kansas and county sheriff cars lit up the countryside before killing their lights.

Snell and Foster met Jake and Bear by their truck, waving the warrant. "I hope this pans out. It's the best lead we've had yet."

"Even a blind squirrel finds a nut every once in a while," Jake said. "What'd you find out about this guy?"

"Wallace Humphrey," Foster read from a notepad with a penlight. "Age thirty-eight, white, six feet, two inches weighing two-thirty. Earned a DUI five years ago along with resisting arrest. Other than that, he's been clean. He's pinged on the radar with the 2A Militia. They're local, only twenty members, but they peg the scale on the alt-right radar when you start digging into their on-line presence."

Snell handed them a picture of Humphrey's mug

shot. He was a handsome man with high cheekbones, piercing eyes, and a thick, but trimmed beard. A long, horizontal scar ran down his check.

"What'd he do?"

"Army vet, honorable discharge a few years back. Now he's a plumber. Has his own business. Tax records show he does okay. The property he lives on was passed down to him from his parents who died while he was in the service."

"Does this 2A Militia have ties to bigger groups?" Bear asked.

"Some chatter of support of the Proud Boys, but they mostly bluster about second amendment rights, thus their name. Like I said, they've shown up in a few inquiries after clashes with Black Lives Matter protestors downtown a few months ago, but nothing came of it."

Two burly guys walked up, decked out in so much protective gear Jake was surprised they could move. "We're ready to roll."

"What do you want me and Bear to do?" Jake asked.

"Nothing," Snell said. "Let us handle serving the warrant. You guys did a great job getting us here, but I don't want another shit storm like the stockyards."

She was referring to a couple years ago when Jake tracked a bioweapon to a meeting in Kansas City's old stockyards district. While Snell and Foster were involved, Jake took center stage. When the copious amount of smoke cleared, the terrorists and associated bad guys were dead and the bioweapon contained, but Snell took the political brunt of allowing Jake to do what he did.

"We've got this," she said. "Officially, you and Bear

should leave the area and let us handle it. Go to the casino down the road and play some poker."

Jake winked. "Gotcha. If you're rolling in dark, watch the driveway. Has ruts as deep as the Grand Canyon. Can we at least listen in?"

"There may or may not be an extra radio in my trunk." Snell said, returning the wink. She twirled her finger in the air. "Let's roll."

Minutes later, the stream of cars rolled past them. Two KCK squad cars blocked off traffic on Leavenworth Road a quarter mile in each direction. Bear trailed the last SUV as it turned onto the blacktop. Once the caravan turned into Humphrey's driveway, their taillights bumped and bounced. Bear resumed his spot at the driveway opening. Jake turned up the radio and trained the binoculars on the house.

"You good with staying back here?" Jake asked.

"You heard Snell. Besides, I've had enough guns pointed at my head for one night."

"You going to tell Maggie about Lenny's garage?"

Bear snickered. "She'd cut off my balls before she cut off yours."

Everything proceeded smoothly as the law enforcement vehicles approached the house. Two of the SUVs emptied, and dark shadows took up positions in the front or disappeared around the sides of the house. Low voices emanated through the radio as people checked in from their positions.

A minute later, a figure in an FBI jacket that appeared to be Snell climbed the porch steps along with one of the county deputies. Jake scanned the cars and spotted Foster tucked safely behind Snell's Fusion with her gun drawn. Snell and the deputy stood on either side of the front door and pounded. The deep voice of the deputy announced their presence and they had a warrant.

There was no answer and no movement in the lighted windows.

The deputy pounded again.

Two seconds later, the front door exploded, glass shattered, and gun fire sparked through the upstairs windows of the house, lighting up the night. Wallace Humphrey had company and a ton of firepower.

CHAPTER TWENTY NINE

The radio erupted with chatter, the teams calling out positions of the shooters. Unknown voices cried out they were hit. Those in the front of the house were pinned behind their cars as bullets slammed into the metal bodies. From the end of the driveway, Jake spotted one body sprawled in the middle of the dirt. He scanned the porch and saw a body lying still and another crawling away, but he couldn't tell which one was Snell.

In front of the house, agents and cops periodically rose above the protective cover of their vehicles and returned fire, but a hail of bullets from machine guns spewing fire from the upper floor windows locked them in place.

"Jesus Christ," Jake said. "It's like trying to storm a German bunker at Normandy. Those guys are pinned down and outgunned. We gotta do something."

Bear jumped from the truck and pulled his .308 Winchester rifle from the back, propping it on the bed of his truck. He peered through the scope. "Tell me where, Jake."

Jake raised the binoculars, the spotlights from the law enforcement vehicles that hadn't been shot out yet providing the details. His whole body buzzed with adrenaline. "There's a dude at the left window, two on the right. Man and a woman. Any of them works."

Over the radio, Snell barked orders to the ground troops. Another voice yelled for reinforcements. Chatter from those covering the back of the house said they took fire as well.

Bear exhaled and squeezed the trigger. The head of the long-haired man at the trigger of the mounted machine gun exploded, his body tumbling back. The woman at the window screamed and disappeared.

"One down," Jake said. "Get the guy on the left."

Bear slid the rifle barrel and growled. "Stupid tree is blocking me."

Bear snatched up the rifle and ran to the right of the truck a few yards, dropping to a knee. He raised the rifle and zoned in on the upper window.

Out of the corner of his eye, Jake spotted a figure dart from the side of the house toward what he could now see was a barn.

"Snell, right side of the house. Got a runner heading toward the barn."

"Got him," a male voice said.

The runner flinched as shots whizzed his way before returning fire with an AR-15. One of the FBI guys rose and squeezed off several shots before spinning like a top and crumpling to the ground from shooters in the upstairs window. Bear's rifle cracked and wood exploded from the bullet-ridden wood frame, but the shots continued to pour down on the officers on the ground.

Bear fired again but missed. "Goddamn it. Can't

get the right angle on the son of a bitch."

Seconds later, a four-wheeler burst from the side of the garage, its headlights quickly disappearing as it rode away from the firefight. Jake tracked the lights as they headed west across what he assumed was a pasture. None of the cops would be able to get to him.

"We got a runner, Bear," Jake yelled. "I'm going after him. Get the shooter."

Bear pushed to his feet and ran to his left. "Ten-four. Don't wreck my truck."

"No promises," Jake said as he slid to the driver's side.

Slamming the pedal to the floor, the tires screamed against the pavement before gaining purchase. He cranked the wheel to the left and spun into a one-eighty turn. The truck's headlights split the night on the road as he tracked the four-wheeler bouncing a hundred yards away through the darkness.

The engine roared as Jake swerved to the left, missing a deputy standing in the middle of the road by less than a foot. In his rearview mirror, the cop jumped into his car and followed.

Jake checked to the left. He'd passed the runner, the four-wheeler peeling to the south, its headlights dimming as it turned away. Fifty yards ahead, Jake spotted a north south road, and he slowed before skidding into the turn. Gravel crunched under Bear's tires and pinged into the body of the truck as Jake flew down the fence-lined road, gaining on the four-wheeler. If the cop trailed, Jake couldn't tell as dust billowed behind him.

The four-runner's headlights bounced through the ruts of the pasture, revealing a structure ahead. As the headlights spilled up the side, the image of an old barn took shape. Jake slammed on the brakes, the truck fishtailing as an opening appeared in the fencing along the road. Jerking the wheel to the left, he followed a narrow dirt path, a patch of grass splitting two tracks. Fifty yards ahead, the truck's headlights spilled over the empty four-wheeler parked in front of the barn. Blue and red lights swirled in the distance behind Jake.

He called on the radio. "Runner's in a barn southwest of the house. I'm in Bear's truck with an officer in pursuit of me. Let him know I'm one of the good guys."

"I got you," a voice said. "I'm thirty seconds behind."

Jake stopped in front of the barn, threw the truck in park and jumped out, drawing his Sig Sauer. If the runner had one of those machine guns, he was in deep shit. It would be like bringing the proverbial knife to a gun fight. He stayed behind the truck's open door, gun trained on the open barn door hoping the cop would get there soon.

Before that happened, a meaty engine roared and headlights flashed on. An old Camaro blasted from the front of the barn heading straight toward Jake. With his heart in his throat, Jake emptied his magazine into the windshield. The Camaro swerved at the last second, a cloud of dust covering Jake, and the runner gunned the engine toward the open slot in the fence. The squad car's sirens wailed and lights whirled as the officer barreled toward them down the fence-lined road. It was a coin flip which of them would get to the opening first.

"Cut him off at the road," Jake yelled into the radio as he leapt back into the truck. "He's going for the fence opening."

The Camaro tore for the opening as Jake slammed the truck into drive and took off after him. The squad car made it there first and blocked the opening. The cop opened the door and climbed out when shots rang out from the driver's side window of the Camaro as it passed. The cop dove back inside the car as the Camaro looped around. It straightened and barreled toward the squad car. It was going to try to ram its way through.

Jake floored the truck, the hefty engine responding as he yelled into the radio. "Get outta there, man. He's going to ram you."

Jake shot north toward the opening as the Camaro bore down on the squad car from the east. To his left, the cop tried to clear the squad car but was hung up, his eyes as wide as full moons as the Camaro bared down on him.

The cop was dead if the Camaro ran into him and Jake wasn't going to get there in time to cut him off. But there was one option left. He steered with one hand and snapped his seatbelt into place as the truck careened toward the opening.

"Sorry, Bear," he muttered.

Bear's truck smashed into the rear of the Camaro sending it spinning and tumbling. The seatbelt bit across Jake's chest, and the smoky smell of the deployed airbag filled the cab. Jake wrestled the truck to a stop and released the seatbelt, his breath coming in gasps. He clutched his chest for a moment, sucking in air until the immediate pain subsided to a dull roar. Opening the door, he stumbled to the ground toward the overturned Camaro. It lay on its roof, the tires spinning and smoke seeping into the night air.

The cop turned a spotlight toward the car and

approached with his weapon drawn. He glanced to Jake. "You okay?"

Jake rubbed his chest with one hand as he approached the Camaro. "I think so. You?"

"Might've shit my pants a little," the officer said.

Jake slipped his Sig Sauer free. He remembered it was empty and fished his spare magazine from the holster. He slapped it into place and racked a round into the chamber. "I can't say I blame you, and I promise I won't tell anyone. You see him?"

The officer bent toward the Camaro's driver's side. "I think he's—"

The cop exploded back as three shots barked into the night. He crashed to the ground, and Jake dropped to a knee and raised his gun, his complete and utter lack of cover raising the hairs on his arms.

Jake duck-walked toward the back of the Camaro, twenty yards away. The runner's gun appeared over the bottom of the car, and three more shots echoed in the night toward the truck where Jake was moments before.

He continued creeping around the back of the car, thighs burning from the prolonged crouch, chest rising and falling quick as his pulse raced. As he cleared the back of the wrecked Camaro, he spotted the runner crouched, his face bloodied as he panted.

Jake raised his pistol and put the man in his sights. It would be better if they took the guy alive, but given the events of the last twenty minutes, he knew the guy wouldn't go down easy. Still, he should give him a chance.

"Drop it or you're dead," Jake yelled.

The runner's eyes widened with surprise before a sad smile crossed his lips.

Jake's finger tightened on the trigger.

"I know not what others may choose but, as for me, give me liberty or give me death," the guy said, spitting a glob of blood on the ground. He jerked the gun in Jake's direction, and Jake squeezed the trigger three times. The man didn't get off a shot. He slumped back against the body of the Camaro and stilled.

Jake moved forward, his gun locked on the runner's body. The cop lay at his feet, eyes pointed up into the night sky. Jake checked his pulse but knew he wouldn't find one. He hated being right. Creeping forward toward the runner, he kicked the man's gun away. Bloody bubbles popped from the man's lips and onto his beard. His breath came in gulps as blood seeped from the bullet holes in his chest and streaked across the scar along his check. Wallace Humphrey.

"Where's the C4?" Jake asked. "What's your plan for it? Come on, man. Do one last good thing here."

"Anarchy Road," Humphrey wheezed. "It's... gonna...be...beautiful."

His head dropped to the side and his eyes dulled. Jake didn't bother to check his pulse.

Anarchy Road. What the hell was that?

CHAPTER THIRTY

The collision with the Camaro crumpled the front of Bear's truck, but the vehicle was drivable. Three bullet holes in the driver's door added to the damage. With the road blocked by the squad car, Jake followed the four-wheeler's tracks the best he could in the darkness, bouncing along ruts and hoping Bear's suspension wasn't damaged in the wreck.

Halfway to Wallace's house, he spotted a gun lying on the ground in the truck's headlights. Hopping out, he picked up the AR-15 by the strap. He cranked his head toward the house, nothing but sirens and flashing lights. The fire fight must be over. He hoped the good guys were still standing.

"I'm coming in from the west in Bear's truck," Jake announced over the radio. The clock on the dash turned to midnight.

"Hurry," Snell's voice cracked.

Jake stiffened in the seat as his foot pressed down on the pedal. He didn't like the sound of her voice and had an awful image of Bear lying in a bloody pile on the ground. "What's going on?"

"Just hurry," she said.

Squeezing the truck through the narrow opening of trees along Humphrey's property line, Jake turned the truck toward a gathering of people near the front of the house. Bullet holes lined the vinyl siding and the windows were shattered. He jumped from the truck and around the dead body of one of the Wyandotte County Sheriff's men, eyes darting around for Bear. His heart pounded like a drum during a solo as he tried to remember the last thing he said to his best friend.

Jake rounded the end of a bullet-ridden SUV, boots crunching against the broken glass. Snell knelt on the ground next to Bear, and Jake's thundering heart stopped, his throat closing and tears pressing against his eyes.

Between Snell and Bear was Foster, tears running from the corner of her eyes as Bear pressed a blood-soaked cloth to her chest. More blood trickled from the corner of her mouth, spraying in a fine mist as she coughed.

"Oh Jesus," Jake whispered. He dropped to a knee and grabbed Foster's raised hand. "How bad is it?"

"She's going to be fine," Snell choked.

"It's bad," Foster panted, trying to smile but doing a piss poor job of it. Her eyes were wide with fright. "You should see the other guy. Did...you...get him?"

"Yeah. I got him. It was Humphreys."

"Good," she said, her face arresting in a grimace as she fought to draw in a breath. "Snell owes me ten bucks."

"I'll pay you when you get outta the hospital," Snell said. She barked at one of the deputies. "Where's the goddamn ambulance?"

"Three minutes out," the man said.

"Hang on, Foster," Bear said. "Three minutes. You can make it three minutes."

"If you don't…crush me first," she wheezed. "You did…good, Jake. Finding this place. I always said… you'd make a good field agent."

"Too many rules," Jake said, stroking her hand. "I'd get shit-canned in the first week."

Foster grunted as a wave of pain wrestled through her. Bear took the towel handed to him and pressed it to the chest wound on top of the blood-soaked one, but Jake thought it wasn't going to be enough. Her head lifted off the ground, eyes darting between Snell, Bear and Jake, turning from fearful to fire. "You guys…gotta get them. Every…last…one of 'em. Will you do that for me?"

"You got it, partner," Snell said, her voice cracking. "I love you, you know?"

Tears poured from Foster's eyes as her head dropped. "I know. I love…"

As her voice trailed off, her eyes dimmed and her head lolled to the side.

"No, no, no," Snell whispered, tapping Foster's cheeks. She shoved Bear back and began chest compressions and blowing into her mouth. Bear slumped against the car, and Jake put his hands on his knees, dropping his head as Snell tried to will life back into her partner. In the distance, sirens penetrated the night, heading in their direction.

Jake had been through a lot with Foster: recovering the bioweapon Ares, at her side when she gunned down a Russian spy and hand in hand as they retrieved Snell when she was kidnapped a few months back. They'd fought together, drank together, laughed together and formed a good friendship. He wiped away the forming tears as needles stabbed his throat.

A minute passed and Snell crumpled to her partner's chest, her body heaving with quiet sobs. Jake gathered Snell up and held her to his chest, stroking her hair as three more police cars and an ambulance rumbled into the clearing in front of the house. When the cars stopped, Snell pulled back, wiped her eyes and turned toward the newcomers. She took a deep breath and nodded she was okay.

Bear tugged on the hood of the car to pull himself to his feet.

Jake stepped over and wrapped his arms around his best friend. They patted each other on the back and stepped away as the paramedics checked Foster's lifeless body. Jake peered around the yard. He spotted two bodies other than Foster's near the line of shot up cars. A half-dozen cops and Feds moved in and out of the house.

"What happened?" Jake asked.

Bear wiped his eyes, turning so he didn't have to look at Foster's body. "After you took off, I angled around to the front of the house. The guy in the window rained fire down on the cops, kept ducking behind the wall and I couldn't get a shot on him. One of the cops near the front of the car made a run for the house and the window guy lit him up like a fuckin' Christmas tree. Foster darted out and tried to pull him back to cover. That's when she was hit."

"Can't believe she's gone," Jake said. He turned away, eyes squeezed shut and let a wave of emotion roll through him. Taking a deep breath, he shook off the immediate pain. Foster would want them to nail the bad guys, not stand around and cry about it.

"What happened to the window guy?"

Bear turned his eyes up to the window. "I splattered his brains along the backwall five seconds later. If I woulda moved my fat ass faster."

"Don't start that crap," Jake said. "You took both those shooters out and saved a lot of lives tonight."

Bear's chin hung above his chest. "How about you?"

"Humphreys made a run for it in an old Camaro he stashed in a barn a mile from here. I rammed it before he took down a cop. I trashed your truck. Sorry."

"Screw my truck," Bear said. "Like I'm gonna worry about some twisted metal tonight."

"And three bullet holes in your driver's door."

"Better than three in you, partner. But you got him?"

Jake drew his lips in tight. "After he shot the cop, but yeah. He said something weird though before he died. 'Anarchy Road. It's going to be beautiful.' That mean anything to you?"

"Nope. Maybe it does to Snell. I hope they find something in that shithole which helps us get these bastards."

"Oh, we're gonna get them," Jake said, setting his jaw. "And they're gonna go down hard. For Foster."

Bear's lip curled. "For Foster."

CHAPTER THIRTY ONE

Hunter drove in the silence of midnight, nothing but his thoughts and the hum of the truck's tires chewing up I-70 as he headed home toward Kansas City. The adrenaline of the protest wore off and Mara slumped against the passenger window, her coat balled up against the doorframe as a pillow. She'd fallen asleep past Columbia, halfway between St. Louis and Kansas City. Lance managed to stay awake a little longer, re-telling his version in St. Louis. Neither one of his team members had to fire a single shot. By design, Hunter had been the only one to pull the trigger.

He flipped on the Fox News Channel on his Sirius radio as the late-night anchor prattled on about the bloody night. Authorities were still trying to sort out what happened from various witnesses and videos popping up on Facebook, Twitter, and TikTok. Hunter supposed someone, somewhere might have captured video of him firing into the crowd, but he doubted it. Plus, he was masked the whole time. Though he couldn't watch the footage, he listened as they played a clip and heard the symphony of pops from his pistol over the raging crowd. The Fox crew blamed Antifa and the BLM protestors for the violence, speculating which one was responsible. In truth, they more or less lumped the two groups together.

He clicked to the CNN broadcast and then MSNBC. Those anchors justified the BLM protestors and said the night was mostly peaceful. They blamed the police and the Proud Boys. Hunter cocked an eyebrow. He didn't even know if the Proud Boys were there. CNN reported six dead from the shooting near the church, another two dead and three others in critical condition from the fighting and ensuing stampede. Eighteen arrests and more were expected as the City of St. Louis burned, spiritually and physically.

In the end, Hunter did what he set out to do. Get in, let them catch themselves in the crossfire, wreak havoc and get out. The progressives on the left continued to scream police brutality despite the lack of statistical evidence and the desire for gun control, while ignoring the riots in their streets that set cities ablaze for months. Those on the right blamed the bleeding hearts while ignoring the history and policies which landed them in this place, drawing a line in the sand they would be pulled across anyway.

The country was being torn apart, the extremes of both sides claiming they were trying to save it, and neither side realizing they were both sharpening their claws on the social fabric while they blindly tried to gouge out the eyes of the other side. The saps in the middle were paralyzed like deer in the headlights, afraid to move in any direction and praying things would get back to normal, whatever passed for normal these days.

Hunter's father always told him that eventually you had to pick a side. He said you can walk safely on the left side of the road or the right side of the road. It's when you chose to walk down the middle of the road that you'd get crushed. When Hunter accused his father of stealing the line from the Karate Kid, his old man put Hunter's head through the living room wall.

Normal wouldn't see the light of day again if Hunter had anything to do with it. The country had a good run, but all good things must come to an end, especially when there wouldn't be anything good to go back to. It was time for a hard reset, and Hunter planned on pushing the button.

You happy with yourself? Eddie's hooded eyes shined red from the backseat. I mean, that was something else back there.

"Yes, it was," Hunter whispered. "It was perfect."

Eddie laughed. His voice hollow and raspy, like he swallowed a mouthful of dirt. At least you did the deed yourself this time. Unlike Ramadi.

"Shut up, Eddie," Hunter said, strangling the steering wheel. Mara stirred, but settled back in the seat.

His phone dinged. He had a message on his Signal app. Mister X allowed limited communication through Signal, because the app provided for encrypted messaging, calling and video chat which no intermediary could view. Supposedly. It was still owned by Google so somebody could be watching. Hunter pulled up the app and checked the message while he drove.

Nice work. Call at 0800 tomorrow. BX25GY. Hunter knew what the code meant.

Lance snored in the back. Mara murmured

something as she twisted in her seat before settling back again. It sounded like Eddie's name. Did she know what really happened in Ramadi? He suspected she might. If Eddie appeared to him, did he talk to Mara as well? Would she tell Hunter if he was? Hunter shook the crazy thoughts away. Eddie was his ghost, not hers, and Hunter knew Eddie wasn't really there no matter how real he seemed. Still, Hunter's eye crept toward the rearview mirror. His chest loosened at the empty seat.

Hunter batted away thoughts of Eddie and focused on the plan. With Anarchy Road's final task within their sights, he had to focus. He'd worry about whether he was going crazy later.

CHAPTER THIRTY TWO

The sun broke over the horizon as Jake, Bear, and Snell nursed cups of coffee at the Waffle House off I-70. Sleep and grief dragged at their features as they slumped in a booth in the corner of the restaurant waiting on their food. None of them had much of an appetite but agreed they needed fuel. The restaurant was less than half full—a few old timers reading the paper over eggs and pancakes near the door and a group of construction guys in the opposite corner.

Jake took in Snell's red-rimmed and bloodshot eyes. "Anybody get hold of Foster's family?"

"I talked to her parents and her sister," Snell said.

"I didn't know she even had a sister," Jake said, scratching at the table. "How'd they take the news?"

Snell paused and swallowed. "About like you'd expect. Can we talk about something other than Foster? I'm going to lose it if we don't."

"What'd you find in the house?" Jake asked. He and Bear gave their statements and got out of the way as soon as the FBI brass showed up. Jake had been there with Snell the last time an agent was killed. Agent

McKernan. The same pissed off boss showed up, so they slipped away while Snell went to work. They'd managed a couple hours of restless sleep in the cab of Bear's truck, awakened by Snell's call to meet.

She twisted around to make sure there was nobody in earshot. "There were enough guns in that house to arm a platoon. You know how there's an ammunition shortage right now? It's because these assholes had all the bullets."

"What about the C4?"

She took a sip. "Found a couple of pounds in the gun safe."

"A far cry from sixty," Bear said. "Where the hell is the rest of it?"

"That's what we're trying to figure out. The 2A Militia isn't a large outfit in terms of membership or reach, and our file on them is pretty thin. I have agents working with the local police to track down and bring in any known members. Up until last night, they've been all talk with little action."

"What's Lenny saying?" Jake asked.

"Nothing. He lawyered up. His basement was full of incriminating evidence. Gun parts, outlawed guns, a couple pounds of C4 and coded records in ledgers. Guy didn't have a computer on site. Says he doesn't trust them before invoking his lawyer. Unless we break the ledger codes, or we get him to cooperate..."

"Then we're nowhere," Bear finished.

She swirled a spoon in her coffee, adding a little more creamer and watching the white spin. "Did you know there's been four other bomb related events in the last five months linked to protests?"

The waitress dropped off their breakfast. Waffles and bacon for Jake and Bear, scrambled eggs and toast for Snell. They just nibbled and picked as they talked.

"I don't remember four," Jake said. "Then again, there's been so many riots, they run together."

"The first was four months ago in Dallas," Snell said. "They found a local activist against police brutality in his house with a bullet between his eyes and a noose around his throat after someone beat the shit out of him."

"I heard that one," Bear said. "Spurred the riot in Tulsa a couple nights later. What's that got to do with a bomb?"

Snell picked at her eggs and dropped the fork. "A wad of C4 was wired to the chair they found the guy tied to in Dallas. We think it was supposed to blow when anyone moved him. Fortunately, the local cops spotted it before anyone moved the guy. Then in Tulsa a couple nights later, a car bomb blew up near the police precinct and killed two members of the Proud Boys. The protestors cheered like Romans at the Coliseum, which was like pouring gasoline on the already raging fire. Fifteen people died that night."

"The car bomb was C4?" Jake asked.

"Yup. Six weeks ago, the Seattle March for Peace. Managed to be peaceful until the sun went down. We suspect Antifa caused most of the rioting and looting. Twelve people dead on the protestor side from a bomb in a backpack, including a mother and her ten-year-old daughter. C4."

"That was sad," Jake said. "Her picture was blasted across the airwaves."

"We thought putting an innocent face to the chaos might calm people down, show it wasn't just the nutjobs on the right and left getting killed. Innocents were getting caught in the crossfire, too."

Bear clucked his tongue. "Not when these fuckers get in a mob. My daddy used to say none of us is as dumb as all of us. He was right."

"Then there was the abortion clinic bombed in Chicago two weeks ago. God's Avenging Angels claimed responsibility at first before changing their tune. The bombing here the night before last. Death To Religion claimed responsibility then denied it. All done with C4. We're spinning our wheels tracking down these leads but keep coming up with nothing substantial and it's pissing me off."

Jake chewed on a bacon strip, the timeline running through his head. "Do you think it's weird these different groups used C4?" Jake asked. "I mean, how easy is it to get this stuff?"

"We've talked about it," Snell said. "C4 is great because you can mold it into any shape, shove it in cracks and holes. It's stable and not subject to physical shock. Hell, you could light the stuff on fire or shoot a bullet through it and it won't blow. Detonation has to happen from extreme heat and a shockwave like a detonator."

"But how does some lowlife like Lenny get a hold of so much of it?"

She shrugged. "That's what we're trying to track down. It's only made in the US at an ammunitions plant in Tennessee, and you can't lay hands on it unless you're licensed through the ATF and have a valid end-use permit. But, like anything else, you can get it elsewhere with the right connections."

Bear dropped his napkin on his empty plate and stole a piece of Jake's bacon. "Could Lenny have made it himself?"

"Highly doubtful," Snell said. "Our guy says the RDX, the explosive component, is hard to obtain and would be expensive. The FBI and ATF are turning over any rock we can to find the source. And we don't know if the C4 used came from the same supplier."

"But it feels that way," Jake said.

"It sure does. We have the radical left and radical right killing each other along with innocent people but using the same means of mass destruction. I'm surprised nothing blew up in St. Louis last night."

Jake and Bear had listened to the news while waiting for Snell to finish things up. A mass riot in St. Louis when left and right clashed in the streets. Shots fired and seven or eight dead at last count.

"What about this Anarchy Road?" Jake asked. "Humphrey toasted it with his dying breath."

"That was interesting, and we've been digging, but we have as little on Anarchy Road as we had on the 2A Militia."

"Same outfit?"

"Anarchy Road is more of a movement than a specific group, at least as far as we can tell. We found a couple of videos on the dark web. Someone dressed in black in a non-descript concrete room with a digitally manipulated voice. What they preach is true anarchy. Not the bullshit anarchy these asshats tout and spray paint on buildings during a riot while filming with their iPhones after downing a latte from Starbucks. These guys want to bring down the whole system and go back to living in caves kinda anarchy. Each man for himself and only the strong survives."

Jake raised his eyebrows. "Sounds like a bunch of wackos."

"Dangerous wackos. They could be all talk, but the

chatter has grown exponentially in the last six months. We're having trouble finding anything substantial. It's like trying to lasso smoke."

"You talk to the surviving 2A Militia members at the house?"

"There weren't any. The one survivor of the firefight was a woman who shot herself in the head before we breached the bedroom door where she holed up."

"Where does that leave us?" Bear asked.

An elderly couple sat two booths over, behind Jake and Bear. Snell leaned in, her voice low. "I got my ass chewed so bad at Humphrey's house that I'm going to have to buy a new wardrobe."

Jake winced. "About us?"

"Your favorite Special Agent Murphy has chunks of my pretty little derriere stuck between his dentures with your name on them."

"A disturbing analogy."

"Your saving grace was the work you did to find Lenny, which led us to the 2A Militia house. More than anyone else has accomplished on this. But, you're still in the shithouse with him. He'd send me through the sausage grinder if he knew I was here with you now."

Jake sank back in the booth. "Why am I in the shithouse?"

Snell pointed to Bear. "Bear's an actual law enforcement official, though out of his jurisdiction. You're not and you killed our one major lead."

Jake's temple pulsed. "After he shot a cop and shot at me."

"I know, I know. Like I said, you're in the shithouse, but not the stockade."

"How do I get in the clear?"

Snell leaned in. "Officially, stay the hell out of our

way. Unofficially, help us find out where the C4 went and what it's going to be used for. I'll help where I can, but I'm on a short leash after what went down at the house."

Jake's mind spun the possibilities as he rubbed the puzzle piece in his pocket. He found it helped him think, like a lucky rabbit's foot. He could ask Keats what he knew about the explosives market, but Keats was a guns and drugs guy. Not once in the time Jake worked for him had he ever mentioned any heavy artillery. Lenny was the only connection he'd found, but now the cops had him. No way Murphy would let Jake and Bear within ten feet of the guy.

An idea raised its head, but he'd need some info from Snell.

"What about other 2A Militia members? You know where they are?"

"Most of the group was in the house," Snell said. "It was like a commune. We have a list of five other people, but it's pretty dated. We're working on tracking them down."

"Give me the names," Jake said. "I have an idea."

Snell pulled out her phone and scrolled through some emails. "You going to tell me what this idea is?"

"You want the rest of your ass chewed off?"

She pulled a napkin from the dispenser on the table and dropped a pen on top of it. "You obviously didn't get this from me. Write." She held the phone out in front of Jake, and he jotted the names on the napkin. When he finished, she slipped the phone back in her pocket. "Don't make me regret giving this to you, Caldwell."

Bear snagged the napkin. "Don't worry. I'll keep an eye on him."

Snell rolled her eyes. "Oh, I feel so much better."

CHAPTER THIRTY THREE

Jake and Bear left the Waffle House and settled in Bear's truck. Bear slapped the wheel and cranked his head to Jake. "Now what?"

Jake held up the napkin. "We have five names to track down."

"Which the cops and feds are already doing. You have a secret weapon I don't know about?"

"Two actually," Jake said, pulling out his phone.

Bear chewed on his beard for a bit. "Keats and Cat."

"You're smarter than you look."

"Don't tell anyone."

Jake doubted Keats would have any connections to the guys on this list, but it was worth a shot. Keats was a night owl and wouldn't be up this early and if Jake called and woke him up, he'd be less likely to help. As a happy medium, he sent Keats a text to call him when he woke up.

Cat was a computer hacker Jake employed on occasion with a knack for uncovering things nobody else could find. Jake didn't understand what the dark web was, but if these guys operated out of it, Cat had a magic light he could shine in those shadows and corners.

"Drue Stambaugh, Wyatt Tate, Drake Ackerman, Cooper Plume and Maxwell Watterson," Jake read while Cat crunched on something, as usual. Jake hadn't laid eyes on Cat in two years, but he pictured the overweight man hunched over a computer in a dark basement, hair flying everywhere and Cheeto stains on his fingers. As if on cue, Cat crunched again.

Jake put the call on speaker so Bear could listen in. "Jesus, Cat. Isn't it a little early for Cheetos in my ear?"

"It's shredded wheat that tastes like fucking cardboard. My doctor says I should drop a few pounds and, for the record, I haven't had Cheetos for breakfast in months. What's this for?"

"They're known members of the 2A Militia and might have something to do with the bombing at the Sprint Center two nights ago."

"T-Mobile Arena," Cat corrected. "You probably still call the amphitheater in Bonner Springs Sandstone."

"Old habits die hard. See what you can find."

Cat clicked his tongue. "Militia guys, huh?"

"They're supposedly communicating through the dark internet or something."

Cat snorted. "Dark web, you dolt."

Bear clamped his smiling lips together as he backed up the truck and headed toward the highway.

Jake wasn't amused. "Don't make me break your face for being a smartass, Cat. Yeah, the dark web."

"Can this wait until I get back from church?"

"Since when did you find religion?"

Cat groaned. "I didn't. The wife did and she made me promise to go with her at least twice a month."

"Play your skip card. I have to find these guys and

fast. Local cops and feds are looking, too."

"I could run circles around those guys."

"Prove it. Start digging and call me back."

Jake ended the call and turned to a grinning Bear. "What?"

"Dark internet? Even I'm not that big of a noob."

"What the hell is a noob?"

Bear pulled onto I-70. "My point exactly."

They headed toward downtown, listening to the news. Twenty minutes later after a slow down for a wreck, the Kansas City skyline rose up and Jake's cell rang. Cat.

"That was fast," Jake said.

"Leave it to the feds to waste resources tracking a dead guy and a prisoner. Drue Stambaugh died two years ago in car crash, and Cooper Plume is serving ten to twenty for armed robbery. You don't need a dark internet search for that."

"It's dark web, dickhead," Jake said. "Good work."

"I'll start digging on the other three, but I hope it's more challenging than this. At this rate, I'm still going to have to go to church with my wife."

Jake ended the call and tapped the phone against his leg. "I can't believe Foster's gone."

Bear bit his lip. "I'm numb. Like it isn't real."

"I'm not numb, I'm pissed off. Not knowing where to go or what to do isn't helping."

"Any ideas?"

Jake imagined Foster's bloody body. He tried not to imagine getting that call in the middle of the night that Foster's parents just received from Snell. Nobody told him when you had a kid that a phone call could represent your worst nightmare. Hell, he'd almost been witness to the ultimate loss at the arena. At that moment, Jake wanted nothing more than to wrap his arms around his wife and daughter. "We're in limbo until Keats or Cat calls us back. Let's check in at the hospital. I'm sure Maggie could use a little relief."

"You going to tell her about the shootout?"

Jake shot a sideways squint. "You're responsible for me. You think I should tell her?"

Bear covered his crotch with his hand. "Good point."

"We have to make a stop first."

CHAPTER THIRTY FOUR

When Jake and Bear entered the room, Maggie's smile couldn't overcome the exhaustion dragging her features to the floor. Even though her make-up was washed away, her blonde hair frazzled, and quarter-sized dark bags hung under her eyes, she was still the most beautiful woman Jake had ever seen. He tried to avoid taking her for granted in their marriage, though his job sometimes made it feel like he did. She rose from the chair and trudged to him, wrapping her arms around his waist. Jake winced as she pressed against his seatbelt bruise when he rammed Bear's truck. Over her shoulder, Halle slept, the drain still protruding from her head. Bear shuffled to the bedside.

"Hey, babe," Jake said, kissing the top of Maggie's head. "How you doing?"

Her slow speech muffled against his shirt. "I'm tired. I don't know if I've ever been this exhausted."

Jake rubbed her back. "I'm sorry. I should've come back sooner. How's our girl?"

Maggie gazed to the bed. "She's good. Sleeping

a lot. Still has a headache, but it's better than it was yesterday. Doctors are optimistic she can go home in a few days."

"You check on Connor?"

She yawned, blinking slowly, like sleep pulled at her eyelids. "Audrey says he's great and she's keeping him forever."

Jake's vision blurred. Whether it was from missing his son, his own exhaustion, Foster's death, seeing his wife again after a few brushes with death or the news his daughter was on the mend, he wasn't sure. "That's great."

"How's your manhunt going?"

"Making progress."

"No drama?"

Jake flicked his eyes away. "So far, so good."

Maggie's eyes narrowed. "Liar. But I'm too tired to chew you out."

"You bring a change of clothes with you?"

She jerked her thumb in the vague direction of the parking lot. "In Bear's truck. Nabbed some for you too. I didn't know how long we'd be here. I threw them in a bag so quickly, I'm not even sure what I brought."

"Damn," Bear said. "I didn't think to grab anything."

"Your wife did," Maggie said. "She threw it in the back of your truck before we left."

Bear sighed. "God bless that woman."

Jake held up a hotel key card from their pitstop. "Got us a room at the Crown Center Sheraton. You look like you could use a shower and a nap."

She eyed the key with the longing of an alcoholic at a stiff drink. "Oh, God. That sounds so good. What about Halle?"

"I'll stay with her," Bear said, holding Halle's hand.

"You two go get cleaned up and get some rest."

"You sure?" Jake asked.

Bear tossed Jake the truck keys. "On one condition. You bring me back some Lamar's donuts."

"Deal."

Jake kissed Halle's forehead and led Maggie out of the hospital. She held onto his arm, resting her head against his shoulder. She didn't say a word until they reached Bear's truck in the parking lot. Releasing Jake's arm, she examined the crumpled front end, and her fingers ran over the bullet holes in the driver's side door.

"What happened?" she asked.

"It's a long story. I'll tell you on the way to the hotel."

She flicked her eyes between the truck damage and Jake before dragging her feet around the passenger side. "I'm too tired. As long as everyone's okay, you can tell me later."

Jake clamped his mouth shut as he thought about Foster, the 2A Militia and Anarchy Road. Everyone was definitely not okay.

******

Hunter Brenner sat in his 1967 Mustang a mile down the road from his office, eyes locked on the face of his watch, waiting for the second hand to tick to the top of the hour. Mister X demanded punctuality. Given the man's hectic schedule, Hunter wasn't surprised. The Mustang's restored engine rumbled, the heater blowing across his face to fight back the early morning chill.

He listened for the voice of his conscious, to let him know when he was doing something wrong, but the voice grew fainter and fainter the farther down this path they traveled. One of the counselors he'd been forced to see in the military said he had a lack of empathy. Hunter quickly came to the conclusion he didn't care. He supposed killing someone or blowing something up shouldn't be calming, but it was. Well, the first time wasn't, but the ones that followed were, like he'd cauterized his emotional nerve endings.

Sleep the night before had been a long time coming and his eyes burned. After working in the garage boring out lumber and rigging the drone, testing various weight loads with Lance until the wee hours of the morning, he'd headed upstairs to the kitchen and poured two fingers of whiskey.

He'd taken the glass to his home office and pulled the box of letters from a desk drawer. Mara's meticulous handwriting graced the envelopes. He'd read over them while he sipped his drink, remembering the warmth they filled him with while he was overseas all those years ago. The hope they provided. His heart sank as he remembered the betrayal they also represented. How Eddie never found them was a mystery. Hunter had finished the drink, padded to the bedroom and slipped into bed, snuggling against Mara's warmth.

At eight on the nose, he dialed the number from the burner phone and punched in the access code Mister X provided. His call was answered on the first ring, but nobody spoke.

"Who controls the past controls the future," Hunter said.

Mister X's gravel voice sounded. "Who controls the present controls the past."

Each call began with the phrase from George

Orwell's 1984. If either one of them failed to utter it, the call was terminated because it meant one of them was compromised.

"Where are we in preparations?" Mister X didn't bother with idle chit chat.

"We'll be ready. The lumber's prepped. We think the drone is ready."

"The hospital visit is still up in the air, and we probably won't know until the last minute, so proceed with the main plan. You have two days," Mister X said.

Hunter's stomach churned. "Two days? I thought we had five."

"Well, now you have two. The target's schedule has changed."

"But, I don't—"

"Adapt and overcome, soldier." Mister X's tone was biting, far from his usual polished demeanor. "Is there going to be a problem?"

Hunter swallowed back the bile rising in his throat. "No, sir. Not a problem at all."

"You did good the other night. The operation was flawless. I have the other pieces in place for the end game. Don't trip over the finish line."

Hunter reached toward the dash and pressed in the cigarette lighter. "Yes, sir. I won't fail."

The line went dead. With a slight tremor in his hands, he snapped the cover from the back of the phone and removed the SIM card. Snapping it in two, he threw the pieces out the window. The cigarette lighter popped as his brain whirled with panicked thoughts about how the hell he would get this done.

His father loved to help Hunter find his focus when his young mind wandered, whenever Hunter failed at something or didn't do what he was supposed to do.

"Failure of focus" his father called it. Hunter snatched the cigarette lighter and stared at the glowing red coil. Without another thought, he pressed the lighter against his forearm, sweat popping on his brow as he sucked in air through clenched teeth. His stomach turned at the odor of searing flesh, but the panicked thoughts scattered and his mind cleared.

He replaced the lighter and gazed at the raw, circular burn, standing fresh against the scars of dozens of others. Rolling his sleeve down, he put the Mustang in drive and headed back to the house. It would be a busy two days if they were going to blow up the President.

CHAPTER THIRTY FIVE

Maggie collapsed on the bed at the Sheraton. "I'm not sure what I want to do more, sleep or shower."

Jake dropped the overnight bag on the floor and dropped to the bed beside her. "I smell like I was blown up and ran around for two days."

A slow laugh sounded from her throat, her eyes closed. "I'm no prize, either."

Jake turned his head and kissed her temple. "Why don't you hop in the shower?"

"Hopping sounds like a lot of work. You go first. I'm going to catch a nap while you're in there."

Their hands intertwined and Jake closed his eyes, enjoying her cool skin against his. His head grew fuzzy as he tried to think of a way to reasonably spin the tale of the previous night without his wife coming unglued. Less than a minute later, she was asleep, the familiar clicking of the back of her tongue against the roof of her mouth as she breathed. Jake slowed his cadence to match hers. A minute later, he slipped away.

His cell phone rang just as he'd fallen asleep. Jake fumbled in his pocket to silence it before it woke Maggie. As he did, he checked the clock on the nightstand. They'd been out of it for two hours. Checking the display on his phone, the call was from Keats.

Jake bolted up and moved quickly to the bathroom. "Hey, Jason," Jake said, rubbing the sleep from his eyes.

"Wow, did I wake up earlier than you for once?"

Jake yawned as he talked. "I had a long ass night."

"Whatcha need?"

"Hold on." Jake slipped the napkin from his back pocket. "You heard of the 2A Militia?"

"2A is Wallace Humphrey's group. Wait, did the little asshole give you my name?"

"No. He's dead."

Keat's cleared his throat. "Oh. What happened?"

"I shot him."

"He tied to the bombing downtown? Doesn't sound like their thing."

Jake sat on the toilet, keeping his voice low. "Maybe. There was a shootout at his place last night. Me and Bear, Feds and local PD."

"How'd you find him?"

"Lenny Moritz. He's in FBI custody."

Keats hummed. "They tie him to guns or something related to the bombing?"

"C4. He supplied 2A with something like sixty pounds of the shit. We're trying to figure out where it went."

"C4? I didn't know Lenny was messin' with it. And none of the 2A people at Humphrey's house are talking, right? Not a big surprise. Those motherfuckers are wound tight."

"They're dead. Like I said, it was a hell of a shootout.

Agent Foster with the FBI was killed."

"Sorry to hear it," Keats said. "I know you liked her. What can I do? I mean, I never did business with Lenny, Humphreys or any of the rest of those nuts."

Jake scanned the names on the napkin. "Seeing if you heard of any of the remaining three 2A members. Wyatt Tate, Drake Ackerman and Maxell Watterson."

"Not the first two. Watterson sounds vaguely familiar, but I don't remember where from. I know someone I could call."

"Hit me back after you do. And the feds and ATF are all over this shit, especially since an agent's been killed. Be careful poking around."

Keats ended the call and Jake poked his head out of the bathroom door. Maggie was still sawing logs on the bed, the comforter pulled around her. Jake snagged the overnight bag. After shaving, he let the hot water beat on his shoulders while running a toothbrush over his filmy teeth, hoping inspiration would strike about what to do with this situation. He often had revelations in the shower. Maybe it was the solitude and sound of the water. Today, nothing.

Fifteen minutes later, he waved through the steam and slipped on the fresh clothes Maggie packed—a blue t-shirt, gray pullover and a fresh pair of jeans, but no underwear or socks. Crap. His mind rewound the last couple of days of sweat and toil, but going commando wasn't an option.

"Beggars can't be choosers," Jake muttered.

When he emerged from the bathroom, Maggie was awake.

"Well, you look a lot better. Save any hot water for me?" she asked.

"It's a hotel. They never run out. Go ahead."

She slid to the edge of the bed and stood. She kissed Jake on the cheek and clamped her fingers like a vice on his jaw. "When I get out, you get to tell me what's going on. Honey."

She disappeared into the bathroom, and Jake couldn't envision a way this would end up well for him.

CHAPTER THIRTY SIX

While Maggie cleaned up, Jake propped the thin hotel pillows against the headboard and studied the wall, trying to spin a no drama story that told the truth of the last twenty-four hours, but wouldn't land his balls in Maggie's vice. He came up snake eyes. His cell vibrated. It was Cat.

"You love me, don't you, Caldwell?" Cat asked.

"In a strictly plutonic way, sure. What do you have?"

"A lead on Maxwell Watterson. Will it earn me a little bonus?"

Jake's tone sharpened. Cat was an annoying one-trick money pony sometimes. "Have a sense of civic duty, Cat. There's more to life than the almighty dollar."

"Seriously?"

"You'll get paid. What'd you find?"

"Maxwell Watterson, age twenty-eight, Kansas City address off State Line," Cat said, reading off the address and phone number. "Grew up in the area, went to Shawnee Mission North, a year at KU before he dropped out. Employment history at Speedy Car

Wash, some fast food joints and most recently for Reliance Construction. No criminal history other than a couple of speeding tickets."

Jake grabbed a pen and jotted down the particulars on the hotel pad on the nightstand. "You asked if I loved you which implied you found something helpful. What else?"

"Quick Facebook scan shows he leans far right politically, not quite QAnon territory, but close. He likes guns, girls and bar hopping. Looks like he was hammered at Kelly's in Westport last night. I'll text you a picture."

"Any ties to the 2A Militia?"

"Nothing I've seen. I'm not hacking into the FBI database unless you need me to, because that is a pain in the ass."

"Nah, the lead came from them so we're good. You sure this address is good?"

"That hurts, Jake. Of course, it is," Cat said.

"Anything else on the other guys?"

Cat had nothing else yet and promised to call when he did. In the bathroom, the water shut off, and a pit settled in Jake's stomach. He was no closer to a plausible story to tell Maggie. A minute later, the blow dryer whirred on. His phone dinged and he pulled up the picture Cat sent. Watterson was a good-looking kid. Dark floppy hair and brown eyes.

Jake dialed the phone number Cat gave him. He wanted to know if Watterson was home.

A deep, sleepy voice answered. "Hello?"

"Hey, where's Max?"

"Ain't here. Think he's at work. Who's this?"

Jake checked the company name he'd jotted down on the pad. Kid worked construction so popping into the main company address wouldn't produce anything. "Met him at Kelly's last night and found his credit card. Was just trying to get it back to him. He mentioned he worked for Reliance Construction or something like that. You know what site he's at today?"

The voice groaned, as if it took tremendous effort to get his synapses firing. "I don't know, man. We had a hard night last night. Did we meet at Kelly's?"

"Don't know. What's your name?"

"Drake."

Jake sat up in the bed, his brain fumbling to remember the last name from Snell's list. "Acker-something?"

"Ackerman. What's yours?"

"Tim. I was the tall guy. We met pretty late in the night."

Ackerman paused. "The one who bought the shots? You were a mad man. I'm about in a coma because of you."

Jake rolled with it. "And I'm payin' for it today, too. You remember what site he's at? I'm heading out of town for work and want to drop his card off."

The blow dryer shut off in the bathroom as Jake tapped the pen on the pad, waiting for a response.

Ackerman moaned. "Damn my head hurts. Try Union Station downtown. Think he's been there the last coupla weeks."

"Thanks for the info. See you around."

"Later. Think I'm gonna go throw up."

"Good luck with that," Jake said.

He clicked end as Maggie emerged from the bathroom with a towel wrapped around her. She went to the overnight bag and pulled out a pair of underwear, jeans and a sweatshirt. She threw the clothes on the bed and stood in front of Jake.

"You come up with a story to tell me?" she asked.

"I think so."

She grasped the tucked in portion holding the towel in place. "Well, before you tell me, remember one thing." She pulled the towel open and let it fall to the floor, standing nude, her perfect body stirring Jake's libido among other things. "If you ever want this again, tell me the truth. The whole truth and nothing but the truth."

"So help me God." Jake swallowed, his eyes drinking her in. "Before we talk, I don't suppose there's any chance we could—"

"Not a chance right now, sweetheart. Maybe not ever again if you don't start talking."

Jake's eyes swept over her one more time. "Well, you'd better put those clothes on, because there's no way I can think straight like this."

Jake told her the story as Maggie dressed and they headed back to the hospital, with a pitstop at Lamar's donuts for Bear. Well, he told her most of the story. If he told her everything, he'd be taking cold showers for a very long time. Not even God would be able to fix that. Finding out the FBI agent she'd met a day earlier was now dead shook Maggie. It rattled the invincibility cage Jake tried to portray himself in so she wouldn't worry about him so much. Nothing would happen. Everything was cool. He had things under control. Relax. Rinse and repeat. He started to bore himself with his repetitiveness.

His bullshit was well and good until the bullet with your name on it came calling. The shot you didn't see. The person hiding in the shadows with your head in his sights. Jake was good, but he wasn't invincible. When someone died around him, the fact that with a slight twist of fate it could be him in a box hit her hard. And, unfortunately, she'd been hit hard too many times in the last few years.

Halle was awake and playing War with Bear with a deck of cards on the food tray. From the sizes of their piles, she was kicking his ass.

"I surrender," Bear said, tossing his meager pile on the table and snagging the bag of donuts. "You are the official War champion."

"I didn't know you were a quitter, Bear," Halle said, winking at Jake and Maggie.

"There's a difference between quitting and knowing when you're beat, little girl. Besides, looking at your mom and dad cleaned up has made me want nothing more than to see if I can drain the hot water tank at the hotel."

"Make it quick," Jake said. "We have things to do."

Bear flicked his eyes between Jake and Maggie as his lips locked around a chocolate covered donut. "Do we now?"

"Yes, you do," Maggie said. "Jake told me everything that happened since you boys left here."

"Everything?"

She rolled her eyes. "I doubt it. But enough. These people have to be stopped before anyone else gets hurt. And if it's you two knuckleheads who have to do it, then so be it."

Bear left while the getting was good.

Jake walked to the bed and sat on the edge. "You doin' alright, kiddo?"

"Better. My head still hurts and I'd love to get this tube out of my skull. Doctor says a couple more days.

You get the bad guys yet?"

"We're closing in."

"Don't stop 'till you get there."

He kissed her on the forehead. "You got it, champ. Talk to you soon."

"Be careful," Halle said, pointing toward the television on the wall. "It's getting crazy out there. People are losing their minds."

Jake checked the TV. Split screens showed violent clashes between protesters in Seattle, and between protesters and police in St. Louis. Buildings on fire, tear gas clouds, police in full body armor against masked rioters hurling bricks, people huddled in a ball while their fellow citizens hurled punches and kicks. Pure chaos. The chyron scrolling across the bottom of the screen read "Violence erupts across the nation."

Jake thought back to what Snell said. Something was brewing. They needed to figure out what it was before it boiled over.

CHAPTER THIRTY SEVEN

After giving Bear fifteen minutes in the hotel to get cleaned up, Jake called Snell and gave her Ackerman's name and address. He told her he and Bear were heading to Watterson's worksite.

"Like hell you are, Caldwell. You and Grizzly Adams aren't going anywhere near that guy. Let us handle it."

Jake curled his toes. "I do the work and you guys sweep in and get the glory?"

"Since when are you worried about glory?"

"Where are you now?"

"Close to Ackerman's house. We were following up on a lead."

Bear rolled down the hospital ramp and turned north on Holmes, Jake pointing the way.

"You're nowhere near downtown," Jake said. "We're like five minutes away from Union Station. Let Bear and me pick this guy up. You can meet us after you get Ackerman."

"You have no authority to pick anybody up."

"We'll find one."

Snell groaned. "You are an immense pain in the

ass. Fine. Go to the site and get eyes on Watterson, but don't engage with him. Just sit in Bear's smelly truck and wait for us. I'll call you when we're on the way."

Bear glanced over as Jake dropped his cell on the dash. "What'd she say?"

"We find Watterson, lay eyes on him and wait. They pick up Ackerman and meet us at the construction site."

"That's boring."

"But I'd like to avoid pissing in the face of her boss any more than we already have."

Bear popped a tobacco pouch between his cheek and gum. "Those punks should be kissing our feet for doing their job for them. What else did she say?"

"Your truck smells."

Bear drew back. "It does not. I cleaned it…like a week ago. Maybe two. Does it smell?"

"Just like you, my man."

Bear cut his narrowed eyes to Jake. "I can't tell if you think that's a good thing or a bad thing. And I showered."

Jake rolled down his window, and the cool morning wind blew inside the cab. "One shower can't make up for years of upholstery abuse. Just sayin'."

Bear rolled up Jake's window from his side and engaged the lock. "You think you're funny, you little shit, but you're not."

Ten minutes later after a stop off at Crown Center to grab some coffee, Bear parked his truck on the downslope of Kessler Road, a blacktop running alongside the World War I memorial overlooking the historic Union Station. Jake once ran a half-marathon whose route took him up that slope, and he was glad they were in a vehicle.

Across the road, Union Station spilled east to west, an architectural masterpiece built in 1914 and renovated in the late 1990s. There was even a gangland shootout in the 1930s called the Union Station Massacre when convicted mobster Frank Nash was gunned down along with four law enforcement officers. It was 850,000 square feet of history housed in tanned stonework anchoring the corner of Pershing and Main. Jake once ventured on an Amtrack train ride out of there to Hermann, Missouri with Maggie for a winery tour. They drank their entire haul on the way back and had to take a cab to the hotel.

Bear scoped the construction site on the west side with his binoculars. A large crane hoisted steel, and trucks rumbled over tracked ground hauling dirt and debris away. A dozen workers in hardhats and bright vests over long-sleeved shirts hustled around the site.

"What are they building?" Jake asked.

"Beats me. Looks like an amphitheater or something."

"See Watterson?"

Bear looked at the photo again on Jake's phone and pressed his eyes back to the binoculars. After a minute, he popped his tongue off the roof of his mouth. "Winner winner, chicken dinner. Got him. Driving the Bobcat on the west end of the site."

He handed Jake the binoculars and pointed. Jake found Watterson in a couple of seconds. "Yup, that's him."

They sat in silence, watching Watterson push piles of dirt and sand around with the Bobcat. By the time they finished their coffee, Watterson had done nothing but drive and smoke cigarettes with a bunch of other workers.

Bear groaned. "The kid's going to die of lung cancer before the day's out. Maybe we should go talk to him."

Jake wanted nothing more than to do that very thing but shook his head. "Snell told us to wait."

"Since when are you such a rule follower?"

"Since Foster was killed. Besides, I don't want these guys to have any kind of technicality they can slither off the hook with."

Bear's chin dipped. "Foster isn't on us. Don't start carryin' that burden around on your shoulders."

"Isn't she though?" Jake asked, staring out the windshield. "She wouldn't have been there if we hadn't cowboyed our way into Lenny's garage."

Bear poked Jake hard in the shoulder. "Listen, Caldwell. She was doing her job, and the job came with risks. I didn't do anything wrong and neither did you. It's bad luck. We'll get these assholes, but you don't get to carry her death around your neck like some fucking albatross. She'll come back from the grave and haunt you if you do, because that'd be the last thing she would've wanted. How could we have known they had enough firepower and ammunition in the house to blow a hole in the world?"

"You mean besides the fact they were a self-proclaimed militia who bought C4 and AR-15s on the black market?"

Bear opened his mouth to reply, then snapped it shut.

In his head, Jake knew Bear was right. Foster was in the FBI and put her life at risk on a regular basis. He shouldn't feel guilty for Foster, but he couldn't shake the image of her lying on the ground in a pool of blood.

"He's getting a call," Bear said.

Jake snapped his head back to the construction site. Watterson stepped away from the other workers, a cell phone pressed to his head. He hung up, checked around and power walked across the lot. Long, quick strides. A man with a purpose.

"He's been tipped. He's gonna run," Bear said.

"Start the truck."

Jake's cell rang. Snell. He put it on speaker. Before she could speak, Jake blurted, "We have eyes on Watterson on the construction site. He's booking it across the lot."

"We nailed Ackerman," Snell said, her excited voice climbing an octave. Her cell signal was spotty. "He…shot at us with…gold-plated Desert Eagle. Ran to his car…bag in hand when we pulled up."

Across the lot, Watterson reached a mid-nineties black Mustang GT with frayed racing stripes across the hood. Bear put the truck in drive, waiting for Jake for the go ahead.

"You're breaking up a bit. Did you capture him or kill him?"'

"One of our guys…knocked his ass out. But, if he got a heads up—"

"Then Watterson did to. What do you want us to do?"

"Don't shoot him, Jake," Snell said. "I want you to…"

Her cell signal bit the dust. Watterson's car backed up. Jake tried dialing Snell again and it went straight to voicemail.

"Shit," Jake muttered.

"What do you want to do?" Bear asked.

"Let's take him down."

Bear slammed the pedal to the floor, and the truck shot forward toward the construction site. Watterson's back tires spit up dirt, and he fishtailed toward the entrance. The Mustang beat Bear to the gate and squealed across the lanes of traffic, heading east.

"Get him, Bear," Jake yelled over the roar of the truck, screeching tires and blaring car horns. He called 9-1-1 and told the dispatcher what was happening. "I'll call out directions. Black Mustang GT, white racing stripes, Missouri plates, heading east on Pershing."

Jake grabbed his "Oh Jesus handle" above the window on his side and hung on as Bear swerved around on-coming traffic, chasing after the Mustang as it skidded north on Main Street. The truck's engine roared as Watterson's lead grew.

"We have a problem," Jake said.

Bear swerved, narrowly missing an old lady in a Buick the size of a boat. "You mean besides going seventy in a thirty-five zone in heavy traffic?"

"How did Ackerman and Watterson know to run?"

Bear tilted his head back and forth. "Good question."

NOW

CHAPTER THIRTY EIGHT

"Tell me something, Jake," Dr. Tate asked. "You've done a lot of things, things many people would call excessive, to get what you're after. Do the ends justify the means?"

Jake pulled at a loose thread on the leg of his jeans. That thread released another which released a third. He could probably unravel his jeans completely if he kept it up. That's the way things worked—one pull of a thread could start the process of everything falling apart. If he answered wrong, would it unravel everything and put him in the crosshairs of the judge?

"That's a loaded question," he answered.

"How so?"

"Because it's designed to serve your agenda."

Dr. Tate's brow furrowed. "I don't have an agenda. I'm not sure what you mean."

Jake stretched his hands out wide before dropping them. "Of course you have an agenda, Doc. Everyone does. The question is loaded because it puts me in a defensive position since the assumption you make in the question puts pressure on me to answer in a certain way."

"I still don't follow you."

Jake leaned forward. "It's like when someone asks a politician 'Have you stopped beating your wife' because it presupposes the guy beats his wife. If he answers yes, it confirms he has beat her in the past but stopped. If he answers no, it confirms he beat her in the past and is still doing it. If I say yes, the ends justify the means then it means I'm this dangerous individual who will do anything to get what he wants. If I say no, I was wrong for every…what you call excessive thing I've done."

Dr. Tate tapped her pen on her pad. "Or, it means you're dodging the question by trying to deflect my attention to the way I'm asking it instead of giving me an honest answer about what you think of the question itself. I'll ask it again. In your opinion, does the means you use to get to your goal justify getting there?

Damn this woman was good. He supposed he'd have to answer the question as honestly as he could. "My answer is sometimes."

"It's a yes or no question, Jake."

"It's really not."

"Fine. Give me an example, please."

Jake studied the floor for a minute, gathering his thoughts. "Breaking a guy's kneecap because he owed my boss a thousand dollars, not justified. Those snapping bones forced me to examine my life and make different choices. I'm far from the same man I was back then. That said, blowing the head off a sadistic psychopath or trying to choke the life out of a murderer who is about to get off Scott free is one hundred and fifty percent justified. Every day of the week and twice on Sunday."

Dr. Tate let Jake's statement sit for a moment. "I thought you said you were sorry for what you did in the courtroom."

"Would being sorry get me out of this therapy session and back on the street sooner?"

"It would help."

"Then I'm sorry. So very, very sorry."

Dr. Tate gripped the pen hard enough to turn her knuckles white. "But you're not really. That's what worries me. That's what worries the court. People have gotten hurt with your definition of justice, when there's no sense of...consideration if what you're doing is worth the damage it leaves behind, even if you accomplish your goal."

Jake clenched his jaw, trying to figure out a way to explain to this woman his modus operandi. He could lie and say what she wanted to hear, but she'd see right through him. The truth might get him in a load of trouble. "We're being honest here, you and I?"

"I hope so."

"Let me ask you something," Jake said. "Answer quick without giving it a lot of thought. Don't think what the legal machinations are or what your psychology training tells you, but what you, as a person, really think. Just between you and me?"

She stiffened her spine and set her pad and pen on her lap. "Fine."

"Justified or unjustified? A man's wife burns dinner and he beats the hell out of her with a belt."

"Unjustified."

"Agree," Jake said. "A guy gets five DUIs and gets his license revoked?"

"Justified, though hopefully he received something worse."

"The same guy later runs over an eight-year-old kid, cripples him and only gets six months in the county jail because his attorney and the judge are pals."

She shifted in her chair. "Unjustified."

"Agreed. Now someone beats the DUI guy with a baseball bat so badly he won't be able to walk again or drive a car, thus preventing him from crippling any more kids."

She blinked for a beat like she tried to send him Morse code. "Unjustified."

Jake let her stew in her answer for a moment. "Same scenario but the eight-year-old kid is your son. The guy served six months, and your son will never walk again, run the bases, dance at prom, or have a family of his own."

Dr. Tate dropped her eyes to her lap and said nothing.

"You see, Doc," Jake continued, "it's not a yes or no. It's not black it's justified and white it's not. There's a wide expanse of gray in the middle. I've been in the wrong where my means absolutely did not justify the end, and I've spent the last few years learning to live with it and make up for it. But there's times when the ends do justify the means, where we have to do what we can to make sure evil doesn't get the last spin of the wheel. We owe that to the people who have been hurt and to protect those who would be hurt in the future."

Dr. Tate raised her eyes and looked Jake square in the eye.

Jake splayed his hands wide again. "Of course, I'm speaking figuratively because I'm so very sorry for what I did in the courtroom."

Dr. Tate stifled a smile. In that moment, the first glimmer of hope shimmered she might kick Jake free.

THEN

CHAPTER THIRTY NINE

"Can't this piece of shit go any faster?" Jake asked, straining his head forward to keep Watterson's fleeing Mustang in sight. The Liberty Memorial faded in the distance on their right as they climbed the Main Street hill.

Bear jerked the wheel and spent a few seconds facing oncoming traffic to get around a minivan. "I could go faster if some ass munch hadn't crumpled my front end."

"I thought you forgave me for that."

Bear tailgated a Taurus and laid on the horn until it swerved out of the way. "I lied. This truck is only six months old. Jesus Christ, this kid race cars on the weekend?"

The Mustang's lead grew to a solid hundred yards as they raced up Main Street. The one factor keeping Jake and Bear in spitting distance was the Friday lunchtime traffic and a smattering of red lights to navigate through. If they didn't catch the kid soon, he would kill someone.

"Heading south on Main Street," Jake said to the

dispatcher. "Just passed 31st Street."

Sirens howled in the distance. They wouldn't be chasing Watterson alone for long.

Up ahead, Watterson swerved into the northbound lane to get around slow moving cars in front of him. Then again, they ran sixty in a thirty-five zone so everyone but them was slow moving. Watterson's maneuver caused a pile up ahead. Jake's seatbelt bit across his chest as Bear slammed on the brakes. He swung the truck to the right onto the sidewalk, blaring his horn to clear a young couple out of their way.

"Sorry," Jake yelled out the window. He received the sidewalk man's middle finger in return. "Don't kill anyone in the pursuit, man."

"Fuck him. I honked. You see the Mustang?"

Bear swung back to the street as they topped the hill and barreled along the downslope of Main. Flashing lights appeared in Bear's rearview mirror.

Jake spotted Watterson a quarter mile ahead. "Got him. Approaching Armour Boulevard."

A couple of KCPD squad cars approached from the south and slid to a stop ahead of Watterson. The Mustang's brake lights flared, and the rear end of the sports car swerved leaving snaking trails of rubber on the road. Watterson tried turning west on Armour but had too much speed and wrapped the Mustang around a light pole outside a U.S. Bank. A few seconds later, Bear skidded to a stop, and Jake jumped out of the truck.

With his Sig Sauer at his side, Jake stayed low as he approached the Mustang, smoke bellowing from under the crumpled hood. The license plate "SYRINX" dangling off the rear. An unwelcome image of Humphrey gunning down the cop the night before flickered, and he didn't want to end up in the same position. Sirens wailed and tires squealed behind him as the cops made their appearance. Across the top of the hood, interested onlookers approached the wreck, but darted back at the sight of Jake with a gun and the cops.

Bear's voice bellowed as he waved his badge. "We're cops. Don't shoot him."

Jake reached the passenger door of the Mustang and swung his gun at the form in the driver's seat. Watterson slumped against his seatbelt, his head lolling forward and blood streaming down the side of his face. On the passenger seat, Jake spotted a Glock 19 and a cell phone. He reached through the shattered window and plucked the gun by the barrel along with the phone. He shoved the phone in his back pocket as he backed away.

"Drop it," a deep voice commanded from behind a few seconds later. "Get on the ground, now. Rose, check the driver. I got this guy."

Jake tossed the Glock and lowered himself to the rough pavement, moving nice and slow. As he drew close to the ground, he gently laid his Sig Sauer on the ground. Screw the plastic Glock. He wasn't going to scratch the stainless steel of his Sig. He spread his arm and legs wide, wincing as the cop kicked his Sig across the asphalt.

Boots appeared under the bottom of the Mustang at the driver's side. Jake spotted gas dripping from the tank.

"This guy's alive, Prichard," Rose said. "Call EMS."

"Don't move," Prichard said to Jake.

Jake lifted his head and peered at Prichard. The cop was thin, wiry with years on the street lining his face.

He had his gun pointed in Jake's general direction, but not at him which meant Bear's proclamation and badge waving convinced them Jake wasn't a threat. He didn't blame them for being cautious.

"Officer Prichard?" Jake asked. The gasoline snaked along the street toward Jake.

"Shut up," Prichard said, calling out particulars on his shoulder mic.

Jake watched the approaching gas and waited until there was a lull in Prichard's information dump. "Officer Prichard? The Mustang's leaking gas. I'd rather you and I didn't blow up this morning."

Prichard flicked his eyes between the gas and Jake. His radio chirped but Jake couldn't make out what was said over the still howling sirens. After a minute, Prichard holstered his gun and flicked his hand for Jake to stand.

Prichard handed Jake his Sig Sauer. "Sorry, had to get verification who you guys were. The fat guy was waving a badge, but we had to call it in. Nice gun, by the way."

Jake checked the Sig for scratches and stuck it in his waist as they backed away from the wreckage. He turned to Rose. "He going to make it?"

"Think so," Rose said. "Unless he has internal bleeding or something. Ambulance will be here in a minute. Why was he running?"

"Feds want to question him over the KCK shooting last night."

Rose's eyes narrowed. "Was this guy there?"

"No, but he was involved with the group that did the shooting. 2A Militia."

Rose's nostrils flared. "A buddy of mine was one of the cops shot. In critical condition."

"Mine too. She died."

Some cops moved in to take care of the leaking gas while Prichard took Jake by the arm and led him away from the crash site. Bear held court with a trio of uniformed cops explaining what happened over the last thirty minutes. The cops took statements from Jake and Bear as an ambulance arrived and loaded Watterson onto a gurney.

Beyond the established police perimeter, Snell pulled up. She showed her badge and made her way to Jake and Bear. "You guys okay?"

"Yeah. Not so sure about Watterson."

"They're taking him to Truman to get checked out. If he's not dying, we'll question him and haul him to the FBI office. Ackerman is already on his way there."

"He say anything?" Bear asked.

"Asked us to call his work and let them know he wouldn't be in this afternoon."

Jake drew back. "That's kinda weird. He must have a ballbuster of a boss."

"Reliance," Snell said. "Same outfit Watterson works for."

Jake played through the timeline. They have a midnight shootout with the 2A Militia. When they decide to make a move on Watterson and Ackerman, someone calls and they both make a run for it. Who made the call? The answer could be in the cell phone in his back pocket.

"You guys want to take a run to the Reliance office with me?" Snell asked. "It's on the way back to the hospital. I'm curious if the last of our missing 2A members works there too."

"That would be a hell of a coincidence," Bear said. "We'll follow you."

They waited for Snell to weave around the cop cars and Bear turned south to follow. While he drove, Jake pulled Watterson's cell phone from his back pocket.

"What's that?" Bear asked.

"Watterson's phone. Picked it up off the passenger's seat."

"Why didn't you hand it over to the cops or Snell?"

Jake hit the power button on the side, and Apple's screen requesting a pin code to unlock the phone greeted him. "I will. I want to find out what's on it and who he called."

"You should've held it to his face. You'll never get it unlocked now."

Jake's mind dashed back to the wreck and the dangling license plate. Watterson was a Rush fan. Syrinx was the name of a priest temple in Rush's epic album from 1976. The name of the album was 2112. It was worth a shot.

Jake punched the four digits and the phone unlocked. "Don't need his face."

Bear's jaw dropped. "Dude, did you conjure the pin number out of thin air? How'd you do that?"

Jake winked. "A magician never tells his secrets."

As Jake and Bear rolled through the Kansas City streets following Snell toward Reliance's office, Jake read off the phone numbers to Cat. "Is there a way to figure out where these calls came from and who they're to?"

"Depends," Cat replied. "I can pull a CDR for the numbers and see what we get."

"What's a CDR?"

"Call Detail Record. Gives metadata on how a phone's used. It'll tell you when the call happened, how long it lasted, who called who."

"I can find that out by looking at the call log on this phone," Jake said.

"That's one piece of the puzzle. I can pull the CDR for the numbers involved. You can only look at Watterson's phone and know who he called, but you can't tell who they called."

"Can you tell me where they called from?"

"Let me see if I can explain this," Cat said.

"And no technical jargon. Explain it like I'm in middle school."

"Oh, so like I normally have to do. When you make a call, the cell phone pings multiple towers at the same time. The calls will be routed through the tower with the best radio-frequency connection to the phone. A switching center figures out where you're calling and calls cell towers in that area. Which tower sends out the signal and which tower accepts the signal depends on the load of the system."

"What if you're moving?"

"You'd be handed off from one tower to another in the middle of a call but you can't tell. It's all handled by software."

"How do you figure out where the person was who made and received the calls?"

Cat said, "When you're stationary, your calls are pretty much going through the same cell tower and sector of the tower."

"Sector?" Bear asked.

"Most cell towers use three antennas covering a hundred and twenty degrees each. You do remember there are three hundred and sixty degrees in a circle, don't you, Bear? One twenty times three equals three sixty."

Bear growled. "Fuck you, you little shit."

"I'm kidding," Cat said. "Just a little friendly banter among friends."

"I'll banter your ass into the ground," Bear said.

"So the cell towers," Jake interrupted, gesturing with his hand for Bear to chill out. "You can use them to figure out where the person is who made or received a call?"

"Yeah. It's pretty unlikely to have more than two or maybe three towers with some level of overlapping coverage at a specific location. Cell phone companies can use the GPS in the handset or triangulate the signal from those towers. With enhanced 911 service requirements, carriers have to be able to trace a call to within a few feet."

Bear followed Snell into a parking lot of a building near the Hallmark Cards headquarters. They bounced over a couple of potholes before parking. A stout man appraised them from the front door before offering an awkward wave and disappearing inside.

Jake thought for a moment. "Would this hold up in a court of law?"

"Depends on the attorney and your expert witnesses. Lawyers have shredded it in previous cases. The guy I did it for got his ass handed to him. But the point is, I can get you there. For a fee, of course."

"What if they're calling burner phones?"

"They're still operating through the cellular network and it's constantly being tracked," Cat said. "It's another layer to the tracing process, but if you give me a name, I can track to see if a burner phone is being carried with a personal number."

Snell stood outside her car and gave an impatient wave for Jake and Bear to come. Jake held up his index finger and pointed to the phone.

"Do it," Jake said. "I don't have any names yet for you other than Watterson, but how long will it take you to get the basic info on the numbers I gave you?"

"Depends on how many numbers there are on the other end. I have a program that backdoors into the major carriers. If it's a personal number, I'll be able to tell you who it belongs to. If it's a burner, unless I can tie it to a personal number traveling together, I won't be able to tell you anything but geography. I built an algorithm for another client that will cross check numbers pretty quickly."

"Do it. Call me the second you get anything interesting."

Jake held high hopes Cat would come through with something useful. If he didn't, Jake wasn't sure what the hell they would do.

CHAPTER FORTY

Hunter sped down Highway 69 heading toward downtown Kansas City, the first pricks of worry peppering his psyche. First Lenny gets busted and placed in federal custody, then the shootout at Humphrey's place that killed most of the active 2A Militia members. They weren't crucial to the mission's success, but it meant the FBI was closing in. When Mister X called to let him know the FBI was on their way to snag Watterson and Ackerman, his level of apprehension went into overdrive. Of the 2A membership, the only ones who could identify him were the now dead Wallace, then Watterson and Ackerman. He wished the little turds would have been at Wallace's house and died in the shootout. But nothing was easy and nothing good was free, as his father used to say.

On his way out of his house, he'd called Watterson on a burner and reached his voicemail, then a hungover Ackerman who he told to get out of town. Ackerman promised to call Watterson. Loose threads. It only took one pull of the string. The analogy wouldn't go away.

He crossed the Heart of America bridge into downtown, reflecting on Mister X's message.

"The targets will be visiting the hospital before the rally at Union Station."

Hunter's grip dug into the steering wheel. "The rally is today? It was supposed to be on Tuesday."

"Change of plan. The President is taking a trip to the Netherlands. Will the stage at the rally be ready?"

"Some of the boards are in place, but not enough. The stage isn't complete, so they can't do it there. Would be a horrible photo op."

"They'll move the rally somewhere else, maybe inside. I'll see what I can find out from my contacts. The hospital's our best shot. Can you pull it off?"

Hunter's mind raced through their supplies, the drone, the C4 they had and the test flights he and Lance conducted with various weights. "How will we know when and where they'll be in the hospital?"

"You'll know when I do. You've got ninety minutes. Air Force One is already en route. Be ready."

The line went dead and Hunter weaved through the one way streets of Kansas City's downtown. At a stoplight, he stroked the stubble on cheek, options whirring through his brain. He supposed he'd been naïve to think this would be easy, but he hadn't counted on the inept FBI getting lucky and closing in this quickly.

He'd held the hope the work of his team would hurl the United States into chaos, shredding the fabric of the nation, allowing him and Mara to drop off the map at Anarchy Road. As it stood now, things were in chaos, but recoverable. The assassination of the President would be the powder keg that would spin the nation into civil war. Anarchy would follow. But the loose ends of Lenny, Watterson and Ackerman could lead back to him. Maybe Lance, too. He could run and he could hide, but for how long? Eventually, they'd come for him and any momentum they'd built would vanish. He needed the loose ends eliminated, but Hunter now didn't have that kind of time.

He passed Union Station and spotted the flashing lights of police cars and a group of protestors gathering. There were a handful of each, but both would grow exponentially by the time the President and Vice-President made their appearance, if that was even where they ended up going. Goddamn it. They should have accelerated the construction schedule. Screw the union and city permit officials holding them up. There might be enough C4 in place inside to make the plan work. Maybe. The one certainty appeared to be the hospital. Mister X was always right about the President's schedule.

Hunter wheeled left on Pershing and rolled up the hill past the Hallmark Cards headquarters. Lance was a worrier and the meticulous planner. He'd want to postpone the op, but Hunter didn't know if they'd get this kind of opportunity again, especially with the Feds tightening the noose. Mara would want to go in guns blazing. As brash and reckless as she could be, Hunter figured her approach was probably right. This was their shot, likely their only shot.

He turned right past Hallmark and down a steep hill. His building lay ahead, a mass of long, low slung brick that used to be a fire station. He pulled into the lot, past some heavy equipment and parked in a reserved spot at the front of the building. As he opened the front door, tires droned on the asphalt behind him and he turned his head. A Ford Fusion with a lady driver. Behind her was a smashed pickup with a giant bearded man behind the wheel and a steely-eyed man in the passenger seat.

Hunter's heartrate picked up, not at the unknown two men in the truck, but the woman behind the wheel. He recognized her from television. Victoria Snell from the FBI. Hunter forced a wave in their direction and darted into the building. They'd found him.

"Feds are here," he said to Mara who occupied the front desk. "Where's Lance?"

"In the shop," Mara replied, her eyes widening. "What're we going to do?"

"Play it cool as a cucumber. Don't panic, direct them to me. You got your gun?"

"In my purse," Mara's voice climbed an octave. "Fuck!"

Outside, car doors slammed shut.

"Don't jump unless I tell you to," Hunter said. "If I do, don't stop shooting until that gun runs dry."

Mara jerked her head toward the door and then back to Hunter. "I love you."

"Love you too, sweetheart."

Hunter ran back toward the shop to warn Lance. He had enough weapons stashed in the building that he could make things very bloody for law enforcement if it came down to it. As he ran, he heard Eddie laughing and singing his favorite Door's song – Five to One. Five to one, baby. One in five. No one here gets out alive.

CHAPTER FORTY ONE

Jake and Bear climbed from the truck and followed Snell toward the front door. Jake considered mentioning something to Snell about Watterson's phone and his direction with Cat but decided to wait and see if anything came of it. He was afraid she, or her stick-up-his-ass boss, would dismiss the effort because of the legality. Jake didn't care if it was legal if it moved them closer to stopping the bad guys. If he got the info they wanted, he'd worry about finding a legal way back to it later.

The three of them crowded into the lobby of Reliance Construction. A fifteen-by-twenty foot waiting area with a coffee table and a couple of chairs in a brick-walled corner, an unoccupied, glass-walled conference room next to it and a reception desk guarding a hallway disappearing to the back of the building. A massive American flag cut from polished steel hung on one wall. The thing would crush someone's skull if it fell.

A woman typed on a computer at the desk—mid-thirties, light brown hair and sharp cheek bones over a pointed chin. She appraised them with cobalt blue eyes as they stepped toward her before throwing on a welcoming smile as fake as a politician's on the campaign trail.

"Can I help you?" she asked.

Snell showed her badge. "Special Agent Victoria Snell with the FBI. I need to ask about a couple of employees in connection with a case we're following. What's your name?"

The woman's nostrils flared for a microsecond. "Mara. Mara Wilder."

"Is there someone I could talk to, Mara?"

"Who would you like?" Mara asked, her features turning as cold as a slab of ice.

"Maxwell Watterson and Drake Ackerman. You know them?"

She scratched at her temple. "I think I've heard their names, but I don't know them personally. Let me check if Mr. Brenner, the owner, is available. He just got into the office."

Mara dialed a number on her desk phone, spoke in a low voice and hung up. "Mr. Brenner will be with you in a moment. Have a seat."

"Bit of an icy reception," Bear muttered as they dropped into chairs.

Snell smirked toward Mara. "And her smile was as fake as her tits. I know people don't exactly jump for joy when the FBI comes knocking, but still."

"Must be your charming personality," Bear said.

"Bite me, Bear."

Jake thumbed through a Sports Illustrated as they waited, while Snell texted a novel on her phone. A few minutes later, a man came down the hall and stopped in front of them.

"Hello," he said, offering his hand. "I'm Hunter Brenner. What can I help you with?"

The man's strong grip wrapped around Jake's. He was handsome, mid-forties, a couple inches shorter than Jake, but the man had powerful forearms beneath the buttoned sleeves of a white oxford. His face was tanned and lined from working in the sun with bullish eyes between cauliflower ears. Brenner's teeth blazed white.

Snell made introductions. "Is there someplace we could talk?"

Brenner gestured toward the glass-walled conference room behind them. Jake, Bear and Snell sat at one side of the long conference table while Brenner closed the door and took a seat at the head of the table. Through the glass, Mara tracked them, her eyes locked on Snell. The room smelled musty. Pictures of construction projects lined the brick back wall intermixed with Brenner in military fatigues shaking hands with people Jake didn't recognize.

"Are you from Kansas City, Mr. Brenner?" Jake asked.

"Call me Hunter. Born and raised here."

"Where'd you wrestle?"

Brenner tapped his mangled ear. "Dead giveaway isn't it? After high school, I wrestled at Oklahoma State for a couple of years before I enlisted."

OSU was one of the premiere wrestling colleges in the US. Jake tipped his head toward Brenner. "Good school. You must've been a beast."

"I did okay. It wasn't as rewarding as serving my country, but it was fun. Now, what can I do for you folks? I have a lot of things going on today."

Snell propped her elbows on the table. "You have

a couple of employees named Maxwell Watterson and Drake Ackerman?"

Brenner stiffened. "Yeah. What'd they do?"

"How long have they worked for you?"

"I'd have to check personnel records, but I'd guess a couple of years each, give or take a few months."

"What can you tell us about them?"

Brenner ran a hand through his caramel hair and leaned back in the chair, his charming demeanor melting a bit. "Good workers. Nothing out of the ordinary for either of them that I can think of. Can I get some idea why you're asking?"

"They might have information on a case we're looking into," Snell said.

Brenner's jade eyes darted between the three people opposite him. "I don't know them well other than they're good workers and show up on time. I think they live together if it helps."

"You know of any hobbies they had? People they hung out with?"

Brenner shook his head. "I know their faces and their names. Have talked with them a few times. That's it. You're welcome to check with their respective foremen."

"Oh, we will. Any disciplinary issues?" Snell asked.

"Not that I know of," Brenner said, sweeping his eyes over Snell as if just noticing how attractive she was. It wasn't a casual eye sweep, but slow and methodical. It was an overt, dick move to unsettle her. Jake knew it wouldn't work, and Snell could handle herself, but it pissed him off.

"We noticed Watterson was working at Union Station," Jake said. "What's going on over there?"

Brenner peeled his eyes from Snell to Jake, his

lips pressing into a white slash. "A remodeling job."

"Of what?"

"I fail to see the relevance of what we're working on."

Mr. Hyde poked his ugly head through Brenner's charming Dr. Jekyll persona. Jake pressed. "You ever heard of the 2A Militia?"

Brenner exaggerated a sigh and scratched his nose. "Militia? I don't think so. I've never heard those guys talk about anything like that. Wait, is this related to the bombing the other night at the arena?"

"Why would you ask that?"

Brenner displayed his perfect teeth again. "I'm not an idiot. My military background coming out, I guess. The bombing, the FBI, you asking about a militia. You think these two were involved?"

Snell held up a palm. "We don't think anything at this point, sir. We're chasing down any possible leads, and the names of these two guys came up."

"Have they said anything?" Brenner asked, his cadence slow, eyebrows raised.

Jake blinked, running back the conversation in his head. Nobody said anything about Watterson and Ackerman being in custody. It was a weird leap for Brenner to make. The question wasn't phrased as innocent curiosity. It was like he worried what they'd say. Jake shook it off. Maybe the fact he didn't like Hunter Brenner poisoned his judgement.

"What makes you think we have them?" Snell asked.

"I'm sorry. I assumed you did for some reason. I can get you their address and any other contact information if you need it."

"That would be great. Thank you."

Brenner made a call on his cell asking for the contact information. Through the conference room window, Jake spotted a lean, black man with wire rimmed glasses in dark pants and a grey golf shirt come down the hall. He said something to Mara, glanced to the conference room and left through the front door.

Brenner set his cell phone on the table. "The information you want is on the way. What makes you think these two were involved in the bombing?"

"Oh, we didn't say they were," Snell said, waving off the question. "We're following up on a lead. Given what's happened over the last couple of days, we're making sure the i's are dotted and t's are crossed. But, as far as you know, no mention of 2A, guns, militias or anything like that?"

"Nothing like that. They seem like good guys."

Snell asked a few more questions, but Brenner either was dumb or played dumb. Jake held his suspicions which one it was. They walked out of the conference room and stopped at the front desk. Mara handed them a sheet of paper with Watterson and Ackerman's phone numbers and address. Brenner was right. They lived together.

Snell handed Brenner her card. "If you think of anything else, please give me a call."

"Definitely," Brenner said, a flirtatious smile brimming from his thin lips.

Behind the desk, Jake noticed a fire flare in Mara's eyes as her glare burned a hole through Snell's forehead. She noticed Jake watching her and jerked her head back to the papers in front of her.

Outside the Reliance office, they gathered around the front of Snell's car.

"What a douche," Snell said. "My skin literally crawled as he ogled me. I thought he was going to try and sell me a used car."

"If your skin crawled from Brenner, it must've been on fire from the receptionist," Jake said.

"The green-eyed monster at her finest," Bear said. "This Brenner guy is dicking his secretary. No doubt about it."

Snell's cell rang. She answered it, listened a few seconds and hung up. "Watterson's awake. We can go talk to him. Follow me to Truman."

Jake and Bear climbed back in his truck and pulled out of the lot.

"Did you notice Brenner's reaction when I asked him about the 2A Militia?" Jake asked.

"Yeah. That used car salesman was lying. Probably about Watterson and Ackerman too."

"And he jumps to wondering what Watterson and Ackerman has said to us. Like he was nervous."

"Hmmm. Guess I didn't take that one the wrong way. He coulda just been curious."

Jake drummed his knuckles against the window. "Maybe. Something rubbed me the wrong way."

"That something's probably the fact Brenner wanted to rub something of his own against Snell and you're getting big brotherly."

Jake was protective of Snell. They'd been through too much together over the years for him to feel otherwise. "Maybe."

As they closed in on Truman though, Jake was pretty sure he was dead on about Brenner. The guy didn't pass the smell test, and Jake was going to find out why.

CHAPTER FORTY TWO

As they closed in on Truman, a crowd of protesters were scattered across the road, signs raised and shouting at cars who weaved their way through. The crowd was fifty in number, all races, colors, creeds and genders were represented. As Bear turned the corner into them, they surrounded his truck waving "No Justice, No Peace" and "Defund the Police" signs.

"Idiots," Bear muttered, weaving his way around the group, edging forward at a slow enough speed that he wouldn't run one over but fast enough for them to know they should get out of the way.

"First amendment in action," Jake said, knowing it would trigger a response from his partner.

Bear snarled. "Bullshit. You have a right to protest whatever the hell you want. I have no problem with it. However, you do not get to be a huge pain in my ass and try to get me fired just because I happen to carry a badge. I'd flash it at 'em, but it'd probably make things worse. Hope they don't bang one of those signs against my truck. I'll end up plastered on the news."

"Afraid they're going make it look any worse?"

"Fuck you, Caldwell. Too soon. Keep it up and I'm gonna charge you for the damages."

"Put it on 2A's bill."

They made it past the crowd and into the parking lot, pulling up near Snell. Men in dark suits with ear pieces stopped them at the entrance. Snell displayed her badge and talked to one of them. They waved Jake and Bear through.

"What was that?" Jake asked.

"Secret Service," Snell replied. "Guess the President and Vice-President are showing up for a photo op with one of the survivors from the bombing the other night." Her cell phone dinged. "Oh hell, they moved Watterson, but I don't know where. Give me a minute."

While Snell figured things out, Jake took the opportunity to go to Halle's room to check in with his family while Bear stood outside waiting for Snell.

"How's the manhunt going?" Maggie asked.

Jake dropped on Halle's bed and gave his daughter a kiss on the forehead. "Slow and steady. That's what wins the race, right?"

"So they say," Halle said. "You check out the protesters outside?"

"We waded through them."

"There's similar protests going on in lots of cities," Maggie said. "It's been all over the news. Hope this one doesn't turn violent like the others. St. Louis was crazy last night. Five people died and two cops are in the hospital, one in critical condition."

"Damn country is tearing itself apart," Jake said. "President's supposedly coming to do a photo op with a bombing victim. Guess that's why they're out there."

Maggie glanced at their daughter. "Maybe they can

stop by and see Halle."

Halle's eyes popped wide. "And go on national TV with this tube coming out of my skull? No thanks."

Snell stuck her head in the door, said hello and turned to Jake. "They moved Watterson to the other side of the hospital. Let's go."

Jake kissed his girls good-bye and followed Snell's fast moving feet. They worked their way across the hospital as Secret Service guys passed them moving the other direction, faces stern, all business.

They took the stairs up two flights, Bear grumbling about skipping a perfectly good elevator, then down an antiseptic-reeking hall to Watterson's room. The policeman outside the room held up his hand to stop them before waving them forward when Snell showed her badge.

"I gotta get one of those FBI badges," Bear said. "It's like a backstage pass for cops."

"You have a badge," Jake said.

"Benton County versus the federal government. Not quite the same pull."

Watterson's bed angled up and his black eyes watched a television with the sound muted. A white bandage wrapped around his head, pushing his charcoal hair up like a Troll doll on a bad hair day. Bruises and a half-dozen cuts peppered his face and arms, the equivalent of a boxer who went fifteen rounds with the heavy weight champ and lost, badly.

"Hello, Max," Snell said, stopping at his bedside and fingering the handcuffs chaining him to the bed.

Watterson's eyes danced from her to Jake, who settled at the end of the bed and Bear who camped by a window overlooking the parking lot below, the afternoon sun beating at his back. "Who the hell are you guys?"

"Victoria Snell, FBI. This is Jake Caldwell and Sheriff James Parley. How're you feeling?"

Watterson groaned as he tried to sit up. "Like I got in a car crash."

"You're lucky to be alive," Bear said.

"How would you know?"

"We were in the truck behind you. Why'd you run?"

Watterson narrowed his eyes. "Why were you chasin' me?"

"Why do you think?"

Watterson clenched and unclenched his fists like he squeezed one of those stress balls. "I didn't have a thing to do with what went down at the house last night. I wasn't even there."

"We know you weren't there. How'd you hear about it?"

"I saw the news. So why were you chasin' me?"

"We just wanted to talk to you," Snell said. "You're in a lot of trouble, Max."

"Kiss my tattooed ass. I got nothin' to say."

"Reckless endangerment and probably vehicular manslaughter."

Watterson's eyes blew wide and whipped around the room to see if they were joking or not. Jake had no idea what Snell was talking about but kept his poker face on. There hadn't been a bystander within thirty feet of the crash.

"Man…man…manslaughter? What're you talking about?"

Snell pressed in. "Little old lady out walking her dog. You hit her when you smacked into the light pole. Killed her dog and she's fading. Probably won't make it through the day."

Watterson shrunk into the bed. "Bullshit. There's wasn't no old lady."

Jake loved the lack of conviction in his voice and added to the charade. "She was a black lady, too. We'll get you charged with a hate crime. A jury will eat it up."

"You...you can't do that."

"In today's political climate, it'd be a cinch. You tell us what we want to know, maybe we take the hate crime off the table. Who knows? The old lady lives, and you might lay eyes on daylight again outside of a prison cell."

Watterson pressed his lips together, dropping his eyes to the handcuffs holding him in place. Jake wasn't sure if he would tell them anything, but he could practically hear the gears in Watterson's head turning.

Snell laid a hand on Watterson's arm. "We have Ackerman, too, Max. He's talking, telling us his story about the 2A Militia."

Watterson's face hardened. "Now I know it's bullshit. Drake hates the cops more than anybody I know. Feds even more than that. He wouldn't say shit to you guys. I bet you don't even got him."

"He might not have said shit before he shot a cop with his gold-plated Desert Eagle when we raided your house." Snell held up her cell phone with a picture of Ackerman in cuffs. "Now he's singing like a canary in exchange for leniency. You comfortable under that bus he's driving over you?"

Watterson's face dropped like someone crushed the air out of him. "What's he sayin'?"

"Nuh uh," Snell said. "That isn't how this works. You tell us what you know. Whichever one of you helps us the most gets a better deal. You jerk us around and you won't smell freedom before you're in your eighties. If you make it that long in prison."

Bear made a kissing sound. "And they'd love a pretty boy like you in Jefferson City. I know the warden pretty well. We could make sure you receive special accommodations."

Jake dropped his voice low. "Put Max here in a dress and pop him down on Sodomy Row and ring the dinner bell. You'd be the most popular girl at the ball."

Watterson cringed. "I'll talk to my lawyer and he'll—"

"It's your right," Snell interrupted. "You can absolutely stop talking to us right now and wait for your lawyer. Just know Ackerman's already talking. We get what we want out of him, we don't need you, and you can say bye-bye to any deal. It's your call, Max."

Watterson's skin turned a shade of green, and Jake took a step back in case the kid decided to projectile vomit everywhere. He pressed his head back into his pillow, his eyes watering. Probably playing back every wrong decision he'd ever made in his life to get him to this point.

"He'll kill us," Watterson whispered. "Both of us."

"Who?"

"I can't say."

Snell rattled his handcuff again. "Can't or won't?"

Watterson's voice cracked with despair. "Is there a difference?"

"Tell you what," Snell said. "We'll ask a few questions, you tell us what you can. Let's start with the 2A Militia. What can you tell us about the group?"

"Just a small group of people who believe in the Second Amendment who like to shoot guns. I've been with them for a year. Drake too. They talked a lot of shit in the beginning, and we went to the occasional protest to try and counter the left-wing crazies, but I thought they were pretty harmless."

"Harmless people don't gun down a bunch of cops and feds like they did at Wallace Humphrey's house last night," Jake said. "Why weren't you there?"

"Drake and I went out to Westport for his birthday last night. Besides, things were getting a little weird at Humphrey's anyway."

"How so?" Snell asked.

"More intense. Talk was turning from scenarios of what 2A would do to what we were going to do. I mean, I believe you government authoritarians are coming after our guns. You already know there's no freedom of speech anymore unless it mimics the far left's idea of it. Fuckin' country is going downhill fast. But those guys wanted to take things to another level. Drake and I were starting to get a vibe and had kinda slowed down on our visits out there."

"What do you mean, take it to another level?"

Watterson's eyes shot to his cuffed hand. "I ain't sayin' nothin' about that."

Jake thought back to Watterson's earlier comment. He'll kill both of us. Watterson had to know Wallace Humphrey was dead, so who was he talking about?

"Who was the leader of 2A?" Jake asked.

"Nobody you want to mess with."

That ruled out Humphrey. The news reports already identified Wallace Humphrey as one of the dead from the shootout. Time to start figuring out the names of the other 2A players who weren't on their radar.

"Was Lenny Moritz part of 2A?" Snell asked. "Before you answer, you should know we have him in custody too."

"He was only a supplier," Watterson said. "He made some sweet ass ARs, though."

"What else did he supply?"

"No comment."

"C4?"

Watterson gritted his teeth. "I said no comment."

Jake stepped back to the bed. "Maybe that's what you meant by things moving from potential talk to another level?"

"You do the math, man," Watterson said.

Watterson's body language spoke. He was starting to close down, and Jake figured they had, at best, a few more questions to ask before Watterson realized he should shut up and wait for his lawyer.

"You want to give us a list of 2A members?" Snell asked.

"No."

Snell pulled out a notepad and read off names, adding the word "dead" after all of them. "Then there's you and Drake. Wyatt is the only one we haven't found yet."

Jake had an idea. The giant flag at Reliance. The pictures on the wall of the conference room. Brenner's odd behavior. He decided to stick a toe in the water. "Don't forget about Hunter Brenner and Mara, Snell."

"Oh, right," Snell said, flipping the paper on her notepad. "They were on the next page."

Watterson batted a hand. "Mara isn't a member of the 2A Militia. That chick's crazy. They wouldn't let her in the door."

Jake's eyes locked on Snell's. Watterson denounced Mara but didn't blink at Hunter Brenner's name. Brenner was a patriot and he was the boss of both Watterson and Ackerman.

"Is Hunter Brenner the head of 2A?"

Watterson's eyes dropped. "No. Don't know what you're talkin' about."

If Watterson played poker, he'd be the world's worst bluffer.

"You're lying, Max," Jake said. "What's he planning?"

Watterson squeezed his eyes shut with enough force to wrinkle the sides of his face. "Nope. No comment. I ain't sayin' another word until my lawyer gets here."

"Is he the one who would kill you?" Snell asked.

Watterson refused to open his eyes, shaking his head. "Nope. Nope. Lawyer."

Jake considered applying a little more physical pressure, maybe to a body part injured in the car wreck, but a slim, thin-haired doctor entered the room, reading a chart.

The doctor stopped and swept his eyes across the occupants. "Is there a problem?"

Snell ticked her head toward the door. "No problem. We were just leaving. We'll be back, Max. If you want a deal, you're going to have to give us something. We'll let you know when your lawyer gets here."

Jake, Bear and Snell walked out the door and made it halfway down the hall before Jake remembered the pictures on Watterson's phone. "Wait, I want to ask him about these guys on Watterson's phone. Maybe one of them is Wyatt Tate. He's the only 2A member we don't know about."

"He isn't going to say anything," Bear said.

"It's worth a shot."

Snell scowled. "Where did you get his goddamn cell phone, Jake?"

"Didn't I tell you I had it?" Jake asked, a gleam in his eye. "Give me a second."

He turned back toward Watterson's room as Snell cursed him. After a single step into the room, he paused as something out the window caught his eye. A giant bird flying toward them, moving fast, coasting without a flap of wings. The closer it flew, the realization dawned it wasn't a bird at all. It was a drone. And it had something strapped to the bottom of it. Something with a blinking red light.

Jake's stomach turned rock hard and every drop of moisture evaporated in his mouth. His brain screamed to run, but his feet were locked in place as his eyes tracked the drone closing in, heading right for the window to the room. His brain registered the whir of the blades right before it crashed through the glass. Jake's feet unlocked as he dove back into the hallway before the explosion knocked a hole in the world.

CHAPTER FORTY THREE

Jake coughed out dust and smoke and pushed to his knees, the glass, wood and stone debris falling to the floor. His ears rang and he blinked away the shimmering world around him. He bared his teeth, his muscles and veins straining against his skin as he stood. His hands shook with rage at the fact someone had tried to blow him up twice in less than thirty-six hours.

His brain registered Snell and Bear running toward him. He turned to the massive hole where the walls to Watterson's room used to be. What was left of the body of the slim doctor lay bloodied and crumpled at his feet. The cop stationed outside the room was in a lump at the base of the nurse's station. Jake couldn't tell if the guy was alive, but unlike the good doctor, he at least had all his limbs.

Halle. Maggie. He spun to the other side of the hospital, and his muddled brain ran through the calculations on his location, the damage and condition of the rest of the floor. Maggie and Halle were probably safe given their proximity. Shell-shocked nurses and doctors stumbled around amid the blare of the fire alarm, checking on each other, tending to bodies on the floor.

"Hey," Bear said, grabbing Jake by the shoulders. "You in there?"

Jake blinked his way to Bear's face, shaking away the cobwebs and stopping when pain erupted in his skull. "I think so. Maggie and Halle. I should check on them."

Bear guided him away from the debris. "You need to sit your ass down for a minute. I'll check on them. What the hell just happened?"

Jake's mind rewound. "Drone. It was a drone. Flew through the window and boom."

Snell leapt into action and barked out orders to a couple of approaching cops and jumped on her phone to get to the security office. Bear lowered Jake onto a chair in a nearby waiting area and found a bottle of water. Jake accepted with shaky hands. He managed a couple of swallows and splashed a handful on his face, wiping away dirt and blood he wasn't sure was his.

"I'm gonna go check on the girls," Bear said. "Sit tight."

"Screw that. I'm coming with you."

Bear pressed a hand on his shoulder. "Stay here and get your legs back under you. I got this."

Jake smacked his friend's hand away. "You'll scare the hell out of them if you walk in there without me after a fucking explosion. Help me up."

Bear grabbed Jake's arm and helped him to his feet. By the time they reached the stairwell, the wobbliness left and the cotton between his ears began to dissipate.

"Think it was the same guys?" Bear asked.

"They do love C4," Jake said, pressing open the door to the stairwell.

"Hope they run out of that shit pretty soon. This is getting old."

"You're tellin' me. You get to be blown up next time."

They took the stairs as quick as they could, which was a slow jog for Jake. Seconds later, a thunder of feet echoed above them, and a bevy of Secret Service guys poured down the stairs. Two pulled the guns and aimed them at Jake and Bear. They threw up their hands and the agents pressed them into the concrete wall of the landing. They explained who they were, but the two agents held them at bay while the rest of their party descended. From the corner of his eye, two figures passed within spitting distance. Two figures he thought he'd never be this close to—the President and Vice-President of the United States.

Once the two highest ranking officials in the country passed out of sight, the Secret Service guys grilled Jake and Bear about who they were and what they were doing. Bear's badge helped relax things, and the suggestion to call Snell to verify their bona fides satisfied them. They released Jake and Bear and disappeared down the stairs.

Bear lumbered up the last flight of stairs. "Wish I woulda known the President was coming down. I would've loved to have a word with him about his awful tax and immigration policies."

Jake winced, his old, injured knee barking at him. "I'm sure he would've been thrilled to hear your perspectives."

Halle's floor bustled with activity, but nothing like Watterson's. Probably because it still had its walls and floors in place. They made it to Halle's room where Maggie nearly knocked Jake off his feet with a hug. She cried and it took a minute to soothe her rattled nerves. Halle was marginally better but when Jake leaned down, she wrapped her strong arms around his neck and wouldn't let go.

"It's okay," Jake whispered. "It's okay, baby. We're good."

"What was that?" Maggie asked.

Jake told her what he knew. The girls accepted his explanation in silence but didn't want to let Jake out of touching distance.

"Did you say anything to the President?" Halle asked.

"My face was planted into the side of the stairwell when they passed us, so no."

"He went right by here before the bomb blew up," she said. "He even gave me a thumbs-up when he walked by."

Maggie stiffened. "Wait. Do you think the bomb was intended for your militia guy, or could it have been meant for the President?"

Jake and Bear exchanged looks. It was a damn good question.

CHAPTER FORTY FOUR

An hour later, Jake and Bear found Snell outside the security office at Truman. She confirmed what Jake had begun to suspect.

"The President and Vice-President were here to do a photo op with a cop caught up in the bombing at the T-Mobile arena before going to Union Station for a rally tonight. An hour before the drone exploded, they moved the cop to an intermediate care bed so he could be monitored more closely. Any guess as to what room he was in before that?"

Bear whistled. "Max Watterson's?"

"The one directly above it."

Jake folded his arms and pressed his back into the hallway wall. "Jesus Christ. Did somebody try to assassinate the President and Vice-President? Where are they now?"

"They were scheduled to speak at Union Station but are getting the hell outta town on Air Force One. I'm sure they're in the air by now. It's a media circus outside."

"How'd they know the President's agenda?" Jake

asked. "Where he was going to be? This hospital is confusing enough from the inside. Can't imagine trying to find the right room from the outside while flying a drone."

A bald guy with elephant ears in a navy FBI jacket stuck his head out the door. "Snell, get in here. We have something."

Jake and Bear followed Snell into the room. A uniformed cop tried to stop them, but Snell waved them through. A beefy hospital security guy with a bad comb over sat in front of a bank of monitors while Dumbo the FBI agent hovered over his shoulder.

"Go back to the footage from the west lot," Dumbo said, before turning to Snell. "We've been combing the video feeds from the various cameras for anything suspicious. Spent a lot of time on the protesters but didn't really see anything. We were about to give up when Bob here noticed this."

Bob punched up a video feed overlooking Charlotte Street. "We obviously know the drone struck the east side of the building. This is from a security camera on the side near the emergency room entrance." He slowed the video and pointed to the screen. "There's the drone moving northwest toward the building. I backtracked the flight path."

"You figured out where it came from?"

Bob punched a couple of keys and a new feed popped up. "That and more. This is the outside of the UMKC training facility entrance."

The screen showed the outside of the University of Missouri Kansas City School of Medicine Clinical Training facility. The building sat on the east side of Charlotte Street with six stories of grey high walls of a parking structure facing the street.

Bob backed up the timeline. "Check this out."

The footage showed the drone emerging from the top floor of the parking garage and heading for the hospital.

"Holy crap," Bear whispered. "There it is."

"Wait," Bob said, bouncing in his seat like a kid on Christmas morning. "It gets better. Wait, almost, there he is."

On screen, a face appeared from the spot where the drone left the parking garage. It was a man holding a controller with both hands.

"Zoom in," Snell said. After Bob did, they studied the face of a black man with glasses. "Now we have to figure out who it is. Send a digital pic of the guy to my phone. We need to get an APB out yesterday. Somebody will know who that son of a bitch is."

Jake drew closer to the monitor, wanting to make sure he was right. It took him three seconds to realize he was. "I saw this guy. Today."

Snell snapped to him. "Where?"

"At Reliance Construction when we met with Brenner. This same guy stopped by the desk from the back and talked to the receptionist before heading out the door."

"You sure?"

"Positive. Same wire rimmed glasses and everything. That's the guy."

Snell jumped on the phone to somebody and darted from the room. Jake and Bear followed, feet moving fast.

"Where's she going?" Bear asked.

"Beats the hell outta me," Jake said. "I'm just trying to keep up."

"If I have a heart attack, tell Audrey to sue the

federal government."

They wound their way to the hospital entrance after a couple of wrong turns in the confusing maze of hallways. Another agent named Bryce met Snell at the entrance. Snell yelled for Jake and Bear to follow her to Reliance. She and Bryce disappeared into Snell's Fusion and followed a couple of KCPD squad cars. Bear caught up to the parade of lights and sirens and followed close past the gawking protestors. The explosion had dampened their enthusiasm as they gathered at a safe distance across the street.

Ten minutes later, they screeched to a halt in the Reliance parking lot and jumped out. Snell led the way into the building while a mix of federal agents and cops swept through every inch of the structure. They didn't find the guy in the glasses from the video. Hunter Brenner and Mara were gone as well.

A middle-aged man in a wrinkled oxford shirt and khakis approached the gathering group in the lobby. "I'm Stu Lundgren, the HR manager. What's going on?"

Snell thrust her phone and FBI badge at him. "You know who this is?"

Lundgren adjusted his glasses and flicked his eyes from the badge to the phone. "That's Lance, one of our security guys. What's this about?"

"What's his last name?"

"I have no idea. He doesn't work for us. He's with PHG Security. It's a private firm we—"

Snell pressed forward. "Can you find out?"

Jake jumped in. "Look, Lance just blew a hole in Truman Medical Center the size of Texas with the President of the United States inside."

Lundgren stammered. "I…I…that's terrible. I have a roster in my phone here somewhere." Lundgren pulled out his cell and searched, his hands trembling. "Here it is. Mallory. Lance Mallory."

"You know where he is now?" Snell asked.

"No. I think he left some time ago. I'd have to call the company to be sure."

"I want his full name, address, phone number and any other information you have on him."

"We'll contact PHG."

"Do it." Snell directed Bryce to go with the man.

Jake glanced to the empty front desk, the last place he saw Lance when he talked to Mara. "Hey, Mr. Lundgren?"

Lundgren stopped and waited as Jake approached.

"Where's Hunter Brenner and the receptionist?" Jake asked.

"Hunter left an hour ago," Lundgren said. "We were discussing a project site in my office when he received a call and left. I'm not sure where Mara is. She should be here manning the phones. I'll page her."

"What's Mara's last name?"

"Wilder."

"Hunter friendly with this Lance guy?" Bear asked.

"I have no idea. But, I get the sense Lance has a bit of a crush on Mara. He spends quite a bit of time at her desk."

Jake, Bear and Snell exchanged wary looks.

"Give me everything you have on Brenner and Wilder," Snell said to Lundgren. When he left with Agent Bryce, she turned to Jake and Bear. "Let's get the team together at my office. This shit just got really interesting."

CHAPTER FORTY FIVE

"You failed," Mister X said.

Hunter dropped to the chair in the kitchen as he pressed the burner phone to his ear. "I know. I apologize."

"Failure isn't an option. So don't be sorry, finish the fucking job."

"How?" Hunter asked. "Air Force One is long gone."

"But the President isn't on it. The buffoon won't be intimidated and run away. Especially not during election season. It would be bad optics. He's still going to the rally."

Hunter sat upright. "So, we can still finish this?"

"You'd better finish it, Hunter. Or I'll finish you."

The line went dead. Hunter darted through the house to the bedroom, Mara on his heels. "You release the statement to the press?"

She nodded. "Blamed it on the Freedom Society, like you said. Why does it matter? With the President gone, we're—"

"He's not gone. The original Union Station plan is still in play. Grab your bag, Mara. We're gonna lay low for a while after tonight."

"What's going on, baby? Why are we running?"

Hunter spun to her, teeth bared, his face flushed from her incessant questions. "Why the hell do you think? We just tried to take out the goddamn President of the United States and failed. FBI has Watterson and Ackerman in custody and paid us an office visit. We're going to finish the job and kill these bastards, but—"

She laid a hand on his arm. "But they can't tie us to anything."

Hunter jerked his arm away and yanked his duffel bag from under the bed. "You want to take the chance? So, get your bag and put it in the truck. We'll finish this job and we're going dark until we figure out who knows what."

"Why can't we stay here? They don't know about this place."

"Maybe, maybe not. Better safe than sorry for now. Don't worry, we'll get back to Anarchy Road soon enough."

"What about Lance?"

Hunter growled. "Enough questions, Mara. We have shit to do. Let me worry about Lance. He should be here any minute. Let's go."

Hunter yanked open the zipper to the long duffel bag. He pawed through it, double checking the clothes, toiletries, guns and ammo. Satisfied everything was there, he stopped, closed his eyes and counted to twenty wondering if he needed another application of the cigarette lighter to his scarred flesh. It had been a while. Panic wouldn't get him anywhere. Panicked people made stupid mistakes. Watterson and Ackerman could tie him to 2A, but they didn't know anything about the bombings. That'd been between him, Humphreys and a few other dead 2A members. He should be good, but the FBI showing up at Reliance shook his confidence.

You actually think you're gonna get away with this? Guilt is clouding your vision, man. You're running the wrong way down a one-way street, Eddie said. He propped on the bed watching Hunter, a flap of raw skin from his head drooping over one eye.

"Shut up," Hunter muttered. "Let me think a minute."

They're going to drag you down. You know that, right? And just like me, you know there's gonna be a time where you gotta make a choice.

Hunter said nothing as he slung the duffel bag over his shoulder and stomped out to the truck.

Eddie waited, resting against the garage door. He fixed the hanging flap of skin into his half-caved-in skull, his left eye bulging grotesquely. There's too many loose ends out there, Hunter. And we all know how you like to deal with loose ends.

Hunter threw his duffel bag in the bed of the truck. "We don't know anything, yet. Shut the fuck up, Eddie."

Eddie laughed. Whatever you wanna tell yourself, pal. Watterson, Ackerman, Mara, Lance. All kinds of land mines you gotta dodge.

"I'll dodge 'em."

Remember Bob Sedgewick walking down the road outside Fallujah? He thought he could dodge the mines too and look where it got him. There wasn't enough of him left to fill a cigar box. It's all about choices. You can't dodge what you can't see, and buddy, you ain't seein' nothin' right now.

Hunter pulled the cover over the back of the truck and stole a peek to the garage door. Eddie was gone.

Thank Christ for that. But his words bounced around Hunter's head. It's all about choices.

What would've happened if Hunter hadn't made the choice to kiss Mara at the party when he and Eddie were back on a short leave? Where would they be right now if he hadn't tasted forbidden fruit? He could still feel her soft, moist lips, her taut body pressed against his, knowing she was Eddie's girl but his lust casting that knowledge aside. Hunter had been ready to let it go as a drunken indiscretion, but Mara loved living on the edge and over the coming months had dangled a possible future in secret letters in front of him. Choices.

Goddamn it. Hunter smacked the past away to focus on the task at hand. They were so close. The country was ready to fall. Everyone was divided into their tribal tents, afraid to stick their heads out for fear of getting them lopped off by the opposition. Those who weren't afraid ran around setting the tribal tents on fire and slaughtering the inhabitants as they fled. The few standing in the middle screaming for peace and sanity were caught in the crossfire.

Hunter knew the sad truth—there was no America anymore. The ideals of the founding fathers that managed to raise the United States into arguably the greatest country in the history of the world were in tattered ruins at the feet of the representative republic. Abraham Lincoln's famous quote "a house divided against itself cannot stand" was as true now as it ever was. If the country was going to return to greatness, it had to burn down to the steel frame on which it was built. There could be no rise of the phoenix without a fire. And Hunter knew he held the match.

But will it burn? Eddie whispered.

Lance's headlights spilled across the truck as he pulled into the drive. He slipped from the car and approached.

Lance shoved his hands in the pockets of his jeans, unable to meet Hunter's eyes. "We missed. I'm sorry, man."

Hunter set a hand on Lance's shoulder. "Not your fault. Bad intel. They moved the guy to the other side of the hospital. I just found out on the way here."

"What now?"

"The President didn't bail. He's going to be at the rally as planned, so we're going through with the op. I'll check the ceiling to verify the charges, you and Mara on the ground inside. We blow it and get out of town while the dust settles."

Lance removed his glasses and rubbed his forehead. "What about Mister X. If he—"

"Fuck, Mister X. Fuck him, Lance. His goal and ours was never the same. He's a means to an end. He thinks he's going to use us and throw us away once he gets what he wants, but we're the ones using him. When we're done, there won't be anything left to rule over. Get your gear, grab Mara and get to Union Station. I'll finish up here and meet you down there for the grand finale."

Lance locked eyes with him, the doubt flickering like a candle flame. Hunter thought of Mara's picture under Lance's mattress. Eddie's voice echoed in his head, laughing. *They're going to drag you down.*

"I got a bad feeling about this, man," Lance said. "Maybe we should—"

"Maybe you should quit thinking so much and do your goddamn job." Hunter paused at the hurt in Lance's eyes. He softened his voice and patted

Lance on the back. "I need you, bud. End game time. Let's go."

Lance trudged toward the house, Hunter trailing behind him. Loose ends. Land mines. Eddie's laugh made Hunter want to scream.

NOW

CHAPTER FORTY SIX

Dr. Tate scribbled notes on her pad. Judging from the way the pen moved, Jake surmised she wasn't writing, but doodling because she couldn't think of what else to say. He'd hit her right between the eyes with the justice analogy of taking a bat to the knees of the guy crippling her theoretical kid.

"What do you think, Dr. Tate?" Jake asked. "Am I a danger to society?"

Her pen halted, but she didn't look up. "I haven't fully decided yet."

"So, you've partially decided. Some part yes and some part no. The question is how large is the gap?"

She thought about the question for a moment. "More no than yes, but that no—"

"Is weighing on your mind."

Her eyes met Jake's. "Yes, it is. I don't know you, Jake. I can only judge from what I see in front of me, what you've done in the past that I know about, and what others have told me."

An empty, hollow sensation took residence in the pit of his stomach. He'd convinced her to cut some of the cords tethering him to the couch, but at least a few remained. In many ways, Dr. Tate reminded him of Maggie. The same steely resolve and uncanny ability to see through his bullshit, but, unfortunately, the same reservation of the path he walked. For the most part, Maggie worked her way past it, but now he had to convince the good doctor.

"Back in high school, there was this guy named Ray," Jake said. "Lowlife scumbag, but I suppose back then so was I. We were poor white trash and my drunken father didn't do anything to dissuade people from thinking that. But Ray didn't bother me, and I didn't bother him. In reality, our crappy home lives weren't that different. Anyway, Ray used to harass my wife Maggie, who was my girlfriend at the time. Later on, Ray stopped coming to school. He broke both of his legs. Well, I broke both of his legs. And his arms."

Dr. Tate's brow furrowed. "Because he harassed your girlfriend? I fail to see how that's helping assuage my doubts."

"No. I broke them because I caught him molesting a grade school kid named Scotty Turlbuckle in the woods near my house. Ray had Scotty pressed up against a tree with one hand down the kid's pants while he jerked himself off with the other one."

"Jesus."

Jake pressed his lips into a line, the image playing an unwelcome movie on the carpet of Dr. Tate's office. "My father showed me, repeatedly and with great passion, how the powerful can physically damage and scar the weak with fists, belts and bottles. But I'd never considered the psychological scars the powerful can leave behind. Scotty saw me coming, tears running down his face, a mix of pleading for help and…and this utter shame at what Ray was doing to him, something he was completely powerless to stop. The kid couldn't do a thing, but I could."

"And you did. Was that justice, Jake?"

He jerked his eyes to hers, heat flushing his neck. He was sick of this justice discussion. "Your fuckin' right it was justice. Ray's lucky I didn't kill him. I don't have a single regret to this day over the beating I gave him. His bones would heal, but Scotty will be haunted every day for the rest of his life. It's probably why Scotty's a meth addict living in a beat-down trailer." Jake paused and took a calming breath. "I may have lost my way for a long stretch, and I did things I'm ashamed of, things that haunted me, things that still wake me up in the middle of the night. But not that. I don't regret doing that. Those…those things, those past deeds, remind me of who I don't want to be and who I no longer am. I might crack some skulls and do things skirting your shadowed line between right and wrong, but I do it because it's right. I do it for those who can't do it themselves. I did it to that fuck-stick in the courtroom because who else would stand up for the people he killed? Who else would stand up for their wives, their husbands, their children? Because it was pretty obvious the goddamn justice system wasn't going to."

Dr. Tate tapped her pen on her pad. It had the same effect on Jake's psyche as a dripping faucet in the middle of the night. "That was an impassioned speech."

"I'm an impassioned guy."

"But, what if you—"

Jake pressed to his feet the second the "but" escaped her lips. "With all due respect, Dr. Tate, you could 'what if' shit all day long. And don't take this personally because I like you, I really do. You've forced me to think about things from a different perspective and I appreciate it. That said, I've explained how I operate, and I've given you numerous examples of how I've learned from my past mistakes. As to my danger to society, I would never, ever knowingly put innocent lives at risk no matter what the goal is. There is no end justifying the means if it results in hurting or killing an innocent individual. You go ahead and write what you have to write to the judge, but this therapy session is over. Have a nice rest of your day."

With Dr. Tate's jaw hanging in surprise, Jake turned and left the office. He hoped he hadn't just screwed himself.

THEN

CHAPTER FORTY SEVEN

Fifteen minutes after they left the hospital, Jake, Bear and Snell gathered in a conference room at the FBI headquarters on the northwest side of downtown. Mounds of paper, computers and empty coffee cups littered a laminate table seating ten, half the chairs occupied by bleary-eyed agents. Maps and pictures lined a bulletin board along the north wall.

Snell darted from person to person, checking in on their status with various tasks after telling Jake and Bear to hang in the corner. They spent the time studying the bulletin board. Jake focused in on the section with the 2A Militia. They had the known member names and pictures posted, a giant red X crossing out those who were dead. They put Wallace Humphrey at the top of the hierarchy, and there was no mention of Hunter Brenner yet. He scanned the rest of the board. There was a section for Reliance Construction, but just Post-It notes with Hunter Brenner, Lance Mallory and Mara Wilder's names. Given how fast things proceeded, it wasn't surprising.

"What are they doing here?" boomed a voice from the door.

Jake and Bear turned. Special Agent Murphy pressed his liver-spotted hands against the sides of the door frame, his balding head turning pink.

Snell crossed the room with a purpose. If she was a dog, her back hair would have been standing straight up. "Jake saw the drone hit the hospital. He identified the guy flying the drone. They tracked down Watterson, which led us to the lead on Hunter Brenner. We need them and it's my call they be here. Sir."

Murphy's nostrils flared and handed her a thin manila folder. "Whatever they do is on your head, Snell. Here's the files on Hunter Brenner and Lance Mallory. What we could find in this short amount of time. Keep me posted."

Murphy offered one last dirty look at Jake before disappearing out the door. Snell followed him.

Bear whistled. "Jesus. Who pissed in his Cheerios?"

"I did," Jake said. "He still blames me for McKernan getting killed at the Wolf's house over the whole Blackbird ordeal. Probably blames me for Foster, too."

"Well, those weren't your fault," Bear said. "And he seems like an asshole."

"He is," Snell said, returning to the room. "But he means well. Let's see what we have."

She sat on the edge of the table and ran her finger down a page while Jake and Bear took seats in between agents typing on laptops and scouring paper.

"Hunter Brenner, born in Kansas City, forty-five years old, Missouri driver's license listing a condo off Grand. I sent a team over there already. CEO of Reliance Construction. Studied business at Oklahoma

State where he went on a wrestling scholarship. Served two tours in Iraq with the Marines. Record shows they barred him from re-enlisting at the end of his second tour because he suffered from a borderline antisocial personality."

"What the hell does that mean?" Bear asked.

A woman across the table with plump cheeks and brown mousy hair piped in. "It's a mental health disorder characterized by a disregard for other people. They tend to lie, act impulsive and have little regard for their own safety or the safety of others." The woman blushed when everyone stopped and stared. "I was a psychology major."

Bear nudged Jake. "Acts impulsively, little regard for his own safety? Sounds just like you."

Jake ignored the jab. "What about his tie with the 2A Militia?"

Snell flipped through the pages and shook her head. "Nothing."

"Was Watterson lying to us?"

"Watterson seemed to be telling the truth, about that at least," Bear said. "Maybe Brenner keeps a low profile about it."

"Or maybe he's not involved at all," Snell offered.

"Don't tell me you didn't get a weird vibe off that guy, Snell."

"Trying to look down my blouse and checking out my ass isn't a federal crime."

"What about Lance Mallory?" Jake asked.

Snell switched out folders. "Born in Shawnee, Kansas. Shawnee Mission Northwest High School. Went to military right after graduation, served two tours. Honorable discharge. Get this, he was an ammunitions technician."

"Makes sense if he's dealing with C4. What else?"

"Missouri driver's license, Lee's Summit address. Sent a team over there as well. Has worked at PHG for ten years and has an ex-wife named Tiffany who lives in Oklahoma."

"2A Militia tie?"

She tossed the folder on the table. "Nothing in the file. But 2A was such a small potatoes group that our notes on them are pretty thin."

Jake growled. "Goddamn it."

"Got something," Agent Bryce yelled across the room. Snell darted over to his computer and hovered over his shoulder.

Jake grabbed Brenner's file and scanned the contents. Something about the guy struck him wrong. When he reached the military portion of the file, he found what he was looking for. Snatching the Mallory file, he opened them side by side. "There it is."

"What?" Bear asked, rubbing his palms over his eyes and suppressing a yawn.

Jake's chin rose and the corners of his mouth curled up. "Brenner and Mallory served in the same unit in Iraq."

Bear sat up. "No shit?"

"We have to figure out if there are any ties to 2A and these two. Too bad Watterson's in a million pieces or we could ask him."

Snell returned waving a piece of paper. "Bingo. Got a match to the handprint on the dead lawyer's window. Mara Wilder. She got arrested in college for setting some guy's car on fire. Bryce also found footage of Lance Mallory in the crowd down the street from the T-Mobile center before the bombing."

Jake told her about Brenner and Mallory being in

the same unit in the war. "They're working together. If Mallory was on the street, Brenner had to be in the lawyer's office with Mara Wilder. It's all coming together. Too bad we can't spring this on Watterson and see what else he knows."

"We still have Ackerman and Lenny Moritz," Snell said. "One of my guys was supposed to check on it, but I haven't heard back from him," Snell said, pulling out her phone and dialing.

"Good thinking about Lenny," Bear said. "I forgot about him. If he sold the C4 to 2A and can put Mallory and Brenner there, we're set."

"Except we don't know where either of them is," Jake said.

"Ackerman won't say anything without his lawyer," Snell said, jabbing the disconnect button on her phone. "My guy thinks Ackerman recognized the pictures, but he clammed up."

They threw some ideas around, but nothing stuck. The 2A Militia members were all dead except for one they couldn't find and Ackerman who wasn't talking. Brenner, Mallory and Mara were in the wind. There was one person left to talk to.

"Where's Lenny Moritz?" Jake asked.

"Down the hall trying to work a deal."

"Let me have a shot at him."

Snell cocked her head as if considering it, then shook it. "Forget it. Murphy said if I let you anywhere near Lenny, he'd have my badge."

Snell's cell rang. She answered it and listened for a minute, her face falling. "Brenner's place is empty, and the Super said he moved out eight months ago. Mallory's address is an abandoned lot. Damn. We have next to nothing now. We know who they are but have no way to find them."

"They've gotta suspect we're onto them and aren't going to be sitting at home with their legs kicked up." Jake passed her the files on Brenner and Mallory. "Sweeten Lenny's deal if he can tie both Brenner and Mallory to 2A. Bonus points if he can tell us how to find them. Might have an address or a phone number we can trace."

She slid off the table. "I'll see what I can do."

Jake's cell vibrated. He checked the number. Cat. About time. He hoped Cat had something, because if he didn't, they were at a dead end.

CHAPTER FORTY EIGHT

"Tell me you have something," Jake said to Cat.

"You sound desperate. Maybe I should double my fee?" Cat said.

"Maybe I should get you charged with obstructing a federal investigation." Jake laid out the elevator speech of Brenner and Mallory along with Watterson's tenuous tie to the bombing at the T-Mobile Arena and Truman. "So, tell me what you, have or I'll sic the FBI on your fat ass."

Cat grumbled. "Or you could just say 'please.'"

"Cat, I swear to—"

"Jesus, calm down. I emailed you my report. Watterson's calls went to a pizza delivery place, a Chinese restaurant and a Mexican joint near his listed address. Apparently, he's not a big fan of cooking for himself. There's two more calls on his CDR from the residence of a Drake Ackerman, which is the same address he listed on his driver's license and another call to the switchboard number at a Reliance Construction. Those are all in the last three days."

"When was the call to Reliance?"

"Two days ago at noon."

Unhelpful. "Which one is closest to 11 AM this morning?

"The call from Drake Ackerman's residence at 10:58 AM."

Jake jotted down the information on the back of Mallory's folder while Bear hovered over his shoulder. "What numbers did Ackerman call or receive around the same time?"

"He got a call at 10:55 AM from an unknown number. Could be a burner phone. I'm still trying to get the CDR on that phone pulled. The good news is I was able to triangulate the call location."

Someone called Ackerman, who immediately called Watterson, who ran like a bat out of hell. Jake had two suspicions who it might be that placed the call. "A few extra bills for you if you tell me where and a bigger one if you can tell me who."

"How big?"

"Big enough. Don't get greedy. Give it to me."

There was a snap hiss of a pop can opening in the background and Cat slurped. "Call was placed from an area northwest of the airport. Very rural. Three residences within ten square miles. But, there's a problem. One is owned by a seventy-year-old farmer, another by a retired minister and his wife and the third hasn't been occupied for twenty years."

"So what's the problem?"

"The call came from the unoccupied residence. Google Earth shows a pretty large house, a barn and another building a hundred yards away by an access road. The former owner was an Edward Puglisi, but he died a year after inheriting it from his parents."

"Why'd you dig this deep?"

"I was curious. I've been looking for property out of the city and this one seemed interesting. Thought maybe I could snag it for cheap if it was in default. Unfortunately, it's not."

Cat never failed to impress Jake. He was expensive, but worth it, even if he was annoying. "If the owner died and nobody is living there, who's paying for it?"

"A charity called Remembrance. They help military vets."

Jake's ears perked up. "Was this Edward guy a military vet?"

"Killed in action in Ramadi according to his obituary."

Jake's heartrate picked up. "Did it say what unit he served in?"

Cat told him and a surge of adrenaline hit Jake's system. It was the same unit Hunter Brenner and Lance Mallory served in.

"One last thing, Cat. This Remembrance charity, they have a website?"

"That's how I figured out they helped military vets."

Jake gripped his phone tight. "They list like a Board of Directors?"

"Yeah."

"Is the name Lance Mallory on the list?"

Cat paused a beat. "Nope."

"Hunter Brenner?"

Cat clicked his tongue. "Sure is. He's the Finance Chairman."

Jake jumped to his feet. They had their connection.

CHAPTER FORTY NINE

Special Agent Murphy walked in and paused at the flurry of activity at the bulletin board and demanded to know what was going on. Jake thought the prick could have asked like a normal human being, but Murphy had a severe case of short-man syndrome.

Snell led the conversation. "I have a team prepping for a raid on an abandoned house owned by a dead guy both Hunter Brenner and Lance Mallory served with in Iraq that's paid for by the charity where Hunter Brenner is the Finance Chairman."

Murphy's eyes slid around the room. "So?"

Jesus, this guy was a tool. Jake jumped in. "Brenner's address is eight months old and Mallory's address is an abandoned lot. I...we think they're camped out at this abandoned house."

"And you're sure these guys are tied together with the bombings? All we know is this Mallory is the one who controlled the drone."

Snell said, "They both served together in Iraq. Mallory was an ammunitions tech who would be familiar with explosives. Watterson is a 2A member who confirmed Hunter Brenner was in the group. Lenny Moritz sold the C4 to 2A."

"And we have phone records linking Watterson and Ackerman to a burner phone from that house," Jake said.

Snell winced and he couldn't figure out why. Then it hit him.

"And how did you get these phone records?" Murphy asked, drawing each word out like a chastising parent to a toddler.

Snell lied, God bless her. "We pulled them and triangulated them to the house. We have enough for a warrant."

Murphy's forehead wrinkled. "I don't think so. Watterson's dead and you can't connect the dots between Lance Mallory, the C4 and the property," Murphy said. "Connecting a dead militia member to a burner phone isn't going to get you paper to go on the site lawfully."

"Maybe Lenny Moritz can connect the dots," Jake said.

Murphy's face reddened. "Lenny Moritz isn't talking until he gets a sweetheart of a deal, which he isn't going to get. He was manufacturing and distributing AR-15s and C4. We have him dead to rights. The only thing he can do is wait for us to drop the hammer."

"And in the meantime, the guys who used the C4 are going to slip away," Jake pleaded. "Give me a shot at talking to Lenny."

"Forget it, Caldwell. You're lucky I haven't booted you from the building."

"Have you talked to him since the bombing at the hospital?"

"We haven't had a chance," Murphy said. His head

looked like a tomato. "Stay out of this."

Jake's nails dug into his palms, and he was surprised he didn't fracture any teeth given how hard he clenched his jaw. Where was this asshole's sense of urgency? "Agent Murphy, what if these guys aren't done?"

"What are you talking about?"

"They scored sixty pounds of C4 off Lenny, and they've used a fraction of it best we can tell. Where's the rest? What else are they planning?"

Murphy pushed his bulbous lips out like a duck. "We'll figure it out."

"When, sir?" Snell said. "Jake's right. They're planning something. It might not be tomorrow or next week, but if they know we're onto them, they could accelerate their plan."

"Or abandon it altogether and go underground," Murphy said.

Jake shoved his hands into his pockets to prevent himself from punching the old man. Jake looked to Bear and noticed his best friend was fighting a similar impulse.

"Maybe you're right," Jake said. He knew he had to throw Murphy a bone instead of battling him at every turn. "Maybe it'll be a while before they bomb another place. The warrant information is thin. You're right about that too."

A smug little grin crept up Murphy's face.

Jake continued, "But, what if Brenner and Mallory are at the house right now? What if the plans for the next target are there? If you stop it, you're the hero. If they blow up another bunch of innocent Americans and you could have stopped it, it'll be your head on a platter and a permanent blemish on the FBI. Let me talk to Lenny. If I can get him to link the C4 to Lance Mallory, that'd be enough to secure the search warrant, right? You let me do it before with Jerry Hart from the Blackbird case a while back. I did it then and I can do it now."

Murphy pondered the idea. "Fine. You don't make any deals, you don't touch him, and Snell is in the room with you."

"Thank you, sir."

Murphy stepped in. "I'll be watching. If you screw this up, Caldwell, I'll—"

"Yeah, yeah, nail my ass to the wall. I'd expect nothing less."

Before Murphy could say anything else, Snell pulled Jake toward the door. Jake hoped he could come through. Regardless of what Lenny gave them, Jake knew he was going to that house to find Brenner and Mallory. It'd be nice if he didn't have to battle the feds to do it.

CHAPTER FIFTY

As rough as Lenny looked when Jake last saw him—strapped to a pole in the garage—eighteen hours locked down with FBI agents was ten-fold worse. Lenny's wild gray hair poked out like he'd stuck his finger in a light socket. Isolated in a windowless room, Lenny was handcuffed to a plain, scratched table, twisting as he tried to stretch from his unyielding steel chair. Jake winced at the stank in the room. Lenny needed a shower in the worst way.

Lenny snarled as he tracked Jake, Bear and Snell entering the room. "Well, if it isn't the two lyin' sacks of shit that got me in this mess. You bring your mommy to protect you?" Captivity tamed Lenny's crazy eyes, and his voice lacked the venom it possessed when he was on his home turf.

Bear and Snell propped against the wall while Jake pulled up a chair across the table from Lenny and sat backwards on it. He pulled the can of Coke from his jacket pocket and set it on the table. Murphy had mentioned that Lenny had begged for one for hours and now eyeballed it like a teenager seeing a Playboy for the first time.

"You got yourself in this mess, Lenny," Jake said. "Don't try to blame it on us."

"Oh, I can blame it on you. We had a deal. I tell you what I know, and you said you were gonna let me go. Is that Coke for me?"

Jake placed his forearms on the back of the chair. "Well you were also supposed to sell me some guns and decided to rob me at gunpoint instead. Let's call it even."

"I don't think so. Besides, my lawyer said to not say a thing to any of you. That's why the fuckin' feds won't give me a Coke." Lenny shot his eyes to Snell. "They love to play their stupid games."

Jake studied his face. The man still had fire in his belly, but from the looks of him, he was close to cracking. "I'll pop the tab on the Coke myself for a little quid pro quo."

Lenny squinted. "Quid pro what? Is that some kinda sex act you wanna do on me?"

"It means you give me something and I give you something."

"And what exactly do you want?"

Jake reached over his shoulder, and Bear handed him the files on Brenner and Mallory. Jake held them up but didn't show Lenny the contents. "Some bad guys are doing some bad things with what you sold them, Lenny. You like being cooped up in a windowless room?"

Lenny shifted in his seat. "Not especially, but I been in worse."

"Well, imagine a windowless room with less comfortable accommodations for the rest of your life. These guys can tie you to at least twenty-five dead people and—"

"I didn't kill nobody."

"The C4 you sold the 2A Militia did. The T-Mobile Arena and now a bombing at the Truman Medical Center that's killed at least three so far. They're going to make you an accessory to all of it. But there's an even worse part for you."

Lenny rubbed his face and leaned back in his chair, his cuffed arm dangling on top of the table. "I suppose your gonna tell me at some point?"

"The bomb at Truman was meant for the President."

"President of what?"

"The United States. He was in the hospital. It's gonna earn you some special prison time in the worst hell hole you can imagine."

Lenny sat up, fear sparking in his eyes. "You shittin' me?"

"They're gonna hang you for treason," Jake said. "Unless, you help us find the guys behind this."

Now they had Lenny's attention. The man's eyes danced around like a Mexican jumping bean on a hot skillet. "I want to talk to my lawyer."

"Where is he, by the way?"

Lenny's lip curled. "Beats me. Said he'd be right back and that was hours ago."

"Sounds like a shitty lawyer."

"Funny, I was thinkin' the same thing. I gotta get something out of this. I need a deal. Full immunity."

Now Jake dropped back. "No way you're getting out of this with immunity. You did the crime, now you gotta do some time."

"I didn't think they were going to blow people up," Lenny whined. "Can I have that Coke? I got a caffeine headache blowing my skull apart."

Jake smacked the folders on the table. "What did you think they would do with sixty pounds of C4? Make a truck load of cherry bombs and save them up for a little Fourth of July fireworks extravaganza? You knew what the group could do, and you're going to help us get them."

Lenny's pulse thumped in his neck. "Can I get a sip of that Coke while I think?"

"You're stalling."

"My lawyer said—"

Jake jumped to his feet. "Fuck your lawyer. He can't help you wiggle out of this. You play ball with us and answer a few questions to get us what we want, and it'll grease the skids with the prosecutors. They might even take the death penalty off the table if you help us stop these guys before anyone else gets hurt."

Lenny's eyes danced between Jake, Bear and Snell and the can of Coke. The wheels were turning. Jake would much rather get the information they needed to make the warrant on the abandoned house a certainty rather than roll the dice and hope they scored a friendly judge. He was prepared to go after Brenner and Mallory by himself if it came to that but hoped he didn't have to. He popped the top on the Coke can and nudged it forward on the table, still out of Lenny's reach but close enough for Lenny to hear the carbonated bubbles popping.

After a beat, Lenny sat upright. "I guess they can kill me in prison the same as kill me out in the real world." He looked past Jake to Snell. "You'll put in a good word?"

"I'll do it myself," Snell said. "As long as you're not jerking us around."

Lenny's head dropped a bit. "What do you want to know?"

Jake slid the Coke can the rest of the way to Lenny who guzzled half the can and belched loud enough to shake dust from the ceiling. Jake opened up the first folder and pulled out Lance Mallory's picture. "Who's this guy?"

Lenny studied it for a second and wiped his mouth with the back of his free hand. "Lance. Mallomar, Malloway. Something like that."

"Mallory?" Jake offered.

"That's it. He's the guy who bought the C4 from me."

"I thought you said Wallace Humphrey bought it."

Lenny drained the rest of the can and held up the empty. "Wallace sent Lance and supplied the money. Can I get another one?"

"Keep talking and I'll throw in a candy bar, too. So Lance was a member of the 2A Militia?"

"Oh yeah. He was a quiet one. You could tell he was one of those kinda guys who overthought shit."

"You know where we could find Lance?" Bear asked.

"No clue," Lenny said, letting loose another belch. "Only met the guy a coupla times."

"But you for sure sold him the C4. Sixty pounds of it. When?"

Lenny's eyes swept the ceiling. "Maybe five or six months ago? I went a little crazy with that much cash, I ain't gonna lie. Things got a little hazy for me for a while, if you know what I mean."

Jake pulled out the picture of Hunter Brenner and placed it on the table. "What about this guy?"

Lenny studied the picture, his knuckles blanching white as he crushed the Coke can in his hands. "Don't know him. Never seen him before."

Jake poked his tongue into his cheek as he sat back. Lenny wiped beads of sweat popping on his wrinkled brow. The man was terrified.

"That's Hunter Brenner," Jake said. "And judging by your reaction, you do know him and have seen him before."

"Your words, they ain't mine," Lenny said, turning the picture face-down on the table. "I'm not sayin' anything about him."

"Because you're afraid he'll find out."

Lenny's voice quieted. "You'd be afraid, too, if you knew him. I ain't saying anything else."

Jake held his hand back, and Bear slapped another can of Coke into his palm. Jake popped the top and slid it to Lenny.

"Another Coke isn't going to get me to talk about him," Lenny said.

"I won't make you say anything," Jake said, lowering his voice to match Lenny's. "Just nod if you want to."

"Is Hunter Brenner part of 2A?"

Lenny's eyes locked on the table and nodded.

"Is he the leader of 2A?"

Lenny nodded again.

"Was Wallace Humphrey acting on orders from Hunter?"

Another nod.

"You know where I can find him?"

Lenny scratched at the table with a dirty fingernail. "No. But you'd be signing your own death warrant if you did."

CHAPTER FIFTY ONE

"Nice work, Jake," Snell said as they walked down the hall, leaving Lenny to his second Coke and probably wondering if he should have waited for his lawyer after all.

"You have enough for the warrant?" Bear asked.

"I think so. Would've been nice for Lenny to tie Hunter Brenner more directly to everything, but the confirmation of Lance Mallory as the purchaser of the C4 and his immediate ties to Hunter should be enough for the judge."

Bear's stomach gurgled loud enough for Jake and Snell to hear. "How long until you get the warrant?"

"Depends on when Judge Patrick teed off today." She pointed to Bear's stomach. "You have time to go get something to eat."

"Call us when you find out anything. And tell Murphy he's welcome."

Snell huffed. "Hell will freeze over before that man thanks you. I'll have to do."

The sun began its decent to the West as Bear listed off places they could grab a bite. Judging from the potential contenders, he was in the mood for Mexican. They climbed into Bear's truck as he finished off the last of the nominees. Jake had other ideas.

"Maybe we should go scope out the abandoned house while we wait," Jake offered.

Bear cocked his head. "Please tell me you're kidding."

"What? We check it out, get the lay of the land, see if anybody's home. From a distance. Besides, Snell's team is going to want the info anyway."

"Which they can find out for themselves."

"I'm saving us time."

"What if I say 'no way'?" Bear asked.

Jake shrugged. "I guess you'll have to buy your own Taco Bell."

"You think my discerning palette is going to accept Taco fucking Bell?"

"I think your discerning palette isn't that discerning. You love Taco Bell. If they had one in Warsaw, you'd weigh another hundred pounds."

Bear cranked the ignition. "You're probably right, but why don't we do the smart thing for once and let the process work itself out. Let Snell get the warrant, we get a bunch of agents to go out there. We scoped out a house less than twenty-four hours ago, and it turned into the second coming of the Branch Davidian compound in Waco."

Jake pointed north. "It'll be fine because we're just staking it out in case the warrant comes in slow. There's a Taco Bell in North Kansas City. It's on the way. I'll buy while you drive."

"You ever try to eat a taco while driving?" Bear asked, gunning the truck down the road. "Lettuce and hot sauce gets everywhere."

"Like it'll make a difference to this truck. I'll drive while you eat. Just go."

Thirty minutes later, Jake pulled onto a narrow, shoulderless blacktop road northwest of the Kansas City airport. The sun melded to the skyline in a fiery collage of orange and yellow.

"We're just doing recon, right?" Bear asked.

"Just recon," Jake replied, rolling the truck up and down a few stomach-dropping hills. "Probably nobody there anyway. We'll chill and wait for Snell's call. Unless we see something wonky."

Bear crumpled the wrapper of his last taco and tossed it to the floorboard. "What the hell does wonky mean, exactly?"

"I'll know it when I see it."

"You worry me, Jake."

"Relax. It'd have to be really wonky for me to jump in."

"Oh, that makes me feel so much better. Just remember, I am a sheriff and responsible for your actions to your wife. Don't put my ass in a wringer."

Jake followed the Google map Cat provided. On either side of the road, barbed wire fencing tracked them, the base of the fence posts lost in long grass and dying daylight. Save for the occasional shredded rubber tire and empty beer cases in the ditches, there wasn't much out here. Jake dropped the window, the scent of road tar mixed with the country air was a welcome diversion to the gastrointestinal stew Bear started to dish out.

"Ooof," Bear grunted, dropping his own window down. "Those tacos are doing some damage."

Jake skimmed the map on his phone and checked their location. "Tell me about it. My eyes are starting to water."

"Hope it wasn't bad meat."

Jake cranked the wheel and turned north on a gravel road. "I don't think it was the meat in the tacos. I think it was the fact you ate seven of them."

"Seven's my lucky number."

"Unless I'm confined in the cab of a truck with you. There's the house."

Jake pointed to the windshield at a dark shape on the horizon, a good half-mile northwest of their position sitting on a hill. In between the road and the house, a stretch of grass descended and fed into a pond at the base of the hill. On the other side of the water, a grove of trees climbed their way up the hill toward the house. Jake passed a long, winding driveway that disappeared over the hill marked with a hand-painted sign.

"Holy shit," Jake whispered.

Bear perked up. "What?"

Jake craned his head to try to catch a glimpse of the house. No luck. He drove another half mile down the road until he found a cutout where he could turn the truck around.

Jake stopped. "You notice the sign at the mouth of the driveway? Looked homemade."

"Anarchy Road," Bear said. "Why does that sound familiar?"

"Because it's what Wallace Humphrey said with his dying breath. This has got to be the place. Didn't see any lights on, but we had a bad angle. Switch me places."

Jake dropped to the road, the gravel biting into the soles of his boots as he walked around the front of the truck. In the distance, the sound of a chainsaw broke the stillness before a commercial jet roared overhead, dropping toward the ground as it approached the airport.

Bear went around the back of the truck and settled in the driver's seat. "Tell me why we're switching?"

Jake grabbed the taco wrappers off the floorboard and shoved them in a bag. "Because you're going to drop me off near the pond, and I'm going to check out the house. Can't see anything from down here."

Bear put the truck in drive. "You liar. You said only if we see something wonky."

"That sign is wonky."

"But not jump in the shit kinda wonky. We should wait for Snell and the warrant."

"What if they don't get the warrant? What if Brenner and Mallory are up there right now? It'd be nice to know if they're at least in the house. If it's abandoned with no signs of life, it'll save us a lot of pre-planning headaches. Don't worry, I'll stay back."

Bear rubbed the back of his neck as he rolled forward. "Yeah, pull my dick and it plays Jingle Bells. You have as much chance of staying back as I do of skipping bacon at a buffet. Remember, that Agent Murphy prick will have your head on a platter if you screw up this case for them. Mine too."

"That's why you're going to stay in the truck, travel down the road a ways and park until we hear from Snell. Once I check out the exterior of the house, I'll pull back and you can pick me up."

Bear leveled a stare. "I'm going to go on the record and tell you this is a stupid fucking move. There's a warrant coming. Wait."

"And I'm not going to do anything to screw the warrant up. I just want to see if there's any signs of life. We'll need to know that before we storm the gates anyway. I'll stay out of sight."

Bear sighed as he dialed Jake's cell. "Fine. Not like I'm gonna talk your dumb ass out of this anyway. Leave your cell on. Seriously though, do not go in the house."

Jake fished in Bear's glove compartment and grabbed a pocket LED flashlight. He opened the door as Bear slowed near the pond. "Trust me. I won't do anything stupid."

Jake maneuvered down the slope toward the water as Bear's taillights disappeared over the hill. The ground was uneven with plenty of rocks hidden under the grass. Jake navigated best he could, but almost rolled his ankle twice.

The pond stretched thirty yards across and another twenty deep, reeds and long grass standing out of the water. Jake skirted the northern edge of the water toward the tree line, his feet sinking a bit in the soft bank while crickets chirped at his arrival. A frog resting on a waterlogged stick leapt into the still water as Jake passed.

He worked his way through the dense trees and brush, digging the toes of his boots into the musty undergrowth as he climbed. Squirrels rustled leaves as they darted away, the overhead limbs wiping away what was left of the daylight. It was slow going but Jake made it to the far edge of the grove, the house looming above him.

It was a long ranch with newer siding slapped on the side of it. A wide, covered porch stretched along the front, broken by a set of stairs leading to a double front door. Piles of lumber and debris rested at the base of the porch on one end of the house and a light burned in a window on the other. One thing was for sure. The place wasn't abandoned.

Jake ducked behind a tree as an engine sounded. Moments later, a pair of headlights appeared from the left side of the house. They swept across his position as they turned to follow the driveway and disappeared, heading toward the road he and Bear traveled minutes before.

Jake spoke into his cell, keeping his voice low. "Car coming your way. Couldn't see who was in it. Any word from Snell?"

"Nothing yet. What do you want to do?"

Jake thought for a beat. What if Brenner, Mallory or Mara Wilder was in the car? Snell said she heard something big was brewing. What if they were on their way to do it?

"Follow the car," Jake said.

"What about you?"

"I can't make it back to you in time. We don't want to lose Brenner or Mallory, if that's even them. Call Snell and tell her what's up. Maybe they can get another unit tailing the car, and you can circle back here."

"She's going to chew your ass until there's nothing left."

Jake pressed his shoulder into the bark of a tree. Bear was right. If Snell didn't get him, Special Agent Murphy would. "Not much I can do now."

"I want to watch when it happens," Bear said. "There's the car. I can't tell who's in it either. I'll call her while I follow. I suppose you're just going to hang out, wait and do nothing?"

Jake eyed the house. If this was Brenner and Mallory's hideout, the answers to what they'd done or what they planned could be in there. If there was nobody left inside, Jake could scope it and figure out if they were on a wild goose chase, wasting their time when they should be focused on something else.

"That's pretty much what I plan to do," Jake said.

"Pretty much? There's a lot of gray in pretty much. Be careful."

"You too." Jake disconnected, checked the Sig Sauer on his waist. He wasn't going to blow the warrant by going in the house, but he could certainly scout the perimeter. He crept from the trees, heading toward the house.

CHAPTER FIFTY TWO

Jake double checked his cell phone was on silent and skirted along the tree line, moving toward the left side of the ranch away from the light burning on the right. He scanned the grounds and listened for any signs of life before he sprinted up the hill and across the gravel drive circling the house. Pressing his back against the siding of the house, Jake heard nothing but crickets and distant sounds of air traffic from KCI. A charred wood scent wafted from a nearby fire pit.

A dilapidated barn slumped fifty yards back to the west. In the day's dying light, it was a mess of rotted boards marred by the occasional streak of faded red paint. A rusted tractor surrounded by weeds slumped beside the barn. It didn't appear Brenner found the time to remodel that part of the property. Jake thought he'd be better off bulldozing the thing to the ground. Jake jumped as a grey tabby cat rubbed against his leg, his startled movement causing the cat to shoot toward the barn.

Jake crept along the west side of the ranch, splitting glances between the darkening ground and the house. A breeze kicked up from the north, bringing with it the stench of manure. "The smell of money" as one of his father's friends used to say. He reached the corner of the house and peered around to the back of the ranch. Next to a large, white propane tank, a squat shed sat on the far side of the gravel drive, its doors opened to reveal the shadow of a mower and yard tools hanging from hooks. A handful of trees towered over the backyard, the spring leaves rustling in the breeze.

With darkness rapidly falling, Jake continued moving along the back of the house, his heart thumping and lizard brain on full alert. He envisioned Brenner stepping around the other side of the house or out the back door ahead of him and slid his Sig Sauer from his waist—just in case. At the far end of the house, yellow light spilled across the gravel drive. Either somebody was still home, or they forgot to turn off the lights when they left which was plausible given his personal experience with Maggie and Halle.

He walked past three crumbled concrete steps that led to a darkened back door, splitting the wood siding on the back of the house, the white paint chipping and curling with age. At the lighted window, he peeked through the glass.

The window sat above a sink in a tiny kitchen with garish, country wallpaper of chickens and cows running in vertical lines. An old refrigerator and stove with pots and pans hanging above it sat on the far wall, split by a countertop covered with storage canisters and a half-filled coffee pot. Jake ducked under the window and checked the kitchen from the other side. An old wooden table surrounded by four chairs with a vase holding dead flowers in the middle.

Seeing nothing else, Jake continued his perimeter check of the house, past a darkened garage window. He turned the corner, passed the closed garage doors and curled around the corner of the house. A weathered door was set atop a warped set of wooden stairs. Jake climbed the creaking steps, peering through the door's inset window and down a long hallway disappearing in darkness beyond the light from the kitchen. Glancing back toward the yard, he realized he hadn't seen a car, which fed his suspicions nobody was home. Still, the absence of a car didn't mean someone wasn't lurking inside and these people weren't the kind to be taken lightly. It was also possible this wasn't Brenner and Mallory at all, though the evidence and his gut pointed to the contrary.

His cell vibrated. Snell. Jake dropped away from the house and answered. "Yeah?"

Snell's anger bit through the receiver. "Our warrant on the house was denied."

"Are you shitting me? What'd the judge say?"

"Insufficient evidence."

Jake's grip threatened to crush the phone. "What did you say to the judge?"

"I wasn't there. Murphy met with him. We're fucked unless we get something from the car you guys are tailing. Our units catch up to you yet?"

Shit. Bear must've left out the fact Jake wasn't with him. "Not yet."

"Keep me posted. I gotta go figure out if there's another way we can get into that house."

Jake pocketed the phone and crept back toward his previous spot at the door. The smart thing to do was to drop back down the steps, creep back into the woods and wait for either Bear or Snell. But, the image of Halle lying in the hospital bed with a tube sticking out of her head fueled his desire to check out the inside. Since Snell failed to snag the warrant, what he found inside could be invaluable to stopping Brenner, Mallory, and Wilder with whatever they planned. If he did nothing and later found out he could have prevented people from getting killed, the guilt would suffocate him.

His brain screamed at his hand to stop as it wrapped around the door handle and slowly turned the knob. The latch released and the door opened, the rusty hinges squealing for a second before Jake stopped applying pressure. He kept his eyes on the hallway, heart thumping in his chest, scents of onions and garlic wafting through the crack. He knew he should wait for backup, but found himself pushing the door open wider, slow enough to avoid the potential sound of a squeaky hinge symphony, but still too loud for comfort. When the door was wide enough, he slipped his body inside.

What would he do if he found Brenner here? Subdue him and wait for the cops? He could come up with some plausible reason why he went in the house. Let the justice system work and put Brenner behind bars for life. But how had the justice system worked with Shane Langston? Jake was still bothered he didn't shoot Langston when he could have. Would he shoot Brenner? Brenner would certainly deserve it. Frontier justice for what the madman had done to his daughter and dozens of others.

Jake stood in a mudroom with empty hooks and dust-covered shelves, the kitchen visible through an opening to his right. Listening to the silence, he gingerly stepped into the hall, the barrel of the Sig Sauer at his side, finger resting on the outside of the trigger guard. To Jake's relief, the flooring was solid and squeak free as he stepped down the hallway.

Easing open the door to the garage, he let his pistol lead the way. His mouth was dry as he stepped onto the concrete floor, flipping a switch on the wall. Light from a single overhead bulb threw shadows on kidney-shaped oil stains and wandering cracks along the floor. A tool bench rested along one wall below an empty peg board. The smells of motor oil and saw dust hung in the air as Jake stepped toward the saw horses in the center of the garage. Stacks of two-by-fours and four-by-eight boards lay on either side. The ends of the boards were bored out, creating a tunnel down the middle. Weird.

His cell vibrated. It was Bear.

Jake whispered, "What's up?"

"I think they spotted me or they realized they're late for something, because they're hauling ass down I-29."

"You talk to Snell?"

"Not so much talked as got yelled at. They tracked down the judge and were getting ready to go in front of him for the warrant. Man, the guys in this car are hauling ass."

"Warrant got denied," Jake said. "Murphy took it to the judge himself."

"Son of a bitch. Probably explains why it got denied. The guy strikes me as a colossal dipshit."

"That car's our only lead so stay on 'em. I'm at the house. Nobody here that I can see."

Bear paused. "You're whispering really quiet. Are you in the woods near the house or actually in the house?"

"I decline to answer on the grounds my answer may incriminate me."

"You fucking idiot. Find anything good?"

"Still searching."

Tires screeched and multiple crashing sounds pounded through the phone followed by a string of curse words from Bear.

"The son of a bitch swerved across three lanes of traffic and caused one hell of a mess. Shit. I got sandwiched between two cars. They're gone. No way I can catch them by the time I squeeze outta this mess."

"Let's hope the local PD can track their car. Get back here as soon as you can. I'll keep looking."

After disconnecting and spotting nothing else of interest in the garage, Jake stepped back into the house and headed down the hallway. The kitchen was still empty. The same with a darkened living room area to his left. He took another couple steps deeper into the house when something creaked ahead.

Jake bit his bottom lip and tightened the grip on his Sig Sauer, raising it to shoulder level, his elbows close to his body. He turned his ear toward the sound, waiting for it to repeat. It didn't. Maybe just the creaks and groans of an old farm house?

He edged toward the darkness, passing a closed door and the light switch set into the wall without turning it on. If there was someone ahead, there was no sense announcing his presence. Two bedrooms were located at the end of the hall. One was empty, nothing but mouse tracks and droppings set in a layer of dust on the floor. The second held a bed and an old dresser. Rumpled blankets and pillows covered the mattress. A closet stood open with empty hangers save for a couple of t-shirts. The drawers on the dresser were ajar, a handful of male socks and underwear and feminine t-shirts but nothing else. Somebody packed and left in a hurry. A man and a woman. Jake thought of Brenner and Mara Wilder.

Jake turned back to the hall and approached the door near the light switch. He pressed his ear to the wood. Hearing nothing, he opened the door revealing bare wood steps leading to a basement, unfinished drywall encasing the stairway. At least his lower extremities wouldn't be exposed as he descended.

At the bottom of the stairs, he was forced to turn on the flashlight. With the beaming light in his left hand, he propped his gun hand over the top, sweeping the light across the space as he turned a corner. Dust particles danced in the flashlight beam revealing boxes stacked neatly along a wall. A threadbare couch sat in the opposite corner beside an old stereo console unit, identical to the one he had in his house growing up. Phonograph, eight-track player and radio in one monstrous wooden cabinet. In the middle of the concrete basement floor was an empty, long, plastic folding table surrounded by a handful of chairs. A newer flat screen with a HD antenna rested on one end of the table. On the far wall was an empty tool bench and a six-foot metal cabinet set in a wide recess. Jake checked the contents—empty.

To the right of the cabinet was an open door leading to another bedroom. Like the bedroom upstairs, the sheets on the full-sized mattress were rumpled and the closet empty. Jake checked under the bed—nothing. Lifting the mattress, he found a picture of a blonde-haired woman. The photo was old, but it was definitely Mara Wilder. What was it doing here? He supposed if the three suspects lived here together, Brenner and Mara would take the upstairs and Mallory would take the single bed in the basement. The HR manager at Reliance mentioned he thought Mallory had a thing for Mara. This picture would certainly confirm that. Jake slipped the picture back under the mattress.

He went back to the main room, disappointed he hadn't uncovered anything of value. He didn't know what he expected to find but hoped it would be something more than an empty house, something that would lead them to whatever the three of them planned. He headed toward the stairs to call Bear when a piece of paper under the stereo console caught his eye.

He squatted, plucking the corner of the paper. He pinched the paper between the fingers of his gun toting hand and shined the light on the paper with the flashlight in the other. It was an architectural drawing of a large space. A huge open space like a ballroom. The shapes of the blue lines and dimensions were familiar to Jake, but he couldn't place it from the drawing. The boxes at the bottom that would normally identify the space were missing. Someone had written a list of what appeared to be lumber sizes and quantities at the bottom of the page under the initials "US". He reached under the console to see if there were more pages when a scuff sounded behind him. Like a shoe on concrete.

Jake instinctively spun away and raised his pistol. Something whacked his gun arm, causing the pistol to clatter away in the dark, leaving behind sharp pain. A dark figure pounced on Jake's still squatted form and they crashed to the basement floor, the flashlight spinning away as blows pounded around his head. Jake was on his side and tried to rise, but his attacker forced Jake to his back where fists of fury rained down, a couple finding their way between Jake's raised forearms.

His attacker straddled Jake, clamping strong thighs around his waist as he continued to strike, like a ground-and-pound attack of a mixed-martial arts fighter. Another blow connected and Jake's skull bounced off the concrete. Stars danced in the darkness as he tried to wriggle his way free. One thing was for sure, this guy knew how to fight.

His attacker grunted and twisted, bringing his face into the beam of the flashlight. The brown hair, the chiseled jaw and the cauliflower ears. It was Hunter Brenner and, knowing the man's wrestling proficiency and his dominate position, an unfamiliar worry rippled through Jake that he wasn't going to be able to get out from under him alive.

CHAPTER FIFTY THREE

One of the hardest things to do in a fight is to keep your cool and remain calm, especially when your opponent is beating your head like a piñata. Jake managed to fend off the majority of the thundering blows from Brenner, but the few sneaking in along with the abuse his arms took was wearing him down. Failure to come out on top was not an option.

Years ago, he'd gone a few rounds with a semi-well-known mixed martial arts fighter named Donovan who Keats employed for a short stint as a collector. Jake argued with Keats that Donovan had the wrong temperament for the job and was proven right when the man went off on Keats in front of Keats's crew. Nobody saw Donovan again after that night, but he taught Jake his "three important things to control or you're fucked" mantra—your arms, your hips and your head. You let your opponent control those, you might as well tap out.

Jake had given Brenner his hips and, in between fists and elbows tried to get control of his arms and hands. Jake knew it was coming and worked up a defensive counter. Brenner needed space and leverage to land his shots. When Brenner lunged for an elbow, Jake blocked it and wrapped up the man's arm. When Brenner brought the other one down, Jake took another jarring shot to the temple, but managed to grab that one as well, pulling Brenner's face close to his.

Brenner tried jerking his arms free, but Jake held on for dear life.

With his arms trapped, Brenner raised his head and brought it down hard for a head butt. Jake slipped his head to the side, and Brenner's head thunked on the concrete floor. It wasn't a hard blow but stunned him enough for Jake to buck his hips up, get some space and get his boots on Brenner's hips. Jake did a leg press to gain separation, gaining enough to toss Brenner to the side. Both men rolled away from each other and climbed to their feet.

It didn't take long for Brenner to wade in, elbows in tight, hands raised to protect his face before he passed through the light and became a hulking shadow. Jake threw a couple of semi-blind jabs. One missed, but the other connected with a satisfying crunch. Brenner staggered back and Jake plowed forward, driving them both into the tool bench along the wall. They exchanged blow after blow as they grappled, one gaining a temporary advantage before the other overcame it. Blood trickled into Jake's eye and he tasted copper from a split lip.

Jake's heart thundered through his chest, his muscles tiring. Each breath he sucked in hurt like a knife stuck in his ribs. Footsteps pounded overhead but he didn't know if it was Brenner's crew returning or his brain being rocked in its cage. In his life, he'd never fought anyone with this ferocity and skill. Jake knew he delivered as good as he received but didn't know how much longer he could continue do so. His mouth hung open as he sucked in air.

They spun along the workbench before something hard and pointed connected with Jake's jaw, probably an elbow. It was enough to loosen his grip on Brenner and force Jake to stagger back a few steps, stars lighting up the darkness. Something scraped and a second later, searing agony ripped across his forehead. He screamed in anger, frustration and pain. Another punch to the head sent Jake crashing to the floor as a faint voice called his name.

As Jake's face kissed the dusty concrete, he waited for Brenner to finish him. Maggie and Halle's faces danced across his mind. The heavenly smell of his infant son after a bath overrode the scents of the basement. He drew his arms in tight over his cracked ribs, waiting for the death blow, but instead heard the scrape of metal and heavy steps pounding on wood.

Light blasted through his closed eyelids, but Jake was in far too much pain to shrink away from it. His right eye was swollen and blurry. Through his left he spotted a hulking form coming his way.

"Sweet Jesus," Bear whispered. "Jake, you okay man?"

It was the best sound of Jake's life. Jake coughed, doubling over at the pain it caused, and spat a wad of bloody phlegm to the floor. "Brenner's here. Watch out."

Bear's steps pounded the concrete as he covered the basement. More feet pounded the wooden steps coming toward him, and two pairs of shoes stood in front of him. Jake managed to turn his head to the concerned face of Snell.

She squatted down and pulled out a handkerchief, pressing it to his forehead. "Oh my God."

Jake groaned. "You should see the other guy."

"One guy did this to you?"

"Brenner. He's gotta be close. Like 'still on the property' close."

Snell jumped to her feet and clicked her shoulder mic, barking out orders for the team to spread out and find Brenner.

Jake struggled to get to a sitting position, the world a bit woozy, blood dripping down his face. It had been a long time since he'd gotten his ass kicked like that. He peeked to the workbench and spotted the knife lying on floor. Brenner must have dropped it after he sliced Jake with it.

But where was he?

Jake knew he'd been knocked for a loop, but there couldn't have been more than twenty or thirty seconds between Bear pounding down the stairs and Hunter disappearing. Where the hell did he go?

Bear grabbed Jake by the armpits, helping him to a seat in a chair at the folding table. Jake continued pressing the soaked handkerchiefs to his head, his rapid breathing from the fight slowing. Ten minutes later, Snell drew up a chair.

"Please tell me you had a good reason for your stupid, reckless move to come in here."

Jake didn't have a leg to stand on. He knew it and so did Snell. "I heard a woman scream?"

Snell's eyes narrowed. "Is that a question or a statement?"

"Umm...a statement?"

"Jesus, you better be a lot more convincing when

Murphy gets a hold of you. Where's Brenner? You sure he didn't slip past us? There's no doors or windows in this basement."

Jake scanned his surroundings, his cotton candy brain trying to replay the last seconds of the fight and the aftermath before Bear showed up. It seemed like twenty or thirty seconds, but could it have been longer?

"I don't know," Jake said. "I don't think so. Where's my gun?"

Bear retrieved his Sig Sauer from the corner of the room and handed it to Jake as a barrel-chested man in a blue FBI windbreaker thumped down the steps and strode across the floor carrying a first aid kit and a bottle of water. "House is clear. No sign of anyone but us."

"Thanks, Percell. Damn," Snell breathed.

Jake managed a few sips of water, giving them the rundown of what he saw before Percell slapped gauze over Snell's handkerchiefs, sandwiching the compress and Jake's head in between his broad hands.

Jake winced. "Don't crush my skull, man."

"Gotta stop the bleeding," Percell said. "What did you see during the fight? Play it back in your head."

"I didn't see a thing. The lights were out."

"What did you hear?"

Jake cranked up the replay again. "I heard something pounding overhead. Must've been you guys. We fought some more. He cut me. I yelled. He hit me again and I smacked the floor. Then…"

"What?" Percell asked.

"There was a paper. A drawing."

"Of what?"

Jake blinked his eyes rapidly, trying to clear the cobwebs. "I was looking at it when Brenner jumped me. We fought and he cut me. I was on my knees and thought I was a goner. I heard a…a scraping sound, no two scraping sounds. Then you guys coming down the stairs seconds later."

"Scraping sounds from where?" Snell asked.

Jake pointed to the corner to the empty six-foot-tall metal cabinet resting against the wall by the tool bench. "It was over there somewhere."

Snell and Bear walked to the corner. Bear pointed to the floor. "Check out the grooves in the concrete. This thing's been slid out multiple times.

Snell drew her gun and pointed it at the cabinet. The agent stopped crushing Jake's skull to join her. Snell nodded at Bear who pulled the cabinet back along the grooves. The same scraping noise Jake heard after Brenner cut him sounded.

Snell lowered her weapon. "Well, shit."

Jake couldn't see anything as Bear blocked his view. "Bear, you make a better door than a window."

When Bear stepped aside, Jake saw a long, dark tunnel disappearing behind a hole in the wall. Snell shined her flashlight down the hole and across the shoeprints in the dirt leading away. Brenner was gone.

CHAPTER FIFTY FOUR

Jake stood and lumbered toward the hole in the wall, fighting off the wave of nausea rippling through him.

Bear held him up by the arm. "Where do you think you're going?"

Jake stepped toward the hole, but Bear's grip was firm. "After Brenner."

Snell and Percell already had guns out and moved in. "You can barely stand up, Caldwell. Stay here. Bear, watch him."

She lowered her head and moved into the five-foot-tall tunnel, the beam of her flashlight bouncing off the walls. The wide agent pressed into the opening. Jake hoped he wasn't claustrophobic.

The nausea passed and Jake felt better, clearer, but nowhere near normal. He limped to the table and lowered himself into a chair, muscles screaming in protest.

"How'd this guy do this to you?" Bear asked.

Jake winced as he licked blood from his split lip. "I guess I'm not invincible. He's strong, Bear. Fierce. He got the jump on me and caught me off guard, but

I've never fought anyone like that before. I felt like Mel Gibson in Lethal Weapon 4 when Jet Li kicks his ass."

"Remember, Mel earned another shot and came out on top."

"I think I'll shoot the fucker next time and save my ego," Jake said.

Bear checked Jake's compress. He peeled the corner away and whistled. "You're gonna need stitches. Will probably have a bad ass scar if it helps."

"A daily reminder to Maggie about the world I live in. Great. How'd you get in here without a warrant?"

"Snell. I don't know what favor she called in or with who, but she was like a pack of dogs on a three-legged cat the second Murphy told her their judge denied the warrant. She got it and her first words to me were not to ask how." Bear stepped to the stereo console and picked the drawing off the floor. "This the paper you talked about?"

Jake nodded.

Bear laid it on the table between them. "Looks familiar."

"I thought so, too. There's a suspicious amount of white space where key should be. No naming the site, no document version, no company logos. Nothing. It must've been something they're building. Check out the lumber listing at the bottom."

Bear's finger traced the US letters at the bottom before his eyes lit up. "That's Union Station. U.S.— Union Station. This is an architectural drawing of the Great Hall. See, there's Harvey's, the restaurant we ate at in the middle. That leads to the Grand Plaza where we hit the Chiefs Superbowl celebration. This is Union Station. What's Brenner doing with a drawing of it?"

Feet thumped the hardwood overhead and descended the stairs. It clicked together.

The C4.

The hollowed-out boards.

The remodel job Hunter Brenner's company was in charge of.

Snell's comment of something big brewing.

Snell returned, sweat pasting ropes of her blonde hair on her forehead. "The tunnel ran a hundred feet and emptied out by the barn. We've scoured the grounds. No Hunter. He's either on foot or has a vehicle stashed somewhere. Percell and some guys are combing the woods."

Jake handed her his water bottle. "You notice the boards in the garage?"

"A bunch of lumber. Why?"

"The ends are hollowed out."

She showed her palms. "I'm not following. Why do hollowed out boards matter? If we don't find Brenner out here, we're screwed."

"Not necessarily," Jake said. Something Snell mentioned at the hospital came back to him. "They've used C4 in every bombing event we know, even the assassination attempt at the hospital. But Lenny sold them sixty freaking pounds of it, and I don't think they used near that much. You mentioned you've been hearing chatter about something big in the works?"

"Yeah. You don't call trying to assassinate the President something big?"

"It is, but you've been hearing the 'something big' chatter for weeks. The hospital couldn't have been the big target because the bombing at the T-Mobile arena just happened a few days ago, so the White House couldn't have planned the photo op that far in advance."

Snell moved her head in agreement. "I suppose so. But the chatter didn't specify a time, date or place. We have no way of knowing where it could be yet."

Jake jabbed a finger in her direction. "Where were the President and Vice-President supposed to be tonight?"

"There's a campaign fundraising event for a Missouri senator. The President was going to make a speech and give his endorsement."

Jake held up the drawing. "And where was the event going to be held?"

Snell snagged the picture and studied it for a moment. "I don't get it. What's...oh shit. Is this Union Station?"

"Brenner's going to blow it up."

CHAPTER FIFTY FIVE

Hunter sped down I-29 toward downtown, wincing as he shifted in his seat at what were most likely cracked ribs. That Caldwell guy was a brawler with an iron jaw. Hunter connected with punches that would've put most men in a coma. Caldwell took the pounding and managed to throw Hunter from a dominant position and send him scrambling. If Hunter hadn't remembered the knife behind the tool bench, who knows who would've ended on top. Either Caldwell was very good or Hunter was getting old. As he probed the cut on his cheek with a raw knuckle, he realized it was probably a little of both.

Surprisingly, the Friday evening traffic was light and allowed Hunter to make good time while keeping an eye out for any KCPD patrol cars. He wouldn't have long before the Feds put out an APB on him and his crew if they hadn't already. Thankfully, they wouldn't have a bead on the car he'd stashed at the edge of the property for such an occasion.

The tunnel under the farm house was a leftover from the Civil War, a genuine Underground Railroad tunnel used to move runaway slaves. It was one of the features he loved most about the house. He'd been in the process of hauling ammunition and food rations from the barn into the bunker hidden in the tunnel. They had enough supplies to stay at Anarchy Road until the Rapture came. He'd just emerged through the hole in the wall when footsteps came down the stairs. He ducked behind the metal cabinet and watched through the opening as a lone figure with a pistol and a flashlight crossed the basement, using the Graham carry method. Guy knew what he was doing. His face was lit up by the LED beam enough to recognize him as Caldwell, the guy who came with the hot FBI agent to Reliance.

Hunter chewed on his lip as he stuck his head out from behind the cabinet to track Caldwell as he crossed to Lance's bedroom. Why was Caldwell here alone? Was he a rogue? Maybe Hunter was in the FBI's sights and they couldn't get enough evidence together to move on him officially. Or maybe Caldwell was the preview, and the FBI movie would start playing soon. He thought of shooting him, but Hunter didn't know if Caldwell was alone. The temptation to run nagged Hunter, but there'd be noise. The better move would be to stay put. If Caldwell left, Hunter could escape out the tunnel. Besides, there wasn't anything left in the house for him to find.

The flashlight beam swept across the cabinet and Hunter held his breath, drawing back, his heart thudding. If Caldwell found this hole in the wall with Hunter behind it, there'd be a war. But the best battle is the one you didn't have to fight. The best move would be to let Caldwell find nothing, and Hunter could escape through the tunnel.

The jig is up, you know? Eddie said, sitting on the tool bench in the darkness of the basement, hand resting on a piece of two by four and staring at Hunter hiding behind the cabinet. Hunter could just make out the whites of his eyes and his swinging feet. Maybe that's a good thing for you, man.

Hunter bit back a response, his breathing rapid.

I know, you can't say shit, but how did you think this was all going to end? You can't hide here and expect someone else to do the dirty work for you like in Ramadi. We've been dancing around this for weeks, but I gotta ask you something. Why'd you kill me, Hunter?

Hunter blinked and thought, "I didn't kill you. Fletcher did. You were going to fuck everything up. The Horsemen were cooking along, and you were going to fuck it up by pulling out."

Nah. That ain't how it went down and you know it. You honestly don't remember? You can't figure out why I keep coming to see you?

"Fletcher wanted you dead."

Eddie hopped from the tool bench and stalked toward him. Fletcher is what he is, and he's gonna fuck you the same way he wanted to fuck me. But Fletcher didn't keep his mouth shut about the airstrike coming in. You did. Fletcher didn't send me across the street into certain death. You did.

Eddie closed the distance between them. Terror rippled through Hunter as Eddie's gnarled, mangled hand reached toward him, the same way he'd done lying in a pool of blood in the Iraq rubble. Hunter had stood over him, cauterizing those emotional nerve endings and blaming the United States government that launched the rockets and erasing the fact

Hunter knew they were coming. Eddie's raw fingers were inches away.

You knew what was coming, and you sent me anyway. All for her. All so you could have her.

Hunter pinched his eyes closed and shook his head violently. He was going crazy, talking to ghosts. When Hunter opened them, Eddie was gone leaving nothing but a cold sweat and the knowledge that he'd murdered his best friend. The United States government killed Eddie with the missile attack, but Hunter sent him in that building knowing it was coming.

Footsteps across the room broke the trance. Caldwell was back. Squatting down by the stereo cabinet. Holding up a drawing. Shit. Holding up the drawing of Union Station. Mara had removed the identifiers at the base of the drawing, but if Caldwell figured out what it was, everything was over. Any revelations about Eddie would have to wait. Hunter couldn't let Caldwell wreck the plan.

He slipped through the opening, reaching toward the tool bench and latched onto the four foot long two-by-four, turning it so the narrow end would cave in Caldwell's skull as he squatted with his back to him. If only it was that easy.

Twenty minutes and many cuts and bruises later, he'd fled through the woods behind the barn, down the narrow trail he'd run a thousand times. All the way to the car stashed in the shed near the road as the lights and sirens shattered the stillness of the night far behind him.

His cell rang as the lights of downtown blurred by on his left, minutes from Union Station. Damn it. Mister X aka Fletcher. He flexed his swollen and bloodied hands as he answered.

"The FBI has raided your house," Fletcher said.

"You're twenty minutes late with the information. I made it out."

"And the others?"

"Getting in place. Once POTUS is in position, we'll finish this thing."

Fletcher's silky voice was calm and cool. "The final rip in the social fabric. It's tearing and it's vulnerable, Hunter. After tonight, there won't be anything left. The Horsemen ride again."

Hunter gripped the wheel tight. "They know about me."

"Yes, they do. Lance and Mara, too. The FBI has video of Lance operating the drone. You might be able to get away, but three of you? Loose ends, Hunter. Loose ends. You know what you have to do, right? I have a lot riding on this. Call me when it's done."

Fletcher disconnected the call. Hunter turned east on Pershing, Union Station lighting up the night as he rounded the curve. He pulled into the parking lot west of the building and parked along the security fencing separating the stage construction zone his company operated from the parking lot. The stage construction was a throwaway job compared to the renovations to the ceiling of the Union Station Grand Hall. Lumber loaded with C4 ninety-five feet above the heads of the town's political elite, the President and the VP, there for a festive evening of slimy handshakes and crooked checks to further corrupt those in power and drag the country to more depraved depths.

Yet something Fletcher said stuck in Hunter's craw. This coordinated effort to shred the fabric of the United States, to tear down the systems of power, to bring everyone down to the same level was a team effort, a shared vision. Fletcher said I have a lot riding on this. Not we. Not all of us. I.

Hunter knew what Fletcher wanted, which diverged from the overall immediate goal, but at least he'd thought the man shared the same vision. A place where nobody ruled over anyone, where everyone was responsible for themselves, shared when they wanted, helped when needed. And if you wanted to fend for yourself, you could do so.

Anarchy Road.

But, if Anarchy Road was nothing but a pipe dream, what was he doing this for? He didn't mind sacrificing a few virgins to the anarchical volcano gods, but was this killing for the sake of killing to further Fletcher's agenda?

Worries of loose ends and a shaky foundational vision was the last thing Hunter expected to feel as he climbed from the car. His vision locked on Union Station fifty yards ahead, red and blue lights spilling up the grand facade. A giggle sounded behind him. He turned to watch a mother and father strolling across the parking lot, dressed to the nines with a six-year-old between them. They held the boy's hands as they swung him back and forth like a pendulum between them. The boy's smile touched his ears as they passed, heading toward a death under tons of exploded concrete.

He spotted Lance's van a few slots down, parked nose out. A steel ball settled in his gut, like the one that settled there the night Eddie was killed. Hunter checked the surroundings for witnesses and ducked between cars to the back of the van. He gave a "shave and a haircut" knock, and the back doors swung open.

Both Mara and Lance were decked out. Lance in a tux sitting on a bench and Mara on the opposite side in a sparkling red gown with a slit half-way up her thigh. How many lustful looks had Lance stole in her direction over the years? Did Mara enjoy those looks? He thought about her picture under Lance's mattress. Had she given it to him? Was she playing both sides as she had with Eddie and Hunter? Thirty minutes ago, the question wouldn't even have crossed his mind. Now, his entire foundation was ready to crumble.

"Everything alright at the house?" Lance asked, checking the C4 wired to the vest on his lap.

"FBI showed up," Hunter said, his voice distant in his head. "I had to run through the tunnel and take the getaway car."

Mara's smile evaporated and she dropped to the ground. "The feds? At Anarchy Road? What's it mean for us?"

Hunter's attention flicked between his two partners. "It means they know who we are. It means that after tonight, everyone will know who we are."

Lance's shoulders slumped and his head fell back against the side of the van. "We're fucked."

Hunter knew what the plan was, what he had to do. But he didn't want to do it. Every fiber of his being screamed to get in his car and go. Instead, he forced steel into his voice. "We're not fucked. The system is. We're going through with this. Afterward, we go underground until things cool. Mister X said he'll make arrangements for us. We'll set up Anarchy Road somewhere else."

"You sure?" Mara whispered, stroking his arm.

Hunter gazed into her eyes and ran his rough

thumb over her cheek and kissed her electric lips. "I'm sure. The vest ready?"

Lance held the vest up. "Still don't think we need it."

"Redundancies, Lance," Mara said. "If the ceiling doesn't work, we'll need the vest to finish the job. That's why I suggested it."

"And an excellent suggestion it was," Hunter said. "Mister X was impressed with the idea."

Lance's eyes narrowed. "You trust him? Mister X?"

"I do."

Lance gripped the vest tight. "I know who he is. You did a good job keeping it a secret, but even Flet—"

"You always were a smart bastard, Lance. Let's keep it a secret." Hunter nodded toward Mara. "It's safer that way for everyone."

Lance nodded. "So, we stick with the original plan?"

"Yeah. You and Mara go in the back entrance. You wear the vest under your tux jacket. We have a friend at the back door who'll let you in. Go together. A happy couple will be less conspicuous so smile. I'll check the loads in the ceiling. When I give you the signal, drop the vest in the crowd and get the hell out. Signal when you're clear and I'll blow the vest and the ceiling. We'll meet back here. By the time they sort through the rubble, we'll be long gone."

Eddie slumped against the car next to them, arms crossed, head shaking from side to side. The flap of skin slapping his cheek. You're really going to go through with it, aren't you? You haven't learned a damn thing since Iraq.

Hunter ignored him and helped Lance slip on the vest. The open van doors blocked the view of those walking the parking lot from the side, and construction protected them from the back. Lance double checked the quick release straps that would allow him to drop the vest with his jacket still on. It worked like a charm. Hunter checked the signal on the detonator. They were good to go.

"Don't press the button too early," Lance said.

Hunter gave his friend a hug. "Be careful. Move casual. People are going to think you're suspicious already with this beauty on your arm."

As Lance slipped on the oversized tux jacket, Hunter turned to Mara. "I love you, you know. Everything I do, I do it for you."

Mara's eyes shimmered. "I love it when you quote our song. We're going to be okay after this, right?"

"Everything is going to turn out fine," Hunter said. "I'll be right behind you. I love you."

She kissed him softly, drawing his lower lip between her teeth as she pulled back, just like he liked. She let go and whispered, "I love you too, baby. See you soon."

Lance and Mara walked along the driver's side of the van as Hunter slammed the doors shut. Mara hooked her arm through Lance's, and they strolled across the asphalt. Hunter watched them go, an inevitable sadness gripping his chest.

Behind him, sirens wailed, faint but growing close. The drawing. The idiot Feds must've put two and two together.

Mara laughed at something Lance said, the tinkling notes of her voice carrying across the western breeze from a hundred feet away, a whiff of her perfume lingered from their embrace.

I loved her, you know? Eddie said, standing by Hunter's side.

"I do, too. I always have. I'm sorry I killed you,

Eddie. I've carried you around with me for so long. But I won't do it anymore. The past is the past and now I know that if I had a chance to go back to that night in Iraq, I'd do it all over again. For her. My conscious is clear and you can't haunt me anymore. It's done."

A scream of tires into the lot behind him. Hunter checked over his shoulder as a truck slid to a halt fifty feet away. Hunter recognized the faces climbing out and screaming his name. Caldwell and Parley. Beyond them, a wave of red and blue lights closing in.

I'll see you in hell, Hunter, Eddie whispered into his ear.

"Yeah, maybe," Hunter said, turning back but finding Eddie gone. Hunter looked toward Lance and Mara, who stopped and turned toward the commotion. Mara's jaw hung open and Lance tensed, preparing to break into a run.

Mara locked eyes with Hunter.

Hunter raised the detonator, his gut gnawing him from the inside.

"No," Mara mouthed.

Five to one, baby, one in five. No one here gets out alive.

Caldwell screamed at Hunter to freeze.

Hunter's thumb trembled over the detonator button.

Loose ends.

CHAPTER FIFTY SIX

Jake and Bear flew south on I-29, Bear blinking his lights to get slower moving cars out of the way. At the speed he traveled, the cars around him moved like they were bogged down in a swamp. Behind them, Snell and her team tried to keep up.

"Come on, man," Jake said. "Can't this bucket of bolts go any faster? I'm losing my mind here."

Bear ground his teeth. "I go any faster and your mind will be lost—through my windshield when I wreck the truck and kill us both. You sure about Union Station?"

"It's the only thing that makes sense."

"What if you're wrong?"

Jake grabbed the panic handle above Bear's door as he swerved. "If I'm wrong, the worst we do is freak out a bunch of political snobs at an event to pay homage to a bunch of overpaid and underworked dickheads."

They swung south on Highway 169, and a pair of sirens joined the parade. By the time they passed the Charles B. Wheeler downtown airport and crossed the Broadway bridge leading into downtown, there were two more in the rearview mirror.

"You want to go through downtown or skirt it on I-35?" Bear asked.

"Skirt it on 35. Maybe we can stop Brenner and his crew before they blow it. He can't be that far ahead of us."

Bear turned onto I-35, mere minutes now from Union Station. "You're assuming he can't blow it at anytime from anywhere from a cell phone."

Jake thought about Brenner watching from the dead lawyer's office as he blew the bomb near the arena two nights ago. "No way. He'll want to see it. He'll be there somewhere."

Jake's cell rang. Snell. He put it on speaker as Bear closed in on the 20th Street exit.

"Murphy thinks we're on a wild goose chase," Snell said. "He won't clear the event space."

Jake banged the dash. "Seriously? What the hell does he want? A written confession from Brenner?"

"He wants something more than a drawing and some hollowed out boards. His words, not mine. He's at least sending pictures of Brenner, Mallory and Wilder to the security team working the event."

"What about Secret Service?"

"I'm trying to reach the right person. Until then, we're relying on contract security and the KCPD. They'll stop any of those three before they breach the building."

Bear drifted across the pavement as he gunned the truck south on Broadway, speeding toward Pershing Road leading to Union Station. They were sixty seconds out.

"Great plan," Jake said. "Unless they're already inside. We have no idea if Mallory is already there and Brenner gained enough of a jump on us that he could be inside as well. That's also assuming a barely-over-minimum-wage security guard can stop trained military professionals. We gotta get those people out of there, Snell."

"I'm doing what I can," Snell said as she disconnected the call.

Bear screeched through the turn onto Pershing Road, the engine of his truck roaring. Up ahead, the grand Union Station building was lit up in a bath of red and blue lights. A hundred yards closer to them, the Reliance Construction site where they'd spotted Watterson earlier in the day sat under a bank of lights in a parking lot west of the Union Station building. As the sirens blared behind them, a figure in the parking lot turned, his face lit up by the halogen lamps.

Jake's heart skipped a beat as they drew closer. "Into that lot. There he is."

Bear jerked the wheel to the left, and they bounced over the curb.

Hunter Brenner turned his head toward Union Station, a man and a woman some distance from him stopping at the crazy train heading their way. Mallory and Wilder.

Bear slammed on the brakes, and the truck slid to a stop at an angle. Brenner cranked his head over his shoulder at the commotion.

Jake jumped from the passenger side, yanking his Sig Sauer from its holster and drawing a bead on Hunter Brenner fifty feet away over the hood of the truck. Brenner recognized them but made no move to run as he turned his attention back Mallory and Wilder.

"Brenner!" Jake yelled.

Brenner's hand rose to his chest, something clutched in it, his thumb raised. As Brenner's thumb dropped, Jake squeezed off a couple of rounds before Mallory and Wilder disappeared in a blast of light and deafening sound.

Jake dropped behind the truck for cover, ears ringing as glass crashed, metal crunched and distant screams sounded, drowning out the blaring sirens behind them for a few seconds. Did Brenner just blow the Union Station roof? Jake had visions of bodies buried under tons of rubble.

"Bear?" Jake yelled.

"Jesus Christ, what the fuck was that?"

"I'm guessing a shit ton of C4."

Jake climbed to his feet, swinging his gun around the front end of Bear's truck. In the parking lot ahead of them, there was a jagged mess of asphalt where Mallory and Wilder had stood. Crumpled cars around them sat at odd angles, mangled like they'd been through an F5 tornado. Between the blast site and Bear's truck, Brenner lay on his back, spread eagle. Beyond them, a hundred yards away, Union Station appeared unaffected by the blast.

Jake crossed the fifty feet between them quickly, hearing the footfalls of Bear on his heels. He trained the barrel of his pistol at Brenner's still form. If Brenner so much as twitched, Jake planned on emptying the rest of his magazine into him.

Blood trickled from a corner of the Brenner's mouth, glass sprinkled his caramel hair, and his mouth opened and shut like a fish when flopped on dry land. A bloody spot grew in Brenner's left shoulder. Apparently, Jake had tagged him with at least one shot. The heat rose in Jake's neck, pissed he'd shot Brenner in the shoulder instead of between the eyes.

A tear squeezed from the corner of Brenner's eyes as he turned his head to stare down the barrel of Jake's gun. "Lawyer."

"Fuck you, Hunter," Jake said, his finger tightening on the trigger. He wanted to empty his magazine into the man on the ground in front of him, reload and do it again.

Snell ran up and stopped. "Door number one—cuff him? Or door number two—let him bleed out?"

"I like door number three," Bear said. "Let Jake finish the job."

"Lawyer," Brenner croaked. "I wanna make a deal. One you're going to want to hear."

"Cuff him," Snell said, placing a gentle hand on Jake's arm and pushing the barrel down as a group of cops surrounded them. "Get an ambulance over here for this waste of oxygen and clear the building, now!"

She turned and made calls as she walked toward the blast site where what was left of Mallory and Wilder was scattered in a crater of metal, blood and guts.

The cops rolled Brenner to his stomach and maneuvered his hands behind his back. They patted him down before lifting him to his feet. By the time they finished, an ambulance sped into the lot, lights on, siren muted. Jake was thankful. He'd heard enough of them in the last couple of days.

Brenner swayed, head lolling on his shoulders before he steadied. His chin lifted and he locked eyes with Jake. His bullish eyes were black, midnight and unending. Then, the right corner of Brenner's mouth twisted into a crooked grin, and Jake's grip tightened on the butt of his Sig Sauer.

As the cops lugged Brenner toward the ambulance, Bear clapped his meaty hand on Jake's shoulder. Jake winced at Bear's heavy touch, the pressure sending waves of pain through his body. Ribs, shoulder, knees. Hell, even his hair hurt. He felt like he'd been beaten with a bag of door knobs.

"We did it," Bear said. "I can't believe we stopped him."

They'd won. They'd foiled the plan of a madman before more innocent lives were taken. But, as Jake's eyes met Brenner's again and Brenner pasted the same cocky smile on his face, Jake didn't feel like they'd won. It felt like the game was still being played and they didn't know the rules.

CHAPTER FIFTY SEVEN

The next few hours were a flurry of activity. Snell popped in and out of the scene at Union Station after ordering Jake and Bear to stay out of the way and let her team and the KCPD work through what happened.

The police questioned Jake about the shooting of Hunter Brenner, specifically what threat Brenner posed considering they found him empty-handed. Jake remembered something in Brenner's hand, knew it wasn't a gun but thought it might be a detonator to the C4.

"We suspected he was going to blow up the Grand Hall," Jake said to the white-haired cop taking his statement. "I thought I saw something in his hand that could've been the detonator, and as he raised it up, all I could think of was the people stacked inside the building."

The older cop raised his bushy eyebrows and checked over both shoulders for anyone nearby. "I think you mean you saw the detonator in his hand, right? Not something that could've been it, but you saw a detonator. Am I correct?"

The cop waited for Jake to take the bait.

"Of course that's what I meant," Jake said. "I saw the detonator. Did anyone find it?"

"Not yet. We're still combing the area in case he threw it, but there's a lot of debris to sift through."

The cop finished up with Jake and another officer questioning Bear moved along as well. Bear dragged his feet to where Jake stood near the Reliance Construction site. They watched the hustle and bustle outside Union Station, red and blue lights still blanketing the side of the building, but this time from police cars instead of ornamental lights set in the ground. News trucks lined Pershing Road, reporters standing in front of spotlights providing up-to-the-minute coverage to the home viewing audience. Luckily, Jake and Bear were still close enough to the blast site in an area off limits to the media.

"I'm so freaking tired," Bear groaned. "At least I look better than you. You look like you went fifteen rounds with the heavyweight champ with your hands tied behind your back."

Jake gingerly prodded his swollen eye and face. He'd checked his face in a side mirror of a nearby car and knew Bear wasn't lying.

"I feel like it, too. Would love to go to the hospital to check on Maggie and Halle."

"You talk to her?"

"For a few minutes. Gave her the lowdown. Let her know we're both good."

"And Halle?"

"Should be able to go home as soon as Tuesday if everything continues to go well."

Bear slipped a tobacco pouch between his cheek and gums. "Well, thank Christ for that. I'm just glad this is over."

Jake remembered the mischievous expression on Brenner's face. "I don't know that it is. Not yet."

Bear spit on the ground, his face crinkled like an old bulldog. "What makes you say that?"

"My gut. The way Brenner looked at me. He has another card up his sleeve with this deal he wants to make."

Bear batted a hand through the air. "Bah, screw him. Feds have him dead to rights. There ain't a deal to be had that's going to get him out of this mess."

Jake hoped so, but his gut told him something else.

An hour later, Snell re-appeared, talked with agents and cops in the area and walked to Jake and Bear.

"How you guys holding up?" she asked.

"We're tired and getting cold," Jake said. "I want a handful of painkillers and to go see Maggie and Halle. How much longer are we going to have to be here?"

"Not much longer I hope. They cleared the building and everyone, including the President and VP, got out safe. Our team swept every nook and cranny of Union Station and found no sign of the hollowed boards and the C4. That is, until I decided to check into the work Reliance was supposed to be doing. Turns out it was the ceiling above the Grand Hall. Our bomb techs went up there, nearly a hundred feet in the air, and found the boards we were looking for. Lined all around the structural supports for the ceiling in a crawlspace. If Brenner and his team had blown it, we'd be talking hundreds of dead."

"What about Brenner?" Jake asked.

"Your bullet passed through the meat of the shoulder. He's going to be fine. He's under heavy guard getting patched up. Refuses to say anything until his lawyer arrives. I'll tell you what, the guy has cold ass, Ted Bundy eyes."

"He didn't say why he blew up Mallory and his own girlfriend?"

Snell shook her head. "Not a word."

"I think he saw us closing in, and he knew he was done," Jake said. "Brenner knew they could hand us his head on a platter."

"Maybe. We'll get the truth out of him."

Bear slumped against the front of his truck. "Unless his slimeball lawyer gets him a deal."

Snell's lip curled. "No way that asshole's getting a deal. If he even—"

Jake's cell vibrated and he checked it while Snell railed on Brenner. It was Cat. Jake stepped away and answered.

"Looks like I missed the fun at Union Station," Cat said. "Unlike you."

"How'd you know I was here?" Jake asked.

"Saw you on the news. They panned a shot and I saw you and Bear for a few seconds standing by some beat up truck. Looks like my tracking efforts went for naught on this round."

"We wouldn't have found him without you, man," Jake said. "I won't forget."

"What do you want me to do with the CDRs from Brenner's phone?"

"Email them to me and I'll get them to the FBI. Anything interesting?"

"One thing." Cat crunched on something while the sounds of pages being turned rolled through the receiver. "One of the phone numbers Watterson called tracked movement with Brenner's personal phone. Like those same numbers traveled together."

"What's that mean?"

"Probably a burner phone," Cat said. "That burner phone made one call and received one call from a number in Kalorama."

"Where's Kalorama? Never heard of it."

"Washington DC. It's a ritzy northwest neighborhood where a bunch of political muckety-mucks live. I remember the name because 60 Minutes did an interview with Obama a while back. That's where he and the missus set up shop."

Jake stopped pacing. Why would Brenner call Washington, much less to a neighborhood where political people lived? If Brenner was part of the 2A Militia, maybe they were tied to someone higher up the food chain. The money for the guns and explosives had to come from somewhere. Maybe it was a special interest group or some national organization. It had to be something if Brenner made the calls on burner phones. Was Brenner not the top dog of this operation?

"What about any calls the Kalorama burner phone made?"

"Just the two with Brenner," Cat said. "Sorry. That's where the trail ends."

"Is all this in the files you're going to send me?"

"Already on it's way. I can't wait for the giant ass check you're going to send me, Caldwell."

Jake slipped his phone into his pocket and walked back toward Snell, the puzzle working through his head. They would be able to track where the DC calls were made and received, but it wouldn't reveal much without knowing who made them. Then again, Brenner seemed willing to talk. I wanna make a deal. One you're going to want to hear.

Jake planned to pass the information to Snell, and then he was out of it. Let the feds sort through the nitty gritty. He just wanted to wrap his arms around his girls and leave this mess behind.

"I got it," someone exclaimed behind him.

Jake and Bear turned as a technician Jake talked to earlier pulled the detonator from the rubble of the Reliance Construction site, thirty feet from where Jake shot Brenner. The tech tipped his FBI hat in Jake's direction.

"Well, that's good," Bear said.

Jake's chest felt a little lighter. "At least one thing went right tonight."

CHAPTER FIFTY EIGHT

Three months later, Jake swayed on the porch swing of his house, a cold beer in his hand, listening to the summer sounds of the Ozarks as day's dying sun took the heat and humidity with it. Maggie kicked him out of the kitchen while she finished cooking a late dinner, after Jake made three unsuccessful attempts spice up the spaghetti sauce behind her back.

Things had settled down on the home front. Work was steady but uneventful, which was fine with Jake and especially Maggie. Maggie went back to work part-time at Hospice House. Halle was back in action, recovered from the bombing at the arena, though her hair hadn't fully grown back yet, and she still suffered from the occasional headache. Connor's energy levels shot up exponentially once the weather turned warm. He was close to taking his first steps and seemed most content playing in the dirt of their front yard. Jake hoped the kid would learn to run as fast as he could crawl and that it wasn't a good idea to eat dirt by the fistfuls.

Jake got up to grab another beer when Bear called.

"Turn on the news."

Jake headed into the house. "Which channel?"

"Hell, any of them."

"Jesus, what is it?"

"You won't believe it. Call me back after you watch."

Jake strode to the living room and snagged the remote from Halle's lap, changing the channel from some reality dating show. Halle protested, though she'd been watching her phone instead of the TV. The image on the screen showed a man in his mid-fifties in a dark suit being perp-walked from a brick-faced townhome costing more than Jake would ever make. FBI agents blanketed the man as they escorted him down the stairs toward a waiting black SUV. The crawler at the bottom of the screen read "Speaker of the House arrested."

"—all we know at this point," the female announcer said. "Our sources have told us Representative Richard Fletcher, the Speaker of the House, has been linked to bank accounts and communication records tying him to extremist groups on both sides of the political spectrum. Authorities have stated an inside source to the operations turned state's evidence and provided information vital to the arrest of House Speaker Fletcher. The FBI will not specify who the source might be, but they confirmed the existence of bank records that tie Fletcher to a number of domestic terrorism events that rocked this country months ago, including bombings in Seattle, Tulsa and, most recently, Kansas City. We'll stay on top of this major breaking news story and bring you more details as they come to light."

Jake flipped through several other channels. Fox News, CNN and the other major networks covered the same information, along with a bevy of political guests pontificating on what this might mean. Maggie joined him as they stood in the living room.

"Did...was this our bombing in Kansas City?" Maggie asked.

"I think so."

"He looks like a scumbag."

"He's a politician. I think they have to look like that." Jake called Bear. "Holy shit."

"I know, right? You ever hear anything from Snell?"

"Not a word," Jake said, stepping into the kitchen. "Last time I talked to her though, she was getting pushed out of the way. She didn't know why, but maybe this has something to do with it."

"Hunter Brenner has something to do with it," Bear said. "That fucker has to be the inside source. What do you think it means for him?"

A sick lump sat in Jake's stomach. I want to make a deal. One you're going to want to hear is what Brenner said. A deal for Brenner meant he got something in return and anything less than the death penalty would be a gross miscarriage of justice.

Jake's phone beeped. Snell. He fumbled with the phone for a moment before figuring out how to link the calls together.

"Hey, Victoria. Bear's on the line too. What going on with Fletcher?"

"I would've called you sooner, but I didn't know they were moving on him. Murphy pushed me out of the loop. I think to spite me because you and I are friends and you did more to nail Brenner than we did. You and Bear, I mean."

"Thanks," Bear said. "I thought you were going to give Jake all the credit."

"Well, I did do most of the work," Jake said.

Bear grumbled. "Always a bridesmaid, never a bride. What have you heard, Snell?"

Her breath rattled the phone. "Brenner's been granted a special hearing. Apparently, he's spilled everything he knew about Fletcher. He kept detailed records of calls, discussions, bank transactions, everything."

"What were they trying to do?" Jake asked.

"Sow discord. Get everyone fighting against each other until it all fell apart."

"Anarchy," Jake whispered, thinking back to the road sign by the abandoned house.

"That's what Brenner claimed they were doing. He said Fletcher was behind the assassination attempt of the President and Vice-President. If both of them were gone, guess who would ascend to the White House."

"Fletcher. Jesus. You think it's true?"

"His information's credible," Snell said. "The higher ups believe him. Buddy of mine says Fletcher was part of a group called the Six Horsemen. They ran a drug smuggling ring in Iraq using military vehicles. Brenner, Mallory and Fletcher were a part of it. Eddie Puglisi, who owned the Anarchy Road property, was part of it, too. Fletcher has a stash of cash in off shore accounts. They think it's that stash he used to fund Brenner's efforts."

"Who were the other two Horsemen?"

"Couple of guys who've since died."

Bear asked, "What's Brenner say about Mallory and the Mara girl?"

"He pins it on Mallory, of course. Brenner was an innocent pawn who was afraid of what Fletcher and Mallory would do to him."

"Oh bullshit," Bear spat. "The motherfu—"

"I know, Bear," Snell said. "But Brenner's turned a lot of hard evidence over. It led us to Fletcher and helped nail the heads of a couple of domestic terror groups in exchange for leniency."

The hairs on Jake's arms stood. "What kind of leniency?"

"Don't know. That's what the special hearing is for."

"Anything other than the chair is too good for that guy."

"Maybe you should learn to shoot better, Caldwell," Bear grunted. "Head shot next time."

"I've heard quite a few folks say that," Snell said. "But, if you had killed him, we wouldn't have gotten Fletcher. Still, there's a lot of uneasy agents around here who don't like where this is headed."

An image floated across Jake's mind of Brenner strolling out of a courthouse into the sunshine, exonerated from his multiple crimes because he turned into a snitch. "When is this hearing?"

"Next week. That's why I'm calling. You and Bear need to be there, because you may be called as witnesses."

"By which side?"

"Our side," she said. "I'll get back with you, because we'll want you to sit with our attorneys and go over your stories. I don't know it will come to that, but we want to be prepared. I'd say clear your schedule for the next five days."

Jake didn't revel in being called in to testify. He imagined a good defense attorney could poke a thousand holes into his actions. Jake's legal status for shooting Brenner added to the uncertainty. The Kansas City cops had let it go, and Brenner's lawyers hadn't pushed it...yet. Maybe it was part of the coming attractions.

"Oh, and one more thing you might enjoy hearing, Jake," Snell said. "You know how it seemed Brenner always was one step ahead of us? There was a reason for it."

"An insider?"

"Yeah, in the Bureau. They combed through Fletcher's records and found the insider. Your favorite Agent Murphy."

Jake's jaw dropped to his chest. "Are you shittin' me?"

"Fletcher had a file an inch thick on Murphy that he was using as blackmail. Slowing up our investigation was supposed to be Murphy's last act, which explains why he dragged his feet at every turn and why our initial warrant on the house got denied. Murphy didn't provide the judge with even a quarter of the evidence we had. Hell, I would've denied the warrant at that point."

"That crooked son of a bitch," Jake said. "Good thing you knew someone. You ever going to tell me how you pulled that one off?"

"I can't teach you all my tricks, Jake," Snell said. "I gotta run. Just start putting your thoughts together on what happened during this whole ordeal. You may be called to tell the tale on the stand."

Jake glanced to the couch where Halle sat, absently rubbing the scar on the side of her head, the hollowness in her eyes as they locked on the news in front of her and hearing Jake's side of the conversation. One thing Jake knew. Brenner had almost killed him and, more importantly, his baby girl. As long as Jake drew a breath, no way in hell Brenner was getting away with it.

CHAPTER FIFTY NINE

A slimy sweat coated Jake's palms as he waited in the packed courtroom. He rubbed them on the dark pants of the one suit he owned. The lawyers had prepped him over the last three days in case they called him to testify in front of the judge during the hearing. It turned out Jake had many talents, but being a witness wasn't one of them. He'd told the team of lawyers some things, but not everything. He didn't lie, but he wasn't transparent either. He was terrified he would spoil the case, and Brenner would go free because of it. The lawyers peppered him with questions Brenner's lawyers might toss his way, and Jake kept tripping over his half-truths and omissions, anger constantly getting the better of him. Eventually, Jake learned to keep his composure and his answers simple. Still, the witness stand might as well have been an execution station.

"Would you freaking relax?" Bear whispered through the side of his mouth. "You're making me nervous."

Jake tugged at the collar of his dress shirt. "This

shirt is choking me, and it's hot as hell in here."

"You have nothing to be nervous about, amigo. This should be a slam dunk. Besides, we have a front row seat. We'll be outta here lickety-split, and you can buy me a beer."

"Nothing's ever that easy."

Two armed officers escorted Brenner through a side door and to a table beyond a mahogany chair rail. Three-piece suit, slicked back hair and confidence dripping from his lined face. Cuffed in the front with chains attached to his feet, Brenner pulled out the chair to the table before turning, his eyes scanning the crowd of reporters and angry onlookers in the back before settling on Jake. Five feet of air and a hunk of wood separated the two. The son of a bitch had the audacity to draw a line across his forehead. The scar from Brenner's knife burned at the reference. Jake's nails bit into his thighs. Bear laid a calming hand on Jake's forearm.

They stood at the bailiff's "all rise" command. The judge came in, a bulbous man with thick glasses and a red-veined nose. He settled behind the bench and smoothed his combover as he flipped through a thick file on his desk. Jake settled into his chair, ready for a few long days on the hard wood. Brenner snuck a look over his shoulder at Jake again and shucked his eyebrows. Jake wanted nothing more than to hop over the rail and smash Brenner's smug head into the wood railing until there was nothing left but his blazing white teeth and cauliflower ears.

The lawyers and judges exchanged information, but Jake had trouble focusing on their words. Images and sounds bombarded his brain. The explosion at the arena. Halle lying in the rubble bleeding, limp, nearly lifeless. The tube coming out of Halle's head. Bodies on the ground at Humphrey's house. Foster sprawled dead in the dirt. Her blood on Jake's hands, blood that wouldn't wash away no matter how many times he scrubbed them under scalding water. The blasted hole in the hospital and Watterson in pieces. So many dead and the scumbag five feet away from him was responsible.

"And the government accepts the items stipulated in the plea arrangement?" the judge asked.

Jake's head jerked up. Plea arrangement? It was the two worst words he thought he'd ever heard.

Jake leaned toward Bear and whispered, "What goddamn plea arrangement?"

"We do, your Honor," the slick-backed beanpole manning the table opposite Brenner's said as he stood.

"Very well," the judge said. "Hunter Brenner, would you stand?"

Brenner's lawyer stood. Hunter pressed against the table and rose slowly, revealing a hint of teeth as he snuck a peek over his shoulder again at Jake.

Jake's gut tightened as all moisture fled his mouth. He felt light-headed, as if someone had sucked the oxygen out of the room.

The judge scowled at Brenner over the top of his glasses, as if sickened he even had to speak to the man. "Hunter Brenner, do you agree to plead guilty to the counts of inciting a riot and unlawful possession of explosives as outlined in the plea arrangement?"

"I do, your Honor," Brenner said. "I'm sorry for what has happened."

The judge frowned. "I highly doubt that is the case. However, the evidence and testimony you have provided has led to the arrest of numerous individuals involved in a criminal conspiracy. The evidence also showed that Lance Mallory and Mara Wilder were the key players in this conspiracy, and you were coerced into your minor role. Therefore, this court sentences you to time served and house arrest in the witness protection program."

The judge continued to speak, but the heat flushing Jake's face blended with the roar of fury in his ears. Minor role? Fucking house arrest? Hundreds dead at the hands of this psychopath, and he gets house arrest because he handed over a crooked politician? Jake's arms trembled in tense fury, dots spotting his vision. His stomach hardened like steel with the realization Brenner would skate from this, and Jake had helped him get there by missing the kill shot right between the bastard's beady little eyes.

The smacking gavel and uproar from the gallery broke Jake's trance on the mahogany rail.

Brenner turned, wearing a shit-eating grin that reached his mangled ears. "Be seeing you, Caldwell. Say hello to your pretty little girl for me."

In the blink of an eye, Jake sprung from his seat. Before Bear could grab him, Jake's hurtled the railing and wrapped his hands around Brenner's throat. He squeezed with every ounce of strength in his bones, trying to get his hands to meet through Brenner's neck. They crashed to the floor, the chains on Brenner's shackles rattling against the old hardwood. Several hands yanked and tugged at Jake's arms, but he had a death grip on Brenner's throat, watching the man's face redden as his eyes bulged. Nothing short of watching Brenner's head pop off like a top would do.

In spite of the life being choked from him, the grin never left Brenner's face.

Like he expected Jake to do it.

Like he invited it.

Jake managed to bounce Brenner's head off the courtroom floor once before something clubbed him in the back. When he didn't let go, another blow hit the back of his head and the world went dark.

NOW

CHAPTER SIXTY

The afternoon sun draped across Dr. Tate's desk, her highbacked chair casting a shadow reaching to the sitting area where she and Jake had talked a few weeks prior. He recalled storming out after a rather lengthy, self-serving monologue that he hoped didn't sink his chances of remaining a free man. She waved Jake inside. At least she offered a smile. Jake took it to be a good thing. Or was she cushioning the blow for the bad news to come?

Her meticulous desk was clear of contents except for a monitor, keyboard and two white envelopes stacked on top of each other. Jake assumed they were for him. His fate. One for the court and a copy for him. He crossed the room and stopped in front of her desk, breathing in the lilac scent from the air freshener plugged into the wall behind her. It was more suited to her than the cinnamon sticks from his last visit.

"How are you, Jake? Please, sit."

Jake dropped to the chair in front of her desk, happy they wouldn't be returning to the couch for a deeper dive into his psyche. He pulled the puzzle piece from his pocket and spun it between two pinched fingers. "I'm good. Busy, but good. Lots of new cases coming in. More than you'd think after what happened in the courtroom."

She shrugged. "Some people respond positively to vigilante justice."

Jake forced his eyes to remain on her and not roll to the back of his skull. "Is that what you think I am after all this? A vigilante?"

"A vigilante is someone who undertakes law enforcement without legal authority when they think the legitimate legal agencies are inadequate."

"Or inept."

"True," she said. "To be honest, I don't think you're a vigilante, though your actions lean in that direction at that moment. I think you were outraged at what you, and many others, perceived as a miscarriage of justice."

"I was outraged by the fact Brenner got off the hook. Yeah. Let's just say it was the last drop of water causing the dam to break."

"And you have some furious flood waters, don't you?"

Jake cocked his head. Were they still in session or did his fate already lay on her desk? His eyes dropped to the white envelopes, one thick, the one beneath it thin. If she cast her ballot in the wrong box, Jake would be watching the outside world through metal bars. He'd tried to choke the life out of Hunter Brenner in front of dozens of witnesses, some high-priced lawyers and a judge. It wouldn't surprise him in the least if he spent some time behind bars. It didn't mean he wanted to. Too many bad things could happen.

"We all have those waters flowing in us, Dr. Tate. Some navigate them better than others."

Her tanned forearms rested on the desk, her long fingers rubbing the envelopes holding Jake's fate. "I want you to know I thought a lot about what you said when you were here. In light of what's come out in the last couple of weeks concerning Representative Fletcher and Special Agent Murphy, you were dealing with some serious, how should I say it, issues."

"I'm just happy neither one of them is going to skate."

She stared at her hands. "Being tried for treason. I'm hearing death penalty talk."

"I hope they blow them up with C4."

A laugh burst through her closed lips. "Oh God, I'm sorry. It's terrible I laughed at that. I suppose it would be a nice touch of irony, though, wouldn't it?"

"It would." Jake ticked his head toward the envelopes. "What's my fate going to be, Doc? I have a wife and daughter chomping at the bit to find out and a son your decision could impact for a while."

The smile melted from her face as she picked up the envelopes. "I'll cut to the chase. I don't think you're a danger to society, Jake Caldwell. I think you have a strong moral compass that's had its direction set by years of trauma and more years traveling down the wrong road. But the important thing is you recognized the road years ago and had the courage to stop walking down it. That's more than most people do, and I think it's admirable."

The tension in his shoulders melted. She was going to kick him loose. "Thanks."

"Not that I don't think you couldn't benefit from some additional therapy. I think there's a lot of baggage there. Baggage you shouldn't have to continue to carry."

"You sound like my wife."

"Smart woman. But, seriously, consider it. I'd be happy to talk or can recommend someone else."

Jake had zero intention of digging any deeper in his past. "Thanks. I'll think about it."

She handed him the thick envelope. "This is a copy of the report I gave to the judge. He and I talked, and I think you're going to get some community service, but no jail time. You can relax."

He figured that's where this was going, but he let a smile creep up at the official news. "I appreciate the good word you put in. What's in the other envelope?"

She tapped the edges of the thin envelope on her desk. "I don't suppose Agent Foster ever mentioned she had a sister?"

Jake's heart sank at the mention of Foster. When the bloody image of her lying on the ground outside Wallace Humphrey's house rose up, he batted it away with the memories of good times over beers. Her smile and her laugh. He thought back to her funeral but didn't remember meeting a sister. But there'd been so many people, and he'd left as soon as he could after paying his respects to her. Foster knew how he felt about her, and she wouldn't begrudge him for bailing before the end.

"She never told me she had one, but Agent Snell mentioned it. Why?"

"Her sister Jillian and I are old friends. We went to college together, even dated for a brief but fiery period. Luckily, it ended well, and we stayed in touch. You came up in our most recent conversation."

Jake touched his fingers to his lip in an exaggerated move. "Tsk tsk, Doc. What happened to patient confidentiality?"

"I won't tell if you won't. Even shrinks need

someone to talk to. Anyway, she said Foster talked you up quite a bit over the years. She admired you and your resolve. She said Foster told her you were the most decent man she knew. Jillian called me after Brenner's plea deal and I asked Judge Cooper to handle your case. He and I go back a ways."

Jake's throat crumpled like a tin can, and he willed his opening tear ducts to close. "You requested it?"

Dr. Tate slid the envelope across the desk. "Jillian wanted you to have this."

Jake eyed the envelope, curious as to what it said, but scared to pick it up, fearful it would rake the scab off the wound Foster's death caused. "What does it say?"

"I have no idea. She said it's for you and you alone, and you'd know what to do."

Jake reached forward and plucked the envelope from the desk. He and Dr. Tate locked eyes for a moment before simultaneously standing.

"One last thing, Jake. I don't know if you got anything out of our time together, but I'm going to offer one last piece of advice if you're willing to hear it."

Jake braced himself. "Shoot."

"It seems to me you've spent the last several years serving justice as a means to assuage the guilt you feel for what you did in your past. Sometimes that comes at a risk to your family and your emotional well-being. My advice? Let it go. Put the baggage down and move on, because, if you don't, it's going to catch up with you someday."

"Just let it go?"

"Let it go."

Jake thumped both envelopes against his palms, considering what she said. She was probably right, but that didn't mean he felt his debt had been paid in full. "Maybe someday. But not yet."

She offered a tight-lipped smile. It was obvious to both of them their time was up. She reached across the desk and extended her hand. "Call me if you ever need anything."

He wrapped his hand around her cool skin and pumped it a single time. "I will. And thank you again." Jake turned and headed toward the door. He reached the threshold and turned back. "You said even you needed someone to talk to. Is Foster's sister a shrink to?"

"No. Jillian works for the U.S. Marshals Service. Good luck, Jake."

Jake tapped the envelopes on the door and headed out to his truck. As he crossed the parking lot, he wondered why Foster didn't mention she had a U.S. Marshal for a sister. Then again, she'd always been a bit guarded about her private life. Maybe Snell knew. In any case, he was curious what was in the envelope.

When he reached his truck, he pressed against the warmth of the door, heated by the afternoon sun glaring overhead. He ran his finger under the sealed lip of the envelope from Foster's sister and extracted a single piece of paper. There wasn't much writing on it, but what was there put a smile on his face. Foster's sister was right. Jake knew exactly what to do with it.

Jake memorized the page, reached into his truck and pulled a lighter from his console. He flicked on a flame and set it to the corner of the paper. The flame licked up the side of the page as he watched the ink being consumed. When the heat grew uncomfortably close to his fingers, he dropped the remnants to the asphalt and tracked the ashes as they scattered and disappeared.

CHAPTER SIXTY ONE

A month after Doctor Tate granted Jake his freedom, Bear found a conference to attend in Minnesota. Jake told Maggie he was due some much-needed rest and relaxation fishing somewhere other than the Lake of the Ozarks, so he tagged along. There was nothing wrong with the fishing at home, but the change of scenery was nice. Now, in the early summer afternoon, they were as far north as one could get without being in Canada, near the charming town of Two Harbors.

Jake cast a line from the bank of a small lake, Bear to his left doing the same. It was a little late in the day to call it prime fishing time, but they left Minneapolis late. Instead of a drab conference room, they'd traveled three hours north and now inhaled the smells of wet earth, algae on the lapping water, and something grilling on the other side of the lake.

The tree-laden terrain rose on all sides, and mosquitos the size of Chihuahuas whined and attacked. Footing was questionable along the rocky and muddy shoreline and Bear almost bit it a couple of times. He managed to stay upright due to his self-proclaimed "cat-like reflexes". A hundred yards across to the other shore, a band of young teens manned a dock. They were too far away to be identifiable or of any bother other than an occasional yelp when one pushed another one in the warm lake water. A friend had recommended this particular lake, though Jake hadn't caught anything substantial yet. His luck would change soon.

Bear broke the stillness. "Feels weird not to have a phone on me."

Jake cast again. "I know what you mean. Just worried this will be the time when all hell breaks loose back home, and we won't know until we get back to Minneapolis. Besides, we know what CDRs can do. We don't want someone to know you skipped a conference the tax payers of Benton County are paying for."

Bear reeled in his empty line and chucked it out again. "I'm not so sure we weren't better off before cell phones were invented. At least you had an excuse when someone couldn't get hold of you."

"I'm a hundred percent sure we were better off. Definitely was better before they stuck cameras in them."

Bear sighed. "Maybe we're just old, partner."

"Feels that way." Jake checked his watch and ticked his head down shore. "I'm gonna head over this way."

Bear pressed his lips together. "Be careful, man. Holler if you want help."

Jake grabbed his tackle box and pole and made his way to the spot marked by a fallen tree where the shoreline bent north. His friend told him it was the perfect spot to catch something. Jake checked his surroundings. Nobody in sight but Bear. The teens across the lake had disappeared.

He set his pole against the fallen tree and slapped away a biting mosquito as he bent and opened the tackle box. He lifted the tray holding lures and fishing tools and extracted what he needed, glancing up the hill before starting to weave his way through the thick trees brushing the sky.

Jake walked at a normal pace until he drew close to the house, visible through the thick foliage. He checked back over his shoulder, and Bear was no longer visible through the woods. He turned his attention to the path in front of him, littered with decomposing leaves, brush and animal tracks in the mud. When he reached the tree line, he leaned against the rough, cracked ridges of tree bark. Birds called around him and squirrels chattered. It was peaceful.

The house was as his friend described it. A single-story cabin, maybe fifteen hundred square feet. Dark brown wood on the outside and a porch wrapping around the front. From that height, how much of the lake below could be seen from the rocking chair on the porch? Probably a lot of it fifty years ago, now maybe a lick of blue water if the wind split the trees just right. The driveway along the side of the house was bare. An old, rusty white propane tank sat in the sun near the drive, a squirrel sitting on top eating a nut while basking in the summer sun.

Jake stepped from the cover of the trees and climbed the hill to the front porch. He stepped up the old wood steps. A half-filled coffee mug sat on a tree stump coffee table beside the rocking chair. Jake held his hand over the mug. No heat. He leaned toward the window and looked inside, keeping his body pressed against the side of the house as much as possible. No movement, just furniture. It was the perfect getaway.

He walked around the rest of the porch and tried a side door. Locked. It was farthest away from the driveway. Last place someone would enter once they arrived home. Jake slipped on a pair of gloves from his pocket and jabbed an elbow into the glass pane, reaching through the hole to twist the deadbolt open. He tested the squeak-free hinges and stepped into the house, sliding the unregistered Beretta M9A3 from his waistband and screwing in the silencer he drew from his pocket.

Jake crept through the house, gun raised, waiting. It only took a minute to explore the tiny home to find it empty. Which was expected. A nearly complete puzzle of an F14 Tomcat displayed on a black rollup mat on a square breakfast table. Jake grinned as he noticed a single piece was missing. He fished around in his pocket and extracted the puzzle piece he found on the floor in the dead lawyer's office. He snapped it into place.

He searched the living room and kitchen for any hidden weapons, finding a small, loaded Glock G26 shoved in between the cushion and frame of an easy chair. Jake flicked the bullets from the magazine and ensured the chamber was clear. He pocketed the ammo and shoved the gun back in place. He rested against the kitchen counter, out of sight from the front door among the stacks of dirty plates and glasses. Taking in the stale odor of cigarette smoke and sour beer, Jake waited. Thirty minutes later, he was rewarded.

CHAPTER SIXTY TWO

The sound of a truck engine rumbled outside. It silenced a few seconds later.

Footsteps thumped on the front porch.

The scrape of a key as it slid into the slot and the click as the lock popped open.

Door screeching open.

Door squealing shut.

Heavy boot steps pounding the hardwood floor coming toward the kitchen.

Jake's pulse quickened, his chest rising and falling at a quicker pace.

Bags rustling as the steps grew closer, mere feet away.

Hunter Brenner rounded the corner, plastic grocery bags hooked over his fingers in either hand. His hair was longer and wilder, the beginnings of a bushy beard covered his face, but his eyes were clear. As he passed the puzzle table, he stopped, bending at the waist to examine the now completed picture.

Jake's hand tightened on the grip of his Beretta as he placed the sights on Brenner's upper body, finger hovering over the trigger. Brenner straightened like a rod was shot up his spine as his brain calculated what the reappearance of the missing piece meant. His shoulders sagged as he slowly turned toward the kitchen.

Brenner stared down the maw of the gun barrel and the man with his finger on the trigger, his eyebrows rising and holding. He didn't yell or bolt or attack. He did something Jake didn't expect. Brenner tipped his head forward in a nod of appreciation.

"Make a wrong move and you're deader than fried chicken," Jake said. "Drop the bags and move backward slow into the living room."

Brenner regarded the bags in his hands. "I have perishables in here. Can I at least put them in the fridge?"

"I don't think you have to worry about the milk spoiling. I thought you were on house arrest."

"They let me go to the general store at the end of the road. A perk of turning over the Speaker of the House."

Jake waved the barrel of the pistol toward the living room. "Move nice and slow."

Brenner lowered the bags to the floor and stood, hands raised as he stepped back. When he reached the living room, Jake dipped the barrel toward the chair to indicate the man should sit. Hunter dropped slow to the recliner and laid his arms on the rests.

"I suppose I should thank you," Brenner said.

"For what?"

"For finding my missing puzzle piece. It was driving me insane. Where was it?"

"On the floor of the lawyer's office near the T-Mobile arena."

Brenner's head rocked back. "Ahhh, yes. I'm impressed, Caldwell."

"Considering I'm going to splatter your brains all over the walls of this cabin, you can call me Jake."

"Well Jake, you must be part coon dog. To tell you the truth, I expected you a little sooner than this. How'd you find me?"

"A friend with the U.S. Marshal service. You killed her sister. My friend."

"Sorry about that."

"Are you?"

"Not really," Brenner said. "To tell you the truth, I was terrified I'd be forced to live out my days here. I'm not a fan of the water or the woods. They were at the bottom of my list. Guess it was a last 'fuck you' from the government to put me here."

Jake sat on the edge of a couch a dozen feet away, resting the gun on his knee, the barrel pointed at Brenner's chest and finger tight on the trigger. "Hope? You were hoping I'd come?"

"You or someone like you. I don't want you to kill me, though I suppose you have good reason to want to. Lord knows you would have succeeded in the courtroom if they hadn't knocked you out."

"Then why? I'm your worst fucking nightmare."

Brenner crossed his legs and slumped back in the chair. "So I could explain. Don't you want to know why I did what I did, Jake?"

"The fact you want to tell me makes me want to pull the trigger even more. You killed hundreds with your bullshit politics. You and that treasonous Fletcher, along with Lance and Mara. People just trying to live their lives. Innocent men, women and children. Almost including my daughter. And for what?"

Brenner white-knuckled the arm of the chair. "For a chance at something real. Not this bureaucratic fantasy world where politicians lie, the rich get richer and the disenfranchised cry out against a rigged system that's of their own creation."

"Did Mara cry out when you blew her up in the parking lot?"

Brenner's chin dropped. "I really loved her. Her and Eddie."

"Who's Eddie?"

"A ghost from my past. You have any ghosts, Jake?"

"Who doesn't?"

"Exactly. Mara and Eddie. They're my only regrets."

Jake's grip tightened on the pistol. "That's your only regret out of this, you asshole?"

Brenner sighed. "Truthfully? Yeah."

Jake jumped to his feet and aimed the barrel at Brenner's head, his jaw ached from the tension. "Maybe you want to think a little harder about the question."

"You can't make an omelet without breaking a few eggs."

"I'll be sure to let my daughter know she was of no more value to you than a goddamn egg."

Brenner raised his palms. "You're not hearing me. This was no simple task. We tried to create a new world order where there would be no order any longer."

"But, without order, nothing can exist."

Brenner smacked the chair. "Without chaos, nothing can evolve. And we stopped evolving a long time ago. Technology has made us lazy. Greed has driven us to our lowest depths. On the far left, the woke culture warriors are the new royalty, and they're cancelling anyone and anything in the name of including everyone and everything. The far right has their heels dug in, hanging onto delusions over the way things ought to be. And the vast majority is stuck in the middle, too afraid to say anything for fear of repercussions. We are living in the greatest age man has ever known, and we're the unhappiest we've ever been as a society."

Jake glared. "To solve this great social dilemma, to fix the problems of society, you try to blow it up."

Brenner's chin tilted down, and he finger-tapped the arm rest. "I blew it up to fix it. Don't you see that? As the social fabric tears and the things that bind us together fall to the wayside, we're going to truly experience the worst we have inside of us. It's inevitable. This great American experiment has been a complete and utter failure. Better to blow it up than let it bleed out."

"So what? We give up?"

"We don't give up. If we want to save it, we have to go back to the basics. Where there's no government, no fringes, no movement of the day, just existence. Anarchy. Maybe, just maybe when it's all been taken away, we can learn to build it back the right way. What's left in the end is what matters. That's what I'm trying to do. I did what I did to bring about a better world. I won't apologize for it. I may be a sociopath, but I'm not crazy."

Jake stepped closer. "Yeah, you are. You are if you think after everything this country has been through since its founding that some bombings, name calling, finger pointing and riots can really tear us apart to the point of no return."

"It's true. Anarchy is the only justice for what both sides have done. The scales of justice can't be balanced so they have to be blown up. I tried before and I'll finish it someday." A smug grin crept over Brenner's face. That same grin he wore in the courthouse. "They can't keep me here forever."

Jake flashed back to Dr. Tate's office. "So the ends justify the means?"

"Always," Brenner said. "Even if sheep like you and your daughter get slaughtered in the process. The end is all that matters."

Jake sighed and lowered the barrel of the gun as he stepped back. "That's where you're wrong. You know, I heard this story the other day. If you go to the desert in the southwest and catch a hundred red ants and a hundred black ants and put them in a jar together, guess what happens?"

"They try to kill each other?"

Jake shook his head. "Nothing. They co-exist. However, if you violently shake the jar and dump them back on the ground, the ants will fight until they eventually kill each other. The red ants think the black ants are the enemy and vice versa. In reality, the real enemy is the person who shook the jar. That's exactly what's happening in society today. Left versus right. The real question we should be asking ourselves is who's shaking the jar and why. If we can take out who's shaking the jar, maybe there's hope for all of us."

Brenner smirked, his hand slipping from his leg to the space between the cushion. "That's a pipe dream, Jake. There's no hope while people like me are around to do the jar shaking."

Brenner jerked up the Glock and pointed it at Jake's head. He pulled the trigger, and nothing happened. He jerked it again, the smirk falling away as Jake reached into his pocket and dropped the bullets to the floor.

"That's where you're wrong," Jake replied, pointing his gun at Brenner. "There's always hope. There has to be."

Jake squeezed the trigger, there was a puff and a hole appeared between Brenner's eyes. His head rocked back, his jaw fell open, his body slumping in the chair. Jake put two more shots in his chest to be sure.

Ten minutes later, he strolled along the lake shore. Bear spotted him and waved before he dismantled his fishing pole. By the time Jake reached him, Bear had his tackle box packed.

"Done?" Bear asked.

Jake chucked the Beretta into the middle of the lake. "Done."

Bear pulled a flask from his back pocket. He unscrewed the cap and held the gleaming silver to the sky. "For Foster."

He took a drink and passed it to Jake, who raised it toward the sky.

"For Foster. And all the others."

Jake took a hit from the flask, the shit they'd been through over the last few months zipping through his head. He hoped Brenner was wrong about society.

Jake handed the flask back to Bear, and they hiked up the hill toward the car for the long ride back to Minneapolis and home to his family. As they walked, Jake silently said a prayer for the majority in the middle to find their voice and give the world the justice she deserved. Until she got it, Jake would be there to deliver his own.

IF YOU LIKE THIS, TAKE A LOOK AT: RETRIBUTION: A TEAM REAPER THRILLER

EVERYTHING COMES AT A COST...

After he is betrayed and shoots the two most powerful men in the Irish Mob, John "Reaper" Kane is forced into hiding. He thinks Retribution, Arizona, is the perfect hiding place, but he is wrong. Underneath the old, crusty surface of the dying town, hides the Montoya Cartel, for they use it as a funnel to ship their drugs across the border.

Trying to lay low in a town gripped with lawlessness is impossible for the ex-recon marine, especially after the local sheriff is brutally murdered by the Montoya Cartel's sicario, leaving an old friend, Deputy Sheriff Cara Billings, the only person standing between them and the town.

Things go from bad to worse when Kane is arrested by Cleaver, the deputy in the cartel's pocket, for shooting a local gang member.

Enter DEA Agent Luis Ferrero who has expressed to his bosses for a long time the need for a task force to fight the cartels on their own ground. He's about to get his wish, and to head up his team, he wants the Reaper.

A thrill ride that doesn't let you go – Retribution is the first novel in the action-packed Reaper Series.

ABOUT THE AUTHOR

James L Weaver is the Kansas City author of the Jake Caldwell series. He makes his home in Olathe, Kansas with his wife and two children. His previous publishing credits include a six-part story called "The Nuts" and his 5-star rated debut novel Jack & Diane, which is available on Amazon.com and has been optioned.

His limited free time is spent writing into the wee hours of the morning, working out, golfing, running, and binge-watching Netflix, Amazon Prime or Hulu - he's not picky.

You can read his blog at www.jameslweaver.net and follow him on Twitter @jlweaverbooks.